The Devil Wears Orange

The Devil Wears Orange

Anna Newallo

First Canadian trade paperback edition: 2024

First Canadian electronic book edition: 2024

Library and Archives Canada

Newallo, Anna

The Devil Wears Orange: a novel / Anna Newallo

ISBN: 978-1-7382207-1-7 ebook

ISBN: 978-1-7382207-0-0 paperback

Cover designed by Ivonete de Sousa

To Julian and Christian
You are forever in my heart

"Ignominy is universally acknowledged to be a worse punishment than death." – Benjamin Rush, 1787

"Good girls go to heaven. Bad girls go everywhere." – Helen Gurley Brown, 1982

Chapter 1

THE ROOM IS STARK. Ordinarily, I like white rooms, a blank space to clear a chaotic mind, but I find the interrogation room sterile. Had they gone with a warmer hue of white on the walls instead of hospital white, and replaced the bare lighting, I wouldn't have looked like someone coming off a 5-day bender. I turn away from the mirror, horrified by my image – smudged mascara and hair so frizzy I don't recognize the clown staring back at me. At least they didn't put me in an orange prison jumpsuit, so I'm grateful for that.

The door to the small room swings open, and a man strides in. He looks like he's approaching sixty, and handsome. Do French men have that *je ne sais quoi* as well? I note his shoulder strap with three white lines to indicate his rank, and while I haven't a clue how to read it, I assume he must be important given the circumstances.

He pulls a chair out and sits opposite me, places a blue folder between us. I lift my gaze from the folder to his face and wonder how long he's been spying from behind the one-way mirror like they do on TV cop shows. Hopefully, he's better than those inept Keystone Cops who harassed me earlier in the day.

"I am *Capitaine* Favreau." Favreau opens the thick folder between us and peruses its contents. "Ms. Charlotte Elizabeth Milton. American, *non?*"

"For the millionth time, yes. Where'd those other cops go? I told them everything," I say, exasperated.

"They don't speak English."

"I speak French."

"You have been intermingling English with gibberish. Your French is atrocious, *Mademoiselle*."

Even in French, the very reference to singledom irritates me.

"The great American public school system has served you well," he says.

"Ah, *Monsieur*, you are jeopardizing the French reputation for being friendly," I say in a derisive huff.

Here, he looks up at me from the folder, opens his mouth to speak, then clamps it shut. He sits straighter in his chair. "*Mademoiselle*, do you care to tell us where the painting is, or shall we continue with this little charade?"

"What?!" I demand, rankled by the insinuation. I have been in precarious situations plenty of times before, but nothing like this. "*I* am the victim. These armed men stole the painting and *abducted* me." Slumping in my chair, I shake my head. "I thought you would be better at this. Don't you always get your man?"

"You're thinking of the Canadian Mounties."

"Well, then get them to help you solve this case," I scoff.

"*Mademoiselle* Milton, so far, you have refused to cooperate."

He can't be serious. They've been interrogating me all day and treating me like a criminal. I thought I'd be back at my hotel room by now, catching up on the remainder of Paris Fashion Week, apologizing to my boss Pierre for missing that important meeting with Prince Rashid, but things have progressed slowly. I wouldn't be surprised to learn the cops took a siesta (or the French equivalent) that afternoon. Honestly, the entire continent is so laid back, it's astonishing they get anything done.

"I've been cooperating all day. Like I already told those other two detectives, these men threatened my friend Anne and..." My voice breaks, and I take a moment to pull myself together. "... and her baby."

Favreau shuffles papers in the file. He squints and reaches for his bifocals tucked in his jacket pocket and waves his hand in the air dismissively. "Did you tell a curator of the Louvre, *Monsieur* Julian Norbette, and I quote, 'What's to stop anyone from stealing any of these paintings, especially this masterpiece?' And here you refer to *Mistress In A Red Dress*."

"It's called humor," I say and try to laugh it off as the harmless joke I intended it to be. The French loved Jerry Lewis, so they should be used to sub-par humor.

As though I hadn't even spoken, Favreau continues to read from the file, "'Even I could get away with it.' Again, a direct quote. At which point, you mimic removing the painting and hiding it under a raincoat that you chose to wear on a warm, sunny day."

"I can explain the raincoat. Where is it, by the way?"

"I hope better than you can explain the art heist," he says, his words clipped. "Forensics has the raincoat, and it will remain as part of our evidence into the investigation. Before the theft, you took a photo with the painting and posted it to social media, writing that you planned to take the painting, *non*?"

"Why would I take a selfie if I intended to steal it?"

He flips through several statements, and even upside down, I can see my bank's logo imprinted on the top of the page. My heart sinks.

"You are *familier* with Saks on Fifth Avenue in New York? Tiffany's also on Fifth, *non*?" His voice is flat when he questions me, brief and to the point.

I sit up straight, arms crossed, my back pressed into the hardness of the chair. "Is it your turn to joke? I'm editor-in-chief for a fashion magazine. Of course, I'm *familier*."

"Are you also *familier* with Visa and American Express? They seem to know you quite well. You remortgaged your *appartement* a few months back to pay off your credit card debt."

I swallow hard. "Why did you get this information? *How* did you get this information?"

His eyes are steady on me, watching my face with such intensity that finally, I grasp what Favreau is alluding to. All day while I was being interrogated by the other two officers, they had been watching me, listening to my stories, searching out inconsistencies in my answers, and compiling information on me. The two detectives were merely useless decoys. I should have kept my mouth shut, but no, I just had to nervously babble away. I fear my answers make me look guilty, and if I didn't know the truth, I'd believe in my own guilt, too. I swipe a finger along my sweaty brow then press it over my twitching eye as the gravity of what is happening smacks me. I've seen enough *Dateline* episodes to know I'm the prime suspect.

"Well?" Favreau says, and snaps me out of my head.

"I am not in financial trouble to the point that I would steal a painting," I say, trying to keep my voice steady. "This is ridiculous. Why don't you gather fingerprints from the car?"

Favreau clears his throat without answering. I notice the change in his demeanor as he shifts uncomfortably in his chair.

"You don't have anything, do you?" Now it's my turn to be in control. "One of the men sprayed the car with something. It destroyed all DNA evidence... so that means you have nothing on me." The moment I say this, I resent the smugness in my voice, yet I unequivocally repudiate his accusation.

"They are not finished with the car. I'm sure they'll find something."

Or perhaps Favreau's people will fabricate evidence against me. It's happened to others. What's so special about me that the same thing won't happen? I turn back to my horrific image in the mirror. It was only three days ago that I landed in the city to cover Paris Fashion Week for my magazine, staying at the luxurious Ritz. My schedule was inundated with shows and dinners and parties, so how did I end up in jail accused of pulling off an art heist? I may be a lot of things, but I, Charlotte Milton, am not a thief.

Chapter 2

The Day Before

AMONG THE CROWDED VENUE at the Grand Palais, I catch the odious scent of a vlogger's perfume. They must have unloaded the entire bottle. Normally, my olfactory receptors aren't this good – sommelier was never in the cards for me despite all the drinking – but something has my senses running wild. I'm pregnant! But that would mean I had sex recently, so that's out of the question.

Harriet leads Anne and me into the crowd, passing photographers sandwiched against the back wall, gliding past acquaintances, stopping to air-kiss those we haven't seen since Milan Fashion Week days earlier. Standing at 6'2", Harriet acts as a beacon for us as we trail behind, following the path she cuts. Now all I have to do is chase that trail to my front-row seat without getting trampled on, stepped on, pushed, or–

"Charlotte," calls a squeaky voice.

–stalked.

"Charlotte," the woman says again as she catches up and taps me on the shoulder.

I turn and stare into the face of my former assistant, Jane, whom I haven't seen since her Etsy store blew up and required all of her time. I liked her designs, even purchased a few items – pillow covers, totes and a child's knapsack for some future child I thought I'd have by now. "Hello, Jane."

"Charlotte, I tried to reach you all week."

Nodding my head with an apologetic smile, I say, "Yes, I'm sorry. You remember how chaotic Paris Fashion Week can get. We'll catch up in New York." I continue towards my seat.

"Would you do me a favor?" blurts Jane.

Over my shoulder, I casually tell her, "Of course. I'll call you when I get back to New York and—"

"—Remember you said if I ever, ever, *ever* needed anything, I could come to you?"

Damn it! I *do* remember. If it weren't for Jane, I wouldn't be sitting in the front row at House of Firth as editor-in-chief of *Catwalk Style Magazine*. Back when Jane was my assistant, someone leaked information to a rival magazine. All roads led to me, but Jane gathered the necessary intel to prove a fashion editor, gunning for my job, tried to frame me. The editor was fired immediately, with Harriet hired as her replacement. A weird sort of happy ending.

Returning to where Jane stands, I sigh, "Yes, of course, Jane. Anything."

Jane beams and clasps her hands together like a winner on a game show. Even her freckles seem to dance up and down. Eyebrows lifted high, they disappear under bangs. "Fantastic. I'll meet you tomorrow before the Lumière show with an outfit for you to wear. A reporter from *On The Runway TV* will be there, poised to ask who you're wearing. It'll be a great plug for me. Thank you so much." Jane throws her arms around me. Sweet thing that she is, Jane doesn't fit into the cutthroat fashion industry.

"What exactly am I wearing?" I ask, untangling myself.

"It's a surprise," Jane says then flies off to another friendly face.

This favor for Jane will undoubtedly cost me, but I'll worry about that tomorrow. For now, I take my reserved seat between Anne and Harriet in the front row. Being the most prestigious fashion magazine has many benefits, and I accept them all with ease. Janelle Monae takes her place a few seats from me and nods in recognition. She was the cover of *Catwalk* a few months back. In no time, a small crowd forms around the actress-singer.

Covertly, I pull at the Spanx at my waist, a large Hermès Birkin bag on my lap for cover. The fact that my boss, Pierre Papineau, owner of Papineau Publishing, arrives today for our magazine's event that evening had me so frazzled when I dressed in my signature black, I paid no attention to the discomfort.

Pierre. Without disclosing any details, he said there's something important he wishes to discuss, and this has me all jumpy. For all I know, I could be up for the editor-in-chief opening at Pierre's news magazine, which has traditionally been held by men. While it would be a lateral move, I'd love to shatter that glass ceiling. But, Pierre's concern is the bottom line, and maintaining journalistic integrity at the magazine means I've had to push back on advertisers. I'm not one to fall into line. And Pierre Papineau knows this.

Restless, I survey the Palais' celestial glass dome, an imposing work of architecture and grandeur. Pulling out my phone, I snap a picture, run it through a filter, and simultaneously post it on my socials to give my 500,000 plus followers a hint of what's to come. I live-posted the first two days of Fashion Week, in my sometimes cute and sometimes witty self in a finite number of characters. Still, how many times can I say something is #ToDieFor?

An excited squeal emanates from the women directly behind me. To some, I'm edging towards celebrity status, but I'd be the first to shy away from such nonsense, though I do like to tell people that my first word was "Gucci." It makes for an entertaining anecdote, better than boring them with a detailed account of how this Columbia journalism graduate fell into the world of fashion (much to the disappointment of my ethics professor) and eventually landed my present job at the magazine. Or how, under my leadership, the struggling magazine was pulled out of the red and revived. I strapped that defibrillator on and shocked the glossy pages onto the coffee tables of the twenty to forty-something crowd and onto the lips of every designer and Hollywood starlet. It's been a long, arduous road, and for a few years I suffered under abusive bosses. Now, when I'm invited to *the* party, or when I'm lauded for raising a young designer from obscurity, or when my social media blows up for something as frivolous as dating a famous TV star, I feel I've earned respect. *So go ahead,* I'd like to tell the awestruck fans behind me, *gush away.* After all, everyone could use a little adoration from time to time.

Harriet scrounges the freebies in the swag bag that had been on her seat, pulls out nail polish and foldable flip-flops, a look of hapless boredom on her face until she finds something that piques her interest. "Filler discount," says Harriet, touching an index finger to the regions just below her eyes. Her almond-shaped, dark brown eyes, high cheekbones, and heart-shaped face make her a doppelgänger for a young Naomi Campbell. Often, she waltzes past onlookers at fashion shows, and is mistaken for the phone-throwing supermodel. "If we had been late because of Anne, we would have missed out." To me, she says, "Becky had to pry the baby from Anne's arms. She wanted to bring him to the fashion show, for God's sake. Can you imagine her sitting in the front row with a baby suckling her breast?" The lashing sounds harsher in her Queen's English accent.

"It was just a thought," says Anne in a defensive tone. "You make it sound worse than it actually was."

Knowing Anne, it was more than a mere thought, one that would have negatively affected her work. She's been floundering lately, and her behavior caught Pierre's attention. Before we left New York for Paris Fashion Week, Pierre had warned that if Anne screwed up again, I would have to fire her. As far as I'm concerned, that's a hard no, even if I have to cajole Anne to do her job, or cover for her, *again.* Anne has given countless years of professionalism to the magazine; I can't abandon her. It takes a village to raise a child, and without family around, me, Harriet and her au pair, Becky, are that village, though Harriet less so.

Anne twists a finger through her long black hair that cascades past her shoulders, her eyes skirt about the room. "Everyone is so meticulously groomed. I tried to get a haircut last week but the young girl ahead of me insisted Ronaldo give her a cut identical to some Japanese anime character. It was a disaster. When I saw what he had done, I walked out." After a beat, she says, "The cartoon character did have nice hair, though."

Music streams through the venue with a performance by a solo musician playing the Oud.

"What's the designers' inspiration?" I say, my thoughts now returning to the fashion show.

Anne recites almost by memory. "They were inspired by a trip to Dubai, the grand palaces and natural beauty of the country and the people."

"Not to mention the bank accounts of every Sheik buying these designs for their wives," Harriet adds.

"Oh, and look at this. It says a real Prince will join us. I wonder where he's sitting." Anne looks around. "That's odd. The most fabulous seats are taken, and those people don't look, well, Prince-*y*."

"What's his name?" I say, peering over the press packet.

"Prince Rashid Mohammed Salah al-Zayed, eldest son of the King. Mother is the senior wife."

"Senior wife? Just how many wives does this Prince have?" says Harriet.

Anne immediately Googles him on her phone. "No, that's his father who has a senior wife and oh...three others. Prince Rashid isn't married."

"Well, ladies, there are three of us. We could all be one of his wives," says Harriet.

I say, "You would share your husband?"

"At least they're honest, unlike what goes on in New York where the senior wife is dumped once her husband publicly parades his soon-to-be junior wife."

Anne blinks back the tears that a month ago would have poured out, and hisses, "I am not a senior wife."

"I didn't mean you," Harriet says in a thin, defensive whisper, and I give her a scolding look. Instead of avoiding the elephant in the room, Harriet rides the damn thing even if the elephant holds a sign that reads, "Do Not Talk About Anne's Abandonment."

In silence, we shift in our chairs with frayed nerves, and swipe at our phones.

Amid a fever-pitched sea of excited attendees, the lights dim to signify the start of the show. The first model appears and parades down the runway wearing a black tunic and gold lamé harem pants. Countless purple beads drape her arms, and layers of exquisite silk fabric envelop her.

Bedouin-inspired layers is the new volume dress, I post, following a grouping of caftans in vivid hues that fill-up the runway. An idea forms about a future "all sizes" issue, and perhaps these dresses, accepting most sizes, can democratize fashion. Now that really is #ToDieFor.

By the time the final model disappears behind the curtain, the audience is eager for the grand finale. Yet, the models don't return for their last stretch down the runway. Nor is there any sign of the designers, which is odd.

A movement behind the curtain captures my interest, and I strain my neck to see. A male model steps onto a darkened part of the stage, motionless, and then regally strides down the runway carrying a single white rose. He wears a full-length gold lamé jacket, a multi-strand draping necklace in purple crystals, and a chunky silver bracelet with chains that lead to his middle finger. A jewel suspends on his forehead from the center of the turban, and a veil of silver silk swings down his long back. Harem pants tighten around his ankles.

He's beautiful. Dark skin, strong eyebrows, brilliant blue eyes, and an angular jaw covered in manicured stubble. I once wrote an article on the art of attraction, noting men with symmetrical faces, like the model's, are put in the long-term-husband-material-for-procreation category. The model may as well be one giant magnet drawing me in.

"Now *there* is a man," Harriet breathes out in a raspy voice. "Ladies, we found our Prince."

The Prince turns for his walk back, his fingers gently caress the flower he holds. I gulp, thinking it's so loud that the ladies must have heard. Every pulsating fiber of my being wants to reach out, to smell him, lick him, ride him. Hot and flustered, I fan myself with the press kit. As he passes, his eyes fix on mine and hold. *Catwalk* once ran a story that when a man is interested in a woman, he will gaze for 8.4 seconds. Breathlessly, I start counting.

Is it possible for a man to smile without actually smiling? He leans toward me and, his eyes still holding on mine, offers me his white rose. I swipe it too quickly, and scratch him in an inelegant attempt to secure the flower.

Then he is gone.

Eight. It was for eight seconds.

"For God's sake, close that mouth of yours," Harriet snaps.

"Was it?—"

"—yes."

"You don't even know what I was going to ask."

"If your mouth was open the entire time he was looking at you. The answer is yes."

The models and designers continue down the runway for their last turn, while I wait for the Prince to resurface.

Chapter 3

MUSIC POUNDS MY EARDRUMS. Maddening strobe lights trigger a headache, and the DJ massacres my favorite Beyoncé song, deconstructs it to some sacrilegious beat. God, I feel much older than my thirty-three years. When did I stop being that fun person who'd party into the wee hours?

The time on my phone reads 9:40PM, and I'm daunted by the prospect of staying until midnight. I've already made the required introductions, snapped photos for my social media, booked several interviews, and learned about a rival magazine, a new startup with big money from unknown players. Still, I haven't connected with Pierre, though his plane arrived hours ago.

Beside me, Harriet tips a vodka martini towards her lips. Earlier, she snubbed "The Tease," the martini created for tonight's event. It's a Cosmo. Same ingredients. Different name. Harriet doesn't do cosmos. Her eyes gaze out at the room. "How dull."

Catwalk Style Magazine's parties end with scandalous write-ups the next morning. The guest list always includes one member of the British Royal Family and a string of Hollywood starlets, who always pair up together – or triple up – depending on the royal. Yet all this salaciousness is too boring for Harriet.

Harriet glances at me, sneering. "What? What's that look for? You act as though everything I say is wrong," says Harriet, sounding like the aggrieved party.

"I'm afraid someone will hear you," I say, looking to see who's within earshot. A *Catwalk* employee besmirching our own event is the kind of thing that will land Harriet on the gossip column and her head on the chopping block for Pierre's guillotine, but the blank expression on Harriet's face reads to me as *'And?'*

Harriet places her empty glass on a passing tray, gives a once-over look at the waiter wearing a Venetian costume of a larva mask, black cape, and three-cornered hat. Harriet says, "Look at the tawdry purple sofas and red carpet of this manse. Isn't our party's theme sex? Where's the sex? Ugh, this party is more *Eyes Wide Shut* than *Emmanuelle*."

"I think we've achieved an atmosphere of dirty hedonism."

Harriet gives me a side stare. "You must have an unexceptional sex life."

"What's the word most associated with Britain and sex?" I say, placing an index finger to my chin in mock contemplation. "Oh, I remember. Uptight. At least it's not a porn-chic travesty like *Caligula*."

Harriet arches an eyebrow. "Great idea. This party could use some '70s porn projected on the walls."

"That's not what I said," I mumble, but Harriet talks over me.

"We missed out on an entire generation of hairy men. Imagine being balls deep–"

Imagine being silent for just five minutes. My head throbs. My stomach growls. My new, high-heeled shoes are killing me, a sacrifice I'm willing to make trading comfort for style when representing the magazine. Plus, there's the added bonus of my calves looking *sexy AF*, as Harriet often reminds me. Surreptitiously, I slide my foot out to stretch my toes. Slipping my foot back into the torture device, I peer through the semidarkness at a male figure surrounded by women.

Interrupting Harriet's drone, I say, "Is that Michael Fassbender?"

"Where?" Harriet whips her head and, sadly for Mr. Fassbender, she spots him. Seconds later, Harriet steps into the circle, towers over the other women and places a hand on the actor's shoulder.

The one glass of wine on an empty stomach makes me tipsy, and I desperately need to diffuse its power with food. At the seafood and caviar end of the table, I swipe a fresh pink shrimp, dip it into the sauce, and take a bite. Before moving on to the caviar, I grab two more shrimp, and scoop up a dollop of cocktail sauce.

"Charlotte."

Pierre's voice calls from close behind me. Getting caught with my hands full of food won't make the right impression on him. He's a proponent of the fashion fat police who believe you should never eat at work functions. An archaic misogynist mind-set still intact. I search the table for a spot to rest the shrimp and caviar-smeared cracker I'm holding, but it's annoyingly crowded with full platters and abandoned Venetian masks. Finally, I cram the tiny hors d'oeuvre into my mouth and chew quickly.

Turning around, I'm startled by the piercing blue eyes staring back at me. The sight of the Prince renders me speechless and motionless. He smiles slightly and brings his hand up to his face, taps his chin, like he's sending me a secret message in some kind of telepathic language. *Come away with me. I want you as my wife.*

Pierre's voice disrupts our intimacy. "Charlotte, I'd like you to meet Prince Rashid Mohammed Salah al-Zayed, whom I hope will join the Papineau Publishing family soon."

"Enchanté."

Butterflies flutter in my stomach, and I swear my heart is pumping out of my chest like in a cartoon. *Thump-thump. Thump-thump.* Rashid reaches out, his eyes fiercely on me. In a stupor, I place my hand in his, draw it up to his face, dirty napkin and all. The perplexed look on Rashid's face reveals my mistake.

Obviously, he only meant to shake my hand, but there's a playful flicker in his eyes, and he tilts his head forward, kisses the top of my hand.

Pierre breaks the intimate moment by clearing his throat. Speaking in French, Pierre introduces me as his editor-in-chief extraordinaire at *Catwalk Style Magazine* in New York City. Is that who I am? Is that where I live? I'm oblivious to everyone except the man who belongs to those eyes. Besides, the fluency of the French is too quick for me, and I'm lucky to understand every third word. Why do I feel so tongue-tied around the Prince? I've met royalty before, even made out with one but he held an Italian title and, well, those don't really count anymore.

Pierre loudly clears his throat, and I glance his way. He taps his chin, sends his own telepathic message. *Come away with me. I want you to run my publishing empire.*

To my dismay, I finally feel the coldness on my chin – the cocktail sauce. Sheepishly, I dab a napkin at the mess on my face, then rub it obsessively until I'm sure the spot is as raw and pink as the shrimp, or perhaps as red as my face.

I studied French in high school, but my command of the language pales next to the fluidity spoken between Pierre and Rashid. I stare at them with nervous concentration, engage in laughter when Pierre bellows at a joke, then, later, inject reflection when the conversation turns serious. I'm unable to grasp their rapid-fire conversation apart from "gallery" and "Monet" and "Lumière show."

"You will make yourself available, Charlotte?" Pierre says in English.

"Oh *si, ahh oui. Je suis célibataire.*"

Confusion crosses Pierre's face. *"Excusez-moi?"*

Did I just say I'm single when I meant to say available?

"Oh, I mean," I stumble. *"Je suis disponible...and je vais à la galerie...duma."*

"Qu'est-ce qu'une 'duma'?" says Pierre.

"What?" My eyes bounce between a quizzical Rashid and a bewildered Pierre. "What?" I repeat, rather unintelligibly when I meant to convey that I'll be at the gallery *demain*. Tomorrow.

"Yes. Exactly. What?"

Both men stare at me in anticipation. *Say something witty and intelligent and knowledgeable about fashion or politics or climate change. Speak, woman, speak!* I open my mouth to comment on the Lumière show when Pierre interrupts.

"Charlotte, we're booked to meet privately with Prince Rashid tomorrow at 3PM." Pierre's phone beeps with a text, and he pauses to read it. "Ah, my husband has just arrived. I promised him introductions with Prince Rashid. *Au revoir*, Charlotte." Pierre takes the earliest opportunity to guide Rashid elsewhere.

"*Au revoir*," I say in haste. Automatically, my brain skips through the loop in my head, replaying the conversation in its entirety. There's no way to soften the blow. I came across as a bumbling idiot. I'll need to be prepared and informed for tomorrow's business meeting. But, informed about what exactly? Pierre has left me in the dark, which, to be honest, is typical of him.

At midnight, I sit in the town car with Harriet and Anne, heading back to the hotel. I lower the window, tilt my head against the glass, gulp in fresh, cool air while Anne chatters eagerly next to me.

"And I met the Prince. I couldn't believe it when Pierre introduced me to him. He's more beautiful up close and speaks French perfectly. I never thought my French was all that wonderful, but the words just poured out of me."

"Did you bore him with talk of your *bébé*?" Harriet bothers to ask.

"I don't talk incessantly about my baby," Anne says in a tight tone, and her eyes flick to Harriet.

Eyebrow raised, I scowl at Harriet. She's always starting something with Anne.

"I mentioned Chase briefly," Anne confesses, "and the Prince was kind to ask so many questions about him. He said something lovely about the West being backward, stripping a woman of her child to return to work for Corporate America. It sounded poetic in French."

To Harriet, I say, "And how were things with Mr. Fassbender?"

Harriet rolls her eyes. "God, I spent part of the evening standing beside Sasha. She doesn't wear a bra. Her perky titties are like beacons for their penises. How can I compete with that?"

Silence fills the limo. Harriet closes her eyes and sinks into the leather of her seat. I'm sure Harriet is dreaming of Fassbender. Meanwhile, I'm envisioning a game of Blind Man's Buff with my Prince Charming for tomorrow's meeting. Hmmm, but who will blindfold whom?

Chapter 4

TERRIBLE THINGS ARE HAPPENING in the alleys of the Jardin des Tuileries.

Sunglasses resting low on my nose and head tilted forward, I inspect a marbled Theseus slaying the Minotaur. It's a travesty that the Minotaur is defeated for being born a monster, punished for his mother's sin of sleeping with a bull. He never stood a chance in life. And up ahead, a tiger takes pleasure crushing a crocodile; his staunch posture and protruding teeth exhibit a sense of righteousness in the heroic killer. And who best to decide who plays hero, who plays foe, than the storyteller? If it was up to me, I'd turn every myth, every fairytale on its head, give everyone a chance at a happy ending.

Here is where Marie-Antoinette would take her afternoon strolls. Forever immortalized as the wicked Let-Them-Eat-Cake-Queen, I'm sure she'd sue for defamation and probably win if she was alive today.

An overnight rain leaves a heavy scent in the early morning air – of soil and lilacs and grass, the kind of green that smells good after a winter spent hibernating. Life returns to the garden, tricked with the hint of an early spring. Little children, sticks in hand, prod miniature boats along the perimeter of a fountain. Nearby is the tent erected in the Jardin for the Lumière show, a special gallery viewing co-hosted by Musée du Louvre and *Catwalk Style Magazine*.

"This is such a lovely day for falling in love," I say.

"I hate when you're happy," says Harriet, pulling the cigarette from her lips, and adjusting the black Chanel sunglasses that are so big they practically devour her face.

My indescribable bliss in anticipation of my meeting with Prince Rashid, can't be deflated. Not even by Harriet.

"Where is that Anne?" Puff. "She's late, again." Puff. "Oh no, she didn't!" Harriet pushes her sunglasses down her nose, revealing bloodshot eyes.

I follow Harriet's sharp glare and spot Anne beyond a low bush, strolling with a baby carriage, all smiles and laughter until she looks up at us.

Anne recoils. "I can explain," she starts. "I just couldn't leave him today of all days. It's so beautiful outside, and I thought there wouldn't be many events for me to bring him to."

"There are zero events to bring a baby, Anne," Harriet hisses impatiently.

It's tiring to keep up with Anne's erratic behavior, especially when I'm the single remaining thread between Anne and her job. If it was up to me, every day would be bring-your-baby-and-dog-to-work day, but the world has other harsher ideas. And Pierre wants me in charge of enforcing *his* rules.

Harriet continues. "There should be a law about babies in public spaces." Puff. "The Mommy Mafia has overtaken every trendy restaurant in my neighborhood. Now I can't enjoy a meal without some brat slapping his mother." Puff.

Anne covers Chase's ears. "It's okay, sweetie," she says in a sing-song voice. "The mean lady isn't talking about you. She has unresolved issues from her cold British upbringing." A stream of cigarette smoke waltzes toward the baby, and Anne fans it away. "Nasty habit."

"What? Little Parisian babies are born with cigarettes in their mouths. No harm done," Harriet says.

Anne looks at her coolly.

Harriet huffs. "For God's sake, I'm going in." She stubs out the remainder of her cigarette and disappears behind the tent's front entrance's white sails.

Anne is about to follow when an attendant stops her.

"*Pardon moi*, sorry, but is crowded. No room for a stroller," the uniformed man says in a thick French accent.

Turning to me, Anne says, "They're so antifamily in Europe."

"Madame, in Europe we have *un, deux*, sometimes *trois* years maternity," he says, holding up his fingers to illustrate. "*Amérique? Un jour.* One day only."

"Well, that's not true," says Anne, before mumbling, "Not quite, anyway."

"You go in. Stroller outside."

I hold my breath. *Please don't go in and risk Pierre seeing you because then he'll make me fire you and I'll refuse then he'll fire me instead.* "He's too heavy to carry for the duration of the event," I point out.

Frowning, Anne turns to me. "You're right. We'll stay outside and enjoy the weather and the birds and the flowers," Anne coos, bends over, and tickles Chase under his chin.

Masking my gleeful relief, I say, "If you think that's best."

"We'll be around when you're done. Won't we? Won't we? Yes, that's right. We will," Anne says in baby-speak and pushes the carriage away.

For a while, I watch Anne stroll down the avenue with Chase, listen to the soothing sounds Anne makes until she's out of earshot. It's a loving moment, but Pierre will think otherwise if he catches her. Pierre is the reason I have Becky on speed dial, and I immediately text her to meet us here. Though it'll take her an hour, Becky should arrive with plenty of time for Anne to make an appearance at the Lumière show before she needs to set off for her meeting.

"Charlotte!"

I turn in the caller's direction. Jane sprints towards me, a garment bag flung over her arm.

"I'm so glad I caught you before you went in," she huffs, struggling to catch her breath. "Well, here it is. Try it on."

"Try what on where?" I scan the public garden for a private sanctuary to change, and the event's Port-o-Potty, though luxurious, is out of the question.

"We don't even know if it will fit properly," I say, doing my best to prepare Jane for disappointment.

A smile springs to Jane's face. "That's the beauty of it. One size fits all."

***

My head pops through the tent's opening, and I scope out the venue. Swaths of grey fabric drape from the center peak to the cathedral windows, and every twenty feet along the perimeter, a lighted tree shimmers. Crystal chandeliers hang like raindrops. Hordes of guests circulate, lips pressed to cheeks, hands on shoulders, and a cacophony of their conversation carries back to me.

It's no surprise the "must attend" Lumière event is jam-packed. It's the reason Jane picked it for me to model her design. *This* is the defining moment that destroys my career, but then again, I do have a habit of exaggerating. Maybe it won't be so bad. Fashion people are open to new, modern ideas, and, with this comforting thought occupying my senses, I enter.

There.

I did it.

Not. Bad. At. All.

"For God's sake, what are you wearing?" Harriet's question shoots at me in staccato.

Sounding nonchalant, I say, "It's a Parisian raincoat. One of a kind."

"But darling, it's not raining. And we're inside." Examining the outfit, Harriet raises one brow and spins me around. "It's like a bunch of plastic bags sewn together, with patches of polka dots and stripes, and all the colors of a rainbow. It's nonsense. I bet it balloons when you walk. Jog that way, and I'll Instagram it with the caption #BagLady." Harriet gives me a little nudge.

I pull away, weary of Harriet's attempt to humiliate me as though the ridiculous outfit isn't doing that already. But, I made a promise to Jane, and I will wear it without disparaging its design. "Oh, Harriet, it's the next trend, and within a week, you'll ask to borrow it. Have you seen *Monsieur* Julian Norbette?"

"He's by the podium, the one who looks like a young Brad Pitt. Hmmm, not bad to look at, is he?" Harriet says, drawing my attention to Norbette. "He could do something about that hair of his, though." Then back to me, she says, "Come to think of it, so can you."

I swat Harriet's hand away.

"Ow. I was only trying to help." Harriet's eyes scan over me again, and she wrinkles her nose. "Then again, the disastrous hair goes with the outfit."

Harrumphing, I walk away, and ignore the gawking and the whispering and Harriet's roaring laughter, as I attempt to push down the front and sides that keep puffing out. It's too much to hope that Harriet is not posting a video on Instagram right now. There are those in the crowd who snicker with joyful smiles, others whose derisive snorts wash over me. I feel as though I'm tied to a whipping post and the whole village has come out for the show. I brace myself for the throwing of imaginary rotten food.

I approach Monsieur Norbette by the podium. "*Monsieur* Norbette, I'm Charlotte Milton. It's a pleasure to meet you."

"And you, Madame." His eyes hover over my outfit before his face snaps back.

With Monsieur Norbette by my side, I make the rounds, introduce artists with fashion designers, designers with media, and work to escape that vlogger who trails me. Somewhere along the way, I lose Monsieur Norbette to a journalist.

Off on one side, an entrance leads next door to a smaller tent housing the event's gallery portion. I slip away, swiping a blue macaron and drink from a table.

Champagne glass in hand, I pause to take in the art. Some of the paintings are smaller than what I had envisioned. I wish they came with price tags like the Starbucks' artwork, which is the only art I can afford right now. When I first bought my apartment, I had this idea to decorate whole walls with B&W photographs, but the cost was proving to be astronomical. My ex-photographer-boyfriend encouraged the design and slipped his photography onto my wall. After our break up, he sent me an invoice with a PAST DUE notice stamped in red capital letters. I mailed him a check with the word ASSHOLE written in red nail polish. I can't believe I thought he was *the one*.

A few people, milling around the paintings, check the time then scamper off to the next event with a gift bag in hand, validating them as a *Catwalk* VIP. Eyeing a painting of two giant squares and a circle, I try to feel it or let it absorb me or do whatever it is you're supposed to do when looking at art. Instead, I tilt my head sideways for a different perspective and wonder if the painting hangs upside down. *Whatever.* Undecided, I move on to the next one. Finally, I arrive at the exhibit's main attraction and ease my way through a small crowd gathered around *Mistress in a Red Dress*. Monsieur Norbette pulls up alongside me, and the group disperses.

"She is exquisite," Monsieur Norbette says.

"It seems risky to have these paintings in a tent instead of tucked away in the museum."

"We have security." He points to the guardsman behind us.

I examine the Rent-a-Guard's uniform, which looks like a discounted Hallowe'en costume. To Norbette, I say, "But, he's not even armed. What's to stop anyone from stealing any of these paintings, especially this masterpiece? Even I could get away with it." I simulate removing the painting off its wire and hiding it under my roomy raincoat. "It's simple," I tell him, my tone serious.

Monsieur Norbette smiles uncomfortably and purses his lips together.

Continuing, I say, "What a headline that would make – *Unladylike Guest of Honor Steals Mistress in a Red Dress*." I fail to stifle a laugh.

A young woman approaches and says, "*Excusez-moi, Monsieur*," then whispers into Norbette's ear.

Addressing me, Norbette says, "There is a matter I must attend to. I will return *tout de suite*."

Alone now, I look back at the painting and stare hard as if I can somehow pick up a vibe from the *Mistress*. Maybe she can tell me what the fuss is all about because I don't see it. Whipping out my phone, I take a selfie with the *Mistress* and post to Instagram: *Taking her back with me to NYC #LumiereShow #CatwalkStyleMag #ParisFashionWeek #MistressInARedDress*

A waiter, dressed in a white fencing uniform and facemask, strolls past, and I plop down my empty glass. I can't recall who came up with the idea for the uniform, but it had something to do with the artwork of a renowned French fencing master currently at the Louvre.

There's a sliver of an opening in the tent where one flap meets another, and I slide my hand in to open it wider. From here, I glimpse Anne pacing in the Jardin des Tuileries, Chase in her arms, the carriage nearby. It has been a while since I felt it, but I recognize that palpable yearning. I long for my own Chase, but the chase after a father is what I find challenging.

A body presses up against my back.

"Don't turn around," a voice tells me.

"*Monsieur* Norbette?" I say though I don't recognize the accented voice. I've spent enough time in Paris to understand the Frenchman's penchant for lots of PDA, and sometimes I forget I'm not in Kansas anymore. French men express their interest straight away with none of the Western slog of casual dating, of late-night conversations with girlfriends wondering "is he into me?" And right now, I'm thinking *Monsieur* Norbette is most definitely into me, but there's boundaries and consent, *Monsieur*. I tilt my head and, in a sidelong glance, catch snippets of a waiter's fencing uniform.

"Lovely," he says.

"Thank you." I feel a rush of heat. It's sad, really, that one compliment from a stranger makes me flush.

"Look at how she smiles slightly at her lover."

I turn to the painting.

"The woman is Lady of Sheffield, a Lady in Waiting to Catherine of Aragon," he says.

"Yes, I read something about her in a brochure. All very interesting." The small talk is flimsy, my mind preoccupied with the waiter who stands so close that I can smell his minty breath on the nape of my neck.

"Her beauty so transfixed the King that he had to have her. As a gift from a Chancellor, the great painter Mario Foligari was commissioned to paint her portrait. It was during these times spent alone that the painter and muse fell in love. So deep and dangerous was their love that they kept it hidden; otherwise, word would travel back to the jealous King and–"

"–And the King would have him killed." I join in.

The stranger enraptures me with his story. "Foligari knew every detail of her body, so he began to paint by memory, creating shades of red to capture the texture of her dress." He runs his hand gently up the side of my raincoat. "A new shade of white to capture the fine porcelain skin of her neck."

His smooth fingers caress my neck, and a tingle runs down my back. I lean into him. This sizzling chemistry with a stranger confounds me, but this is Paris, and, according to Harriet, hot sex with a stranger is mandatory.

"And a new shade of coral for her lips." He works his fingers along my jawbone.

A heavy breath escapes me. "Please tell me they ran away together."

"Foligari secretly planned their escape to Italy, where they would be free from the King's reach and that of the court's. But on that fateful night, Lady Sheffield was betrayed by her father, who wanted to see his daughter please the King and, in turn, bring favor to himself."

"He'd do so well in Hollywood," I quip. I reach out my hand until I brush against his fingers.

"Out of jealousy, the King dispatched his horsemen and, in a rage, it is said that he had the painting of his Lady destroyed. Thankfully, this proved false. Centuries later, the painting was found in the cellar of a home in Leeds where Catherine of Aragon was once exiled."

"And the lovers?"

"It wasn't their fate to be together. Having lost his muse, Foligari never painted again."

It's been months since a man stood that close to me, his hand pressed against the small of my back. Perhaps it's his accent or his close proximity, but whatever the reason, I'm turned on and want him in my hotel suite right now. Should I ask him to wear the uniform to bed? What am I thinking! Damn the accent. Damn the cologne. I must be ovulating.

"And what of Lady Sheffield?"

"She remained with the King until he tired of her."

"That's not a happy ending," I gripe. It is only then that the significance of the painting dawns on me. Lady Sheffield wasn't looking at her lover, but at the ghost of him, for she knew one day, she would lose him.

The stranger tilts his head towards me and whispers into my ear. "Do you see your friend out there?"

Jarred by the change in topic, I whip my head in the direction he's gesturing to see Anne through the opening I created earlier. I want more of the sexy whatever-is-happening-between-us, and talking about Anne is an arousal kill. How would he like it if I brought up his mother?

"She has a lovely little boy, Chase. It would be a shame if something were to happen."

"I don't understand." I attempt to look at the face of the man, but he pushes my head forward.

"Keep your eyes on your friend. Now, do you see *my* friend?"

As he says this, a short man of medium build and wearing a baseball hat walks up to Anne. My mind races, heart thumping.

"Right now, he is telling her that unless her friend, Ms. Milton, obeys every instruction she is given, her life is in grave danger."

In the alley of the Jardins, Anne holds Chase tighter.

"He tells her that she need not worry, that if her friend loves her and Chase as much as she believes she does, then everything will be fine. Do you understand, Ms. Milton?"

I nod my head weakly, stunned that he knows my name. In the distance, Anne stands rigid, clutches Chase, and looks frantically around her.

"'You can't run or scream,'" he says. "'No one can help except Ms. Milton.'"

Outside, the man opens his jacket. My hand flies to my mouth, suppressing uncontrollable utterings. Does he have a gun?

"My nature does not allow me to be a violent man. However, my partner views things differently." Gently, the waiter twirls my hair that cascades around my neck.

I stiffen. "Don't touch me," I say, trying to keep my voice steady.

He pulls his hand away. "I apologize, my dear, Charlotte. Please, tell me you understand my predicament."

This time, I nod in exaggeration to illustrate how docile I can be. How did things go so wrong? He whispers instructions in a soft intonation then makes me repeat everything back to him, voice shaking. When he is done, he backs away and disappears. As instructed, I count in a quiet murmur…18, 19, 20.

Perhaps this is all a misunderstanding or a prank for a new TV show – God knows, I've seen my fair share of trashy Euro shows – but when I look back at the guard, I notice that, true to the stranger's words, a red laser beam is aimed at his forehead. They mean to kill him. I set the plan in motion and nervously approach the guard.

"I'm sorry to have to put you through this, but a man…"

"Pardon moi?" the guard says, confused. *"Non-Anglais."*

Oh. *Merde.*

Switching to French, I tell him a gun is pointed at his head, but I can tell by the expression on his face, mirroring the Prince and Pierre's at the party, that he doesn't comprehend a word.

"Oh, no," I moan. Exasperated and terrified, I use trembling hands to gesture the shape of a gun, aim it at his head, and cock back my finger. Alarm jumps to his face, eyes wide, mouth open, quickly agitated.

"Ssshh, not so loud." I worry he will draw attention to us. "Stay still and be quiet." I bring a finger to my lips, wear an intense expression on my face.

The guard quiets down. Under his breath, I hear the incantation of a prayer. His eyes look up, almost cross-eyed, to where the red laser shines on his sweaty forehead. Now that he's contained, I swipe his phone from a pouch on his hip and drop it to the ground, stomping until the screen cracks and blackens.

"I'm terribly sorry, but if I don't do as they say, they'll hurt my friend." My quivering voice cracks part-way through.

The guard is riveted by something, and I turn around to follow his gaze. A hand appears in the slit of the tent alongside *Mistress in a Red Dress*.

"I'm so sorry," I say, voice thick with dread. Carefully, I lift the painting off a wire that hangs from the ceiling. It's more burdensome than I anticipate and nearly drop the *Mistress* on my toes. Grabbing onto both sides of the frame, I heave the painting through the opening and hand it to the thief on the other side. The moment he takes it, I thrust my head through, eyes scanning the area for Anne and Chase.

They're gone.

Chapter 5

T UMBLING OUT FROM THE slit in the tent, I search for Anne and Chase. I scan the fountain, the gravel walkway, the benches, but they aren't there. Panicked, I tear across the grounds. I did everything the waiter had asked, and he took them anyway.

As I sprint, I catch swirling images of tourists posing for family photos in front of the fountain. Get out of my way! I want to yell, if only I could quit gasping. A woman is pushing a stroller, but she's blonde.

It takes me several seconds to locate the white of the waiter's uniform, the thief jostled by a tour group. I hunt the man in white like Alice pursuing her rabbit, but Alice never had to do it in heels with blistered feet and a side cramp. I nearly catch him by Rue de Rivoli, but people on the street push past me, shopping bags in hand, and block my view. If I'm having trouble navigating through this crowd, then it must be more challenging for him with the painting.

Horns blare, startling me, and I lose sight of the white rabbit. My head jerks from side to side, eyes darting. Dread rises from my gut and into my throat. What have they done with Anne?

There! I spy the waiter attempt to get into a green Peugeot, but a large family blocks his way. It gives me time to catch up to him. I seize the frame and yank it towards me.

"Where are they?" I shout. His head tilts to me, the fencing mask hides his facial expression, but his body language appears unruffled by my presence. He pulls the painting back to him with little force as though I'm nothing more than a tiny ant.

But ants are strong enough to carry more than twice their weight, and I tighten my grip, pulling the *Mistress* back toward me. My voice comes in hard and loud. "Tell me where they are, or I'll scream for the po–"

Someone smothers my mouth from behind, and my attempt for a blood-curdling scream comes out muffled. My assailant drags me back into the waiting vehicle. I kick back, trying to hook my foot behind his ankle to pull him off balance, but only succeed in hitting his shin. I try again, slam him with my heel, but he hoists me up and all I hit is air. My arms pinned, I thrash and wiggle but he's too strong. Why can't I remember the self-defense article we ran in the health section two years ago? He stuffs me into the backseat, banging my head on the way in and my purse falls to the road. Doors slam shut. Bodies press against me on either side.

Undoubtedly, one photo-snapping tourist witnessed this and is on the phone with the police, right? But when I scramble around to look out the window, I'm stunned by the sight of tourists too preoccupied to notice what transpired. None of them will dial 9-9-9 emergency.

Then, as the car whizzes past a bench, I spot Anne and Chase sitting, unharmed, and playing a game of Peek-a-Boo, seemingly untroubled by the earlier threats. Anne looks up and lifts an arm in a wave; I press my hand against the back window in response, but realize Anne is actually waving at an approaching Becky. Relieved, I relax and suck in measured breaths. They're safe. Oh, thank God. And after a beat, What about me?

Turning, I see the waiter has removed his mask and replaced it with aviator glasses, a Yankees' baseball cap pulled low above a beard and moustache badly glued to his face. He says something in a foreign language to the kidnapper – the same man who had threatened Anne in the Tuileries – who sits on the other side of me. The waiter's tone is biting and coarse in admonishing him, his finger pointing at me. My head whips from one to the other as they bicker. Perhaps the waiter is angry that they can now add kidnapping to their list of criminal activities.

Leaning on its side across the car's floor hump in front of me sits a familiar face – *Mistress in a Red Dress*. Hundreds of years after her death and men are still clamoring for her attention.

I avert the waiter's stare, and have to swallow a few times before I can get any words out. My voice is unsteady. "I kept my part of the bargain. You can't just take me. I'm an American." I cringe as I say it. Such an American thing to say.

The Peugeot merges in roundabouts and rolls through stop signs, driving the same speed as the others. We've blended in so well with traffic that it's hard to spot the vehicle with the stolen painting. I look back. No one is following. *Incroyable!* This is either the most carefully planned art robbery or the luckiest. With that thought comes another realization. If no one is after them for the painting, then no one is coming to save me.

The waiter speaks to the driver, who then tosses a small bag, retrieved from the front passenger seat, back to him. Catching it, he unzips the main compartment – I peer in, expecting to find a gun. Instead, the waiter retrieves a black turtleneck and, bending forward so I can't see, whips off his hat and glasses, and throws the turtleneck over his white uniform. With the disguise back in place, he sits up. He speaks with the driver as he slides black slacks over the white ones stretched taut over his muscular legs. The waiter kicks off his shoes, reaches under the driver's seat for black sneakers, and stuffs his big feet into them. All the men wear similar outfits.

"Listen, you can drop me off here. I won't say anything to anyone. I promise," I say and stare at the thief, trying to unmask his eyes hidden beneath black shades. The beard and hair are fake, and even with sunglasses on, I may still be able to identify them. I've read enough crime stories to know your chance of survival diminishes when taken to a secondary location. I should have fought harder, screamed louder, bitten someone's ear off.

The worst part, I fear, is that when they find my body, I'll be wearing this horrendous raincoat. I hope they don't retrieve my body.

Nee-eu! Nee-eu! The wails of a police siren interrupt my morbid thoughts, but they sound more like an annoying car alarm than the rescuing sound of freedom. I don't care whether they are chasing the lady in red or the lady in the multi-colored raincoat. I can't contain my elation and a smug smile forms on my face.

The driver checks the rearview; concern mounts on his face that is duplicated on the others. The waiter yanks out a gun from somewhere. Startled, I gasp. He had lied when he told me he's a non-violent man. He stares at me; a petrified image of myself reflects back from his sunglasses. After a beat, he replaces the gun in his holster.

The other men shout in their foreign tongue until the waiter silences them. He points to his right, but in the confusion and screaming, the driver turns left. He makes a sharp turn onto a small, cobblestoned street. It's a dead end. The flashing police lights are now behind us. The driver shifts gears and reverses straight towards the police car. I scream.

"Aaahh!" the kidnapper whoops. His primal war scream blasts in my ear, silencing me. He smiles and it's the first time I see his toothy grin.

The Peugeot plows into the police vehicle. The impact throws me onto the waiter. I try to push myself off, but he has wrapped an arm around my waist. Our faces are so close that I consume his familiar smells, the mint on his breath, the bergamot of his cologne. The palms of my hands rest against his heaving chest. There was a spark between us at the gallery; no one can fake that kind of chemistry. *Damn*, he was the beddable type until he asked me to commit high-profile art thievery.

Finally, I manage to push myself off the waiter, my breathing deep and uncontrollable, my body's tingling an affront to my logical mind. Mentally, I lambast the betrayal like the adult me arguing with my horny teen self. Embarrassed, I avert his gaze. Why do I feel as though I'm on an early morning walk of shame after a night of great sex? Though I can't recall the last time that happened.

The vehicle has crammed the police car into a set of parked vehicles. It looks like an accordion, all creased and jumbled. The Peugeot continues reversing down the street until it reaches the end and turns right. The driver shifts the car into gear and squeals off. I catch a smile on the driver's face in the rearview. The thieves got away. I feel my life slip away.

We race down side streets and along the River Seine. Trees flash by, and up ahead is a bridge, its bends made to resemble a woman's curves. Leave it to the French to sexualize architecture. The driver eases on the accelerator as two police cars appear behind them, but by now I feel it's only to torment me with their teasing ways. The Peugeot picks up speed and squeezes into a bike lane, sending cyclists scrambling out of the way. I scream as the car narrowly misses a fleet of riders, then returns to the safety of the street amid a cacophony of horn blows. Along the way, we manage to lose one of the police cars.

The waiter uses an electronic screwdriver to carefully detach the painting from its frame. A sharp swerve causes him to stab his finger with the tool, and he barks something to the driver. Once done, he rolls the picture, inserts it into a tube, and then slips the tube and straps over his shoulder.

The getaway car takes another turn, no longer constrained on a narrow Parisian street. Another police car swoops in to take over the one left behind along the Seine, and we are back to having two police vehicles on us. The driver's hands tighten on the wheel. His eyes dart to the rearview mirror. A quick right finds us back on a narrow street. Uphill. Downhill. Up again. At one point, we are airborne, and I frantically reach for a seatbelt.

Finally, the sirens grow faint. I look back to see the police caught behind drivers clumsily pulling over to the side of the narrow roadway. I breath out a heavy groan, kicking myself for having followed the white rabbit down the hole.

In the brief moment the Peugeot is out of view from the police, and after a few turns, it manages a harsh right into an empty warehouse. The metal garage door clangs shut behind us. Then there is silence, the kind of silence whereby our breathing reverberates in the cavernous space. No one speaks, and in that quietude, the siren of a police car rushes past our secret hiding place.

I close my eyes. Had I known today would be my final day, then last night I would have... What exactly would I have done differently? Demand Pierre give me that job at the news magazine? Aggressively flirt with the Prince?

Someone mutters something that sounds like an order. My eyes flash open. Some of the warehouse windows are blasted out, and a rickety set of wooden stairs seem to lead nowhere like the apartment in *The Seven Year Itch*.

The men exit the car. I fumble with the red release button, and, in frustration, the waiter yanks off the seatbelt and pulls me out, pressing me hard against him. He puts his arm around me, a firm hand on my waist.

"Please, let me go," I whisper so only he can hear.

The driver sprays a fire extinguisher inside the car then rushes up the stairs to join the others. The men are oblivious to the two of us left behind, and the waiter's gaze follows his men up the steps, then back to me. It's a small favor I'm asking from him. I never asked for any of this and was minding my own business. My only mistake was to let the art absorb me, but *Mistress* absorbed me too well and sucked me into this mess.

Light floods the semi-darkness of the warehouse as someone flings a door open at the top of the staircase. A man races down towards them, machine-gun in hand; he is tall and thin and dressed in black with a baseball hat. He claps the backs of the men as they rush past him, but when he notices me, he angrily says something to the other men and points his gun in my direction. I tremble against the waiter.

The waiter shouts something. The gun-toting man hesitates, then heads back upstairs.

Finally, the waiter untangles his arm from around me and takes one step back, then mounts the stairs. He's letting me go. I let out the breath I hadn't realized I held and watch him ascend with the tube secure across his chest. I slide one foot backward, then another to slink out of the warehouse. *Crunch.* I step on the broken glass scattered on the floor and remain still, unsure if it's loud enough for him to hear. His back stiffens, and he stops mid-step, turns, and swiftly heads down, taking them two at a time. He must have changed his mind. I'm not going anywhere.

"No, no, no," I say, backing up until I hit the garage door. I bat at his hands as he reaches for me, but I'm like a kitten swatting at a ball of yarn. Frustrated, he bends, scoops me up, and throws me over his shoulder. The slippery plastic of the raincoat makes me slide down his back, and I grip his belt to avoid landing on my head. As I'm carried up the steps, I lift my head and eye the garage door that grows smaller in the distance. The rooftop is high enough to throw me from. Death by sidewalk is not an outcome I had considered, and, like many, I had hoped for a painless death surrounded by children and grandchildren.

The waiter throws open the door, and it clangs against a wall. A helicopter is on the roof. The swoosh of the blades wind up, idle at first, then spin faster until it's fully ramped up, the wind blows hair into my face as I struggle to look to the Seine beyond. They aren't the fly-by-night thieves I mistook them for. This is a decent Hollywood heist movie, and I'm the token female who maybe gets two scenes in the male-dominated genre.

The waiter puts me down and grabs my hand, dragging me as a stumble behind him. A familiar sound, faint at first but growing, tickles my ears. *Nee-eu. Nee-eu* – the sound had once lulled me into a false sense of security. I dare to have a bit of swelling hope. Will they actually get here on time to save me?

I hear the police smash through the warehouse door, and rushed French voices echo from below. I'm hoisted into the helicopter. The gun-toter sits at the controls while the primal warrior guy lands next to him. Across from me is the Peugeot driver, and the waiter is at my side. My stomach sinks with a heavy thud as the chopper lifts. The police burst through the rooftop door, but it's too late to save me now. They raise their guns and arbitrarily shoot. A bullet ricochets off the metal opening near me. Shock must be settling in because I don't react to what is happening around me. The waiter throws me down on the seat and lies on top of me, hands cupped to cover my head, his shaded eyes squarely on mine. I like the weight of him on me. We could have moved from the flirtation back at the tent to this in three easy steps, so why did he have to go blow what could have been a nice one-night stand?

A barrage of bullets whiz past. The pilot grunts and his body lurches forward. The helicopter dips and rises unsteadily, and my stomach follows the sickening motion. The waiter yells something but who could hear over the sound of the spinning rotor? When the co-pilot places a hand on him, the pilot swats him away as though irritated by the attention and assures every-one he's fine and steadies the machine.

The chopper rolls sideways and flies over the Seine. The waiter lifts himself from me, but I remain flat on the seat. I was supposed to call my parents this morning but forgot, and now my final words to my mother are: "For the last time, the eggplant emoji doesn't mean what you think it does."

I try to sit up, but swoon when I view the vertiginous drop to the water below, and fall against the waiter. Instinctively, his hand goes to the tube across his chest. *Mistress in a Red Dress* is safe against his body just as I had been moments earlier. Is it possible that he doesn't mean to harm me? Then, he would have left me back at the warehouse. I steal glances at my captors, wondering what's next. Do they plan to toss me into the Seine below? I could try to swim, but we're so high up that death seems more likely.

The helicopter glides over the water, edges higher. I discern people waving from boats that litter the water below, tiny people in tiny vessels waving with tiny hands. The chopper pitches nose down, and the pilot slumps forward unconscious, his back soaked in blood. He's bleeding out. My stomach drops like I'm on a roller coaster, and the waiter shouts something at one of his partners.

The man next to the pilot pulls him back into his seat and reaches for the controls. Still, we dip, then plunge, and spin. It reminds me of a ride at Coney Island when I went with a boy I liked. I felt invincible then, but now what is all this vomit-inducing turmoil a prelude to except death? I can't tell which way is up until the co-pilot straightens the chopper with a jerk that pitches me across the seat and out the door.

It feels like an out-of-body experience where I watch my hand reach for the metal legs of the seats, but miss, and my legs dangle over the side. Something keeps me up; my arm, caught in the seatbelt of the chopper, stops me from falling completely. I struggle to grab the seatbelt with my other hand, but gravity has its own idea and drops me a few more inches.

The waiter frantically stretches his arm out for me, motioning for me to meet him halfway. Our hands make contact. "Let her go!" someone yells in English – but the waiter ignores them. His hands tighten around mine. His face reddens, and between clenched teeth, he shouts at his men. The chopper descends.

The Peugeot driver now lies on his belly next to the waiter, his short arms outstretched, but unable to make contact. My legs swing in the air, the revolting raincoat balloons upwards.

I struggle to hang on. My sweaty hand slips. Frantically, I lash out with my arms, grasping at anything, but find only air. The waiter's sunglasses crash towards the earth with me.

"Oh, non. Non!" he yells.

My raincoat balloons out as a parachutist, then flaps wildly about my head, blocking my screams. Icy water cuts through me like glass, slices through my feet, my legs, my arms. The raincoat turns upside down and inside out, wraps itself around my head, arms straight up. An undercurrent pulls me.

I'm not sure how much longer I can hold my breath. I struggle against the copious yards of opalescent plastic.

Remain calm.

Stop struggling.

I don't know which way is up. My arms flap. I take an involuntary breath, and water rushes in through my nose and mouth and into my lungs. This is drowning.

Something grabs me. I tell myself not to breathe, but my body betrays me.

Up.

Air smacks my face.

I'm dragged along a hard surface. People shout.

Something is pushing down on my chest, hurting me.

Now someone is kissing me.

Chapter 6

1. Paris Fashion Week – Trending

#TheDevilWearsOrange

@BitchinDiva8901

OMG moron alert! #EditorInThief Charlotte Milton took selfie before stealing painting #TheDevilWearsOrange #MistressInARedDress

@CondeNasty6758

Arrogance américaine à son meilleur #TheDevilWearsOrange #MistressInARedDress #EditorInThief

@FashionSmasher4367

Hey @CatwalkStyleMag is there an opening? Shame on you if you keep #EditorInThief as part of your brand. If you do, I'll #cancel my subscription #TheDevilWearsOrange #BoycottCatwalkStyleMag

@Anthro4Ever4264

I'm an anthropology major. Back in the day they pilloried peeps in the center of town to shame them. Who needs a whipping post when you have social media? #TheDevilWearsOrange #MistressInARedDress

@FashionSmasher4367
Masthead on @CatwalkStyleMag's web page just deleted #EditorInThief's name. #Fired!!! I'm #liveposting from police station waiting for her release #TheDevilWearsOrange

@PradaButNot4118
Anyone see that clip on YouTube? Did she drown? And what's she wearing? Obviously something #ToDieFor #OOTD #TheDevilWearsOrange

@HarrietCatwalkStyleMag
Drinking game. One shot every time someone posts #TheDevilWearsOrange

@AnneCatwalkStyleMag
Replying to @HarrietCatwalkStyleMag
This isn't funny @HarrietCatwalkStyleMag. The police want to speak with us. OMG what do we tell them?

@HarrietCatwalkStyleMag
OH FOR GOD'S SAKE @AnneCatwalkStyleMag learn to DM properly

@PradaButNot4118
Miranda Priestly be all like "Who is that sad little person?" #TheDevilWearsOrange #EditorInThief

Chapter 7

T HE PARIS POLICE HEADQUARTERS is a large building tucked into a square of Place Louis Lépine in the 4th *arrondissement*. Once a barracks, the 19th-century building sits across public space; stone benches run the length of manicured shrubs outlined by a tree-lined street. Beside it, the Seine laps against the stone walkway of the canal.

When they first brought me in, dripping wet and wrapped in a blanket, I was too shaken to understand the chaos surrounding the front of the headquarters. An officer inside asked if I was okay, to which I mumbled something incoherent. Another officer took my raincoat, and then I was made to sit in a wooden chair. The man next to me had wrinkled his nose and eyed me up and down. I smelled like the Seine, but I wanted to ask him what was his excuse?

Eventually, they escorted me down a corridor and into a stark white room with a white square table and chairs. Hours have passed since then, and now I'm hungry and tired; my hair is frizzy, my makeup smudged, and my damp clothes wrinkled. I look to the now destroyed Jimmy Choos on my feet and shift uneasily in my chair. I'm glad I trashed the wet Spanx earlier when I used the *toilet*, though it was like peeling off blood-sucking leeches. Yet, it's the two interrogating officers across from me, Lieutenants Pascale and Riel, who behave as though their day has been far more taxing. Pascale is the younger of the two, with near white-blond hair to match his fair skin, almost passing for an albino. Riel buries his head in his hands, elbows on the table, fingers raking through his grey hair. When he pulls his hands away from his face, the movement exposes his cheeks, ruby red, and eyes, puffy. They've been slogging away for hours with no relief and, obviously, they're playing at something to deliberately draw out this interrogation. To what end? To wear me down? I've already told them everything I know.

"I don't understand why I am still here," I say in English.

Again, I reiterate my story to the officers and, though I've been at it all day speaking with them in French, perhaps this time they will listen if I speak slower. It is now evening, and I haven't spoken to a familiar face since my kidnapping this morning. My voice grows hoarse. My stomach growls for food, and I crave a baguette with brie and strong French coffee.

I let out a heavy sigh and whine about them wasting time while the kidnappers are still at large, but the detectives look to one another in utter frustration. We have been at a standstill for hours now, with, as far as I can tell, nothing being done about the crime committed against me. Riel places his head in his hands again and wearily mutters something to Pascale. Pascale grows agitated, points to me, and bangs his hands on the table. I jump back in my chair.

"Whoa. Maybe it's time for a break." My suggestion is lost among the raised voices.

Now, Riel turns to bang on the table as the two men turn on one another. I'd like to slink out of the room unnoticed, perhaps find food and a phone to call Pierre and Harriet and my parents – anything to get away from the madness escalating in this room.

A knock at the door draws everyone's attention away from the argument. After a moment, Riel opens the door then steps aside. A new figure, who resembles Anne, appears at the door, and when she takes a timid step into the room, I realize she *is* Anne.

"Anne," I say with great relief and rush to her, wrapping my arms around her. Anne reciprocates with a tight embrace.

"Oh, Charlotte, if you needed money, why didn't you come to me?"

Baffled, I pull away. Did the Keystone Cops get to Anne too? Have they presented her with falsified evidence and turned my friend against me?

"Anne, I didn't do anything wrong. Tell them what that man told you this morning when you were in the Tuileries with Chase."

Skittish, Anne looks down and mutters something under her breath.

I say, "I didn't catch that."

"I'm sorry," says Anne, "but I already told them. No one threatened me."

"I saw that man threaten you. You looked horrified."

Anne's eyes widen, and her mouth falls open. "Oh, *that* man. He didn't threaten me. He told me a frightening piece of news about this toxic material found in baby bottles that becomes dangerous when heated. I stopped breastfeeding after my nipples became chapped and bled, and have been lying to my militant pro-breastfeeding mommy's group ever since. OK, sure, breastfeeding is probably better, but maybe this isn't a one solution fits all scenario, you know? Choosing not to breastfeed doesn't make me a horrible mother."

I blink. I will spend eternity in a jail cell isolated by a cliff overlooking the ocean, with only a spoon to dig my way out, but somehow Anne has made this about herself. "Anne, please listen to me. I need you to speak to someone at the American Embassy."

"I already have. They said they'll keep a close eye on the trial."

"Trial? I haven't been charged with anything."

Riel grows agitated and waves Anne off. As he escorts her out, I try to get in as many words as I can. "Go back to them. Have Pierre get me a lawyer."

Before the door closes, Anne wails, "Oh, Charlotte, the theft is all over the news, and, well, Pierre says you're done at *Catwalk*!"

The door slams shut, the reverberation resonates with those last few words. *Pierre says you're done at Catwalk!* There's plenty of ramifications packed in those tiny words. Now, who will protect Anne from Pierre? Certainly not Harriet. And how dare Pierre fire me? I was at the gallery doing my job for his magazine when I was threatened and literally kidnapped. I need to get my hands on a phone, speak to Pierre, explain the whole thing, and get my job back. Sounds simple enough, but what if he says no? Stupidly, I believed that my friends would rally behind me and that the American Embassy would demand my release, yet Anne has confirmed my worst fears. I'm alone in a foreign jail under some awful lighting that is washing me out.

Chapter 8

P ROFESSOR JACK CAREY LOOKS at his watch, a digital model that does things he has no use for. When he first began teaching, he carried an old pocket watch his grandfather gave him, but it made him look old and stodgy, much like his grandfather had been, so he stopped carrying it. He removes his round-framed glasses, lifts a kerchief from his breast pocket, and wipes his lenses, never mind that they were already clean before this little ritual of his. He inspects them under the harsh, fluorescent lights and, accepting them as clear, rests them high on the bridge of his nose where he likes them. He picks at a thread fraying from his tweed jacket and doesn't know enough to stop before he causes too much damage. It unravels the cuff of his sleeve, and he decides to leave it for Mrs. Getty, his housekeeper, to mend when he returns home.

Finally, he looks back to the other side of the one-way mirror and stares at a dejected woman identified as Charlotte Milton. Her interrogator, Capitaine Favreau, was cold and harsh and left her in a state. Jack was granted partial access to a Parisian police file assembled on her. There's little to indicate her involvement in the high stakes game of cat and mouse in the world of art thievery, at least not as an experienced player. Hollywood's version of an art thief is the Thomas Crown type – dashing and rich, educated, and cunning. This, Jack knows, is an absolute fabrication. There are plenty of thieves who don't understand the game and bite off more than they can handle, stealth-like when breaking into a home to steal a painting but lacking the know-how to dispose of it. They assume if the painting's worth one million dollars, they should clear at least half that when, more than likely, they'll make a small fraction of its true value. Unloading the painting is problematic if they don't know how to filter it back into the legitimate art market without anyone wising up to it. These stupid thieves would do well with Jack's expertise.

Charlotte doesn't fit the profile of an art thief, nor, Favreau has told him, do they consider her the architect behind the daring theft. They believe she was handpicked for an inside job. The masterminding criminals probably uncovered Charlotte's financial mess, just as the police did, and exploited her vulnerability, persuading her that a minor transgression would lead to a significant financial gain.

Favreau appears next to him. Jack hadn't even heard the door open. Both stare at the suspect, her head forward against the palm of her hand, biting her lower lip.

"I trust your flight from Oxford was smooth?" Favreau asks him.

"It certainly was, thank you."

"And you are finished teaching for the year?"

"No." Jack has a couple more weeks left but can rely on his teaching assistant if need be. He had been in the middle of class, watching his Art History students hunched over their desks, furiously writing their final test when he received the call from Detective Chief Inspector Crane of the Art and Antiques Squad in Scotland Yard.

"*Mistress In A Red Dress,*" DCI Crane had said, "was stolen this morning from Paris."

And would he, could he, if at all possible, get on a plane to Paris immediately to help? Jack knew it was on loan from The British Museum in London just as it had been the last time it was stolen.

Montréal was the first time Interpol had asked for Jack's help, flew him over and set him up with a couple of detectives from their art theft unit. Several high-profile paintings were stolen, including *Mistress in a Red Dress*. After nearly a year into the investigation, *Mistress* was the only one found during a sting operation that saw Jack play decoy as a would-be buyer for a Lord in England. With the intelligence gained from Jack's reconnaissance, they followed a group of men into a small town outside Montréal. They discovered the painting hidden in the trunk of an abandoned vehicle on a farm. Jack spent four hours sitting with *Mistress in a Red Dress* at the police station, and the French-Canadian police joked he was courting his new girlfriend. For his involvement, Jack met the Queen and personally returned it to her in a show before the cameras. It was his proudest moment.

"There are no checks and balances in this world of art," says Favreau with weariness in his voice. "The world has gone mad in some way. Criminals behave like spoiled children wandering through a shopping mall with their parents, pointing to a Rembrandt, a Munch, saying I want this and that, *maman et papa, s'il te plaît*. They possess an inherent sense of entitlement. If it's there, it must be stolen." A heavy sigh escapes Favreau. "Nowadays, most of the galleries and museums don't discover the robbery until much later."

"That must make it difficult for you," Jack offers, suspecting Favreau needs to unload his burdens.

"Of course. One must work backward, look into the art world, follow the trail that will lead you to the person or persons of interest. Ah, but this time, we got lucky. We have her."

Favreau points to Charlotte, his index finger pressed against the mirror, paint rubbed on his digits' tips. Favreau strikes Jack as the type of man who fancies himself an artist, painting nudes on his days off. This is personal to him, and he's in it for the long game, patiently biding his time to wait out the thieves for the *Mistress*.

"And we have you," Favreau says. "You have quite the reputation. How do you see this playing out?"

"Well," Jack starts, contemplating his answer, "she won't tell you anything, probably because they kept all the other details from her. It's how they operate; don't tell the right hand what the left hand is doing and you won't get caught. Chances are she knows who they are." Jack mulls it over for a moment. "Offer her a deal. Or get her to trust you, and she will lead you to them."

Jack looks at his watch again, the lateness in the day now taking its toll. This was easy enough, he thinks, surprised the Parisian police haven't asked much from him. Jack has been called upon exactly three other times by Canada, Belgium, and Switzerland. Clearly, Interpol doesn't hold the incident in Belgium against him, for it was someone there who supplied his name to Favreau.

The Belgian authorities approached Jack about a Devereux painting stolen from a museum in Portugal. The plan was simple. An undercover police officer impersonated a buyer, but they required Jack to confirm the painting's authenticity before an arrest could be made. All that was required of him was to establish "yay" or "nay," but when he sat with the undercover cop and the two thieves in the lobby of a hotel, the Devereux wrapped in plastic, Jack became furious. He admonished them for not protecting the work that should have been covered in a velvet cloth and stored flat in a room temperature at 70 – 72 degrees Fahrenheit.

His lecture continued for another ten minutes while the undercover cop next to him grew agitated with each passing minute. Jack finally confirmed its authenticity by the brush strokes and numbering on the back of the painting. They retrieved the painting, arrested the thieves, but the Belgian police refused to use him again after that.

As for the Swiss, well, Jack swore he'd never work for them again after they made him close a transaction in a hotel room without a wire for fear the thieves would search him. He was literally on his own with no way to contact help. Matters worsened when a breakdown in communication between Interpol and the local police had the local authority charge into the room. Wires were crossed, information not shared, and they believed an illegal gun transaction was taking place. The police, fully armed in battle dress uniform from head to toe, peered at him through red goggles. Jack recalls throwing himself to the floor and tried to remember the Swiss-German words for "Don't shoot. Civilian."

"There was a time," says Favreau, interrupting Jack's memories, "when I had more resources, but now between stolen art versus worker protests, violent crimes, and now terrorism, art loses. The resources available to me are limited to listing the stolen painting with Interpol, Art Loss Register, and sending out a media release across Europe, North America, and Asia. These are things people ignore. All this to say, there's another option. The lady won't trust me, however, she doesn't know *you*, Professor."

This sounds too much like Switzerland. Don't the police understand his role is to offer expertise, not to be thrown into the fire? Though perhaps he needs to retrieve that assured cockiness he had with the Belgian job. That would be one way to deal with this Milton woman.

"The timing couldn't be worse," Jack answers adamantly, flustered and shakes his head so hard he's afraid he'll sprain it. "I have tests to mark so I'm afraid I'll have to decline." Besides, he'd like to tell Favreau, he has a planned vacation, which includes a lecture in London on the relationship between Van Gogh's art and his color choices. And before he runs off, he'll need to prep his private garden, which once received an Honorable Mention of Recognition from the Oxford Horticultural Society of Women. Jack is the only male in the group. This year, he's determined to place in the top three.

Favreau doesn't seem to have heard him because he says, "Do a little reconnaissance, track her whereabouts, gather information, and report back to me. After all, it is a little flattering for you, *non?*"

"How so?"

"The thieves, too, admire the painting. They keep stealing your *Mistress*, Professor."

Chapter 9

I WON'T SURVIVE PRISON alone. Chances are I'd make a fine *femme*, a tasty little morsel for the most terrifying female serial killer in the French prison system. Sure, there'd be a learning curve or two, but from there, I'd do quite well. Oh, the power I could wield. The favors I could demand. If boredom settles in, I will hold a fashion show. Or even better, design my own clothing line from behind prison walls. *Chateau d'If Milton*.

Down the corridor from the cell I'm sitting in, a door opens and clanks shut. I lift myself from the hard bench I've sat on for more than an hour now and stretch; my body cracks as I lengthen each limb. A police officer comes to my cell; the name *Coteau* appears in white on a black nameplate.

"Charlotte Milton, you've been released. Follow me, and we'll get forms signed," he says. His English is impeccable. Where was he earlier when I needed him?

Undoubtedly, I've misunderstood, and when he unlocks the cell door and stands aside with the door ajar, I wonder if I should make a run for it. My eyes dart around the room. No, they'd intercept and toss me back in with their maniacal Parisian laughter drifting into my cell.

"Out," he says again.

I follow him out of the cellblock in a daze, down a blue and white corridor, and into the station's central area. Dozens of police officers sit at wooden desks either on the phone or banging away at computer keyboards with all ten digits. My nose catches a whiff of cigarette smoke when an officer returns from break.

"This way," Coteau says and leads me to a desk where a bookish gentleman sits. When I near him, he offers me his chair, and I nod in thanks. He appears to be in his early forties, clean-shaven, with an attractive face tucked beneath circular, old man glasses. He's wearing a tweed jacket with tan slacks I'm sure my grandfather wore in the '80s. Before I sit, I mentally give him a makeover, picturing him in dark jeans, a white shirt, and a checkered Prada jacket. I'd complete the look with white sneakers. That would take care of his civil servant vibe.

"Sign here," says Coteau, sitting at the desk across from me, "and here."

I scan the document he places in front of me. "It's in French. It will take time to read through it."

Coteau sighs. "It says you understand the charges against you are still pending, and further investigation into the matter is required in a shellnut, as you Americans are fond of saying."

I refrain from correcting *shellnut*. "There must be more than that."

Coteau cocks his head. "*Mademoiselle*, it takes ten French words to every English word, but please, feel free to use the *Capitaine*'s private office while you sound out the words for two hours." His facetious tone sounds worse with the accent.

"There's no denying you're French." Turning to the bookish man next to me, I say, "Are you going to allow him to speak to me this way, or does the American Embassy have some backbone?"

The gentleman appears caught unawares, his mouth gapes open, and his eyes flicker between me and the officer. He babbles a response. "I'm afraid I'm not who you think I am. Ms. Milton, my name is Professor Jack Carey, and I teach Art History at Oxford University."

"Oh," I say and take the hand he has extended. "Nice to meet you."

I'm desperate to get out of here, exhausted from the physical and emotional ordeal, so after a beat of hesitation, I sign my name at the bottom. I'm not thinking clearly, and right now, I want a bacon cheeseburger and to soak in that spa tub in my hotel room to get the stench of the day off. Before releasing the form, I say to Coteau, "Now, are you sure it doesn't say anything else that I should know about?"

"Non."

I relinquish the document.

From a desk drawer, Coteau pulls a clear plastic bag of my belongings and slides it across to me. Ripping the bag apart, I dump its contents for inspection. My hands skirt over one purse, two red lipsticks, cell phone, a Dior hand mirror, notepad with pages clipped together, one silver pen, two cheaper backup pens, scarf, sunglasses, and one condom wrapper, its corners worn from being in my purse longer than I'd hoped.

"You found my handbag. What's this powder?" I say, rubbing my fingers together, then toss the items, except for my cell phone, into my purse.

Coteau says, "All items were swept for fingerprints."

"Glad you retrieved my purse from where I dropped it during the kidnapping." I turn on my phone, but the screen remains black. "Is the fingerprint powder known to destroy electronics?"

Coteau shrugs. "Maybe."

"Maybe?" I repeat, aghast. "If it's destroyed, you owe me a new phone."

"Very well, *Mademoiselle*, and you owe us a painting."

Teeth clenched, I think of ways to use my 500,000 followers on social media to unleash fury at the Parisian police for wrongfully detaining me. Then, I remember the 500,000 followers aren't mine but belong to the editor-in-chief at *Catwalk Style Magazine*, a position I've been fired from. I can start over, but how many will be interested in what I have to say without the power and influence I once wielded? I need to persuade Pierre to reinstate me.

"*Mademoiselle*, you signed here that all your personal items have been returned to you in the manner that we found them," he says and holds up the document.

He's right. It's my signature on the page, written in a flourish like a celebrity autograph. I reach over the desk in an attempt to grab the document, but to no avail. Turning to Jack for help, I say, "You saw what he did. He tricked me. Do something."

Jack holds his hands up and shrugs his shoulders with a flabbergasted *what-can-I-do?* expression.

"Useless," I hiss and storm off.

"Don't go through the front," Coteau calls after me.

I stop mid-stride and face the police officer, my head to its side, a hand on my hip. "Why?"

"Press is outside. We have a back exit for this purpose."

"I can handle a few reporters," I say.

"Don't underestimate the Parisian press, *Mademoiselle* #Editor-in-Thief."

In a huff, I storm down the yellow corridor, take a wrong turn and backtrack until I hit a door marked *Sortie*. The cool night air smacks me hard, and I gulp it, listen as the Seine laps against the water's edge. I wonder if I still smell like the river. Pulling at my top, I sniff, then grimace at the stench of sweat and perfume with a hint of urine, which may not necessarily be the river's fault.

"Excuse me, Ms. Milton, a word, please."

I glance over my shoulder to see the Professor trailing behind me. I keep moving without acknowledging him.

"I would like to help you."

The clickety-clack of my footsteps hitting the cobblestones stop. I'm tired and hungry and worn down, and when an absolute stranger says they'd like to help, all instinct tells me to run the other direction, but I'm not in my right frame of mind. I turn, and in the semidarkness, he reminds me of Mr. Pepperman, my eighth-grade science teacher who failed me on an assignment when I refused to cut up a frog.

"Help how?" I say. My voice sounds more irritated than tired, which isn't my intention.

A car turns a corner, heads down the street, and when it comes into view, I note the sign's green illumination. "Taxi!" I scream, but the cab rushes past. I look about distractedly, crossing the empty street, and whistle for the taxi, but it is too far gone.

"May I ask where you're going?" says Jack.

"My hotel," I say and look about to the empty street. "Where are all the cabs?"

"It's after midnight, and they tend not to pick up fares outside a police station. I have a rental nearby. I can give you a lift."

I squint at him, bothered by his eagerness. "Who did you say you are?"

"Professor Jack Carey. I teach Art History at Ox–"

"–Oxford, that's right. And why are you here? At the police station?"

"I'd like for you to help me retrieve the painting. You see, this is the second time it has been stolen."

"Hmmm, you'd think the French would have learned from their mistake the first time around."

"Ten years ago, it was stolen from a museum in Montréal."

"Ah, French Canadian then."

"Yes."

"Still French."

"Technically." Jack mutters.

My eyes hover over him. "Anyway, I don't need your help."

Jack smiles at me, casts a steady, assured gaze, and says, "It's late, Ms. Milton. I'm exhausted, and I have a briefcase full of tests to mark at the office. Still, I believe we can help one another. I'd like to ask you some questions, maybe something will be remembered, something you neglected to tell—"

"—Where is it?"

"The painting?"

"Your rental," I snap. I strain my eyes shut, nod, then look at him. "Sorry, I'm exhausted, and I shouldn't take it out on you," I say in an attempt to eclipse my inelegance.

"Being knackered gets to the best of us. It's nearby."

Jack leads the way down one street, then left to another where little European cars are sandwiched one behind the other on both sides of the road. I tramp past him before I realize he's opened the door to a red Peugeot.

"You've got to be kidding me?" I groan.

"Pardon?"

"Nothing. I love Peugeots. Very roomy in the back. And the shock absorption is marvelous." I slide into the passenger seat and bump my head on the way in.

"Are you alright?"

"I'm fine. The Ritz, please," I say, sounding as though I'm speaking to my personal driver. I dig into my purse, fingers run across my notepad and graze the curled edge of that condom wrapper, and finally I pull out my phone.

"Do you have a car phone charger? I need to see if my phone works."

Jack points to the glove compartment where I find it and set it up for my phone. I'm relieved when the charging symbol displays. Immediately, I dial Pierre's number, but it goes to voicemail.

"Pierre, it's Charlotte." My voice comes on strong and happy though I feel neither. "I'm on my way to my hotel. Let's talk in the morning. I can explain..." I laugh, but it sounds hollow and not at all like my own... "and it's quite funny, really, you'll laugh when I tell you about the ordeal and ineptitude of the police. Anyway, I'll be ready to jump right back into work tomorrow morning. Good night." I disconnect. Perhaps my message will have him forget he fired me.

Next, I call my parents. Mom answers, and Dad gets on the extension. Both speak over the other and ask questions without giving me time to respond, like when they caught me smoking weed with a friend, and they took turns hammering their disappointment. They beg me to come home, and already arranged a meeting with a high-powered lawyer (my father repeats "high-powered lawyer" several times), but I swear one isn't necessary. Besides, knowing my parents, they'd remortgage their home to pay for legal bills if need be. I'm not about to become a financial burden on them at my age. I'm spent, but after ending the call, I contemplate making others to friends. To say what exactly? Everyone will want an explanation, and that will take too long. Besides, it's the middle of the night.

I settle into my seat, and we drive through the dark, narrow streets in silence. I glance at the French apartment buildings that whiz past, the ones that house French people living their French lives and eating freshly baked bread, sipping lattes, and reading good books. The truth is I envy the European *laissez-faire* lifestyle, something that could never survive in a place like New York.

Watching Jack thump his index finger on the steering wheel, I can tell that the silence unnerves him. He motions to the radio and turns the knob. It blares, forcing him to lower the volume in a hurried movement. A late-night talk show fills the car, a caller speaks passionately and eloquently about freedom and novels and the beauty of art. And then the name Charlotte Milton spills from the radio, and my blood runs cold. They speak about me as though I'm a criminal. Of course, the police offered me as a scapegoat to the people of France.

Jack snaps the radio off.

"Thank you," I say, my voice soft.

The Peugeot rounds a corner to the Ritz, where we see a crowd of paparazzi. I strain my neck for a better view and wonder if the press has mistaken Harriett for Naomi. Again. As we edge closer, a photographer glances our way and peers inside the car. His facial expression gives way to recognition, and he snaps photos, though I can't understand what has him so enraptured. His frenetic clicks with his camera garner the crowd's attention and, in no time, all the paparazzi descend on us. Flashes blind us. Some scream my name and, in all the chaos that surrounds us, I realize they are here for me. Something has been happening, has been growing during those long hours I was locked away at the police station. In that absence, I became a celebrity for doing a very bad thing.

"Drive. Drive," I sputter.

Jack throws the car in gear, beeps for people to get out of the way. Panic-stricken, I hide my face from the flashes, pull at my top, and stretch it over my head. Jack reassures me that he will get us out. Sirens appear and grow louder. According to his play-by-play, the police arrive and take over the scene, moving the paparazzi out of the way and waving Jack out.

Once the car is in motion for some time, I pull the sweater away from my face. I look back, but no one follows. The police won't allow a paparazzi chase through their streets again.

"Pull over, please."

Jack obliges.

Clumsily, I reach for the door latch and exit, gulping air, and slump against the car. I thrive on chaos and deadlines and near-impossible tasks, but this colossal misunderstanding is too much for me to fix.

"It's over," I say. My breath becomes shallow. There's a pain in my chest like an elephant has decided I'm a good resting spot. I can't breathe. There's a warm touch on my shoulder, and a calm voice whispers in my ear.

"I think you're having a panic attack," says Jack. "Ride the wave. Don't fight it. Fighting will make it worse."

But I need to fight – for my job, my reputation, my life.

"Look at me."

His voice draws my eyes to his bespectacled face.

"Ride the wave. Understand?"

There's something soothing in the steady calmness of his voice, and I give into his control. I stop fighting against my body and abandon all thought, let myself go to ride the wave like I'm on a surfboard, and the ocean is the problem I just conquered. The chest pain subsides. My breathing returns at a regular pace.

"Okay," I tell Jack, and we get back in the car.

Settled, I scoop up the cell phone that's charging next to me and dial a number. My breath deepens with every ring.

Someone on the other end picks up, sucks in deeply, and blows out what I know is cigarette smoke. Harriet says, "Hello, Charlotte. What do you need, and where should I meet you?"

Chapter 10

J ACK'S INABILITY TO PENETRATE Charlotte's inky sunglasses unnerves him. How can he read her facial expressions if he can't see into the windows of her soul? His blazer, which she borrowed, hangs loosely over her shoulders, its collar flipped up below wisps of her hair tucked beneath a headscarf. Earlier, he witnessed Charlotte pull these items from her purse as a disguise from the paparazzi; not that there are any in this little cafe he has brought her to. No one is here at this time of night, and the waiter seemed ready to close before they threw open the door.

Charlotte reapplies lipstick, a small mirror secure in her hand. She smacks her lips, tucks the mirror away, and scoops up the menu. How can she see anything through those sunglasses? She looks like a giant fly poring over the menu, and instantaneously, his mind retrieves a memory from young adulthood. He's sitting in the TV room watching Cronenberg's Naked Lunch, the *unfilmable* film that his brother, Richard, made him watch, stoned. Richard had fetched a container of brownies from his room and, though Jack questioned the verity of his brother baking anything, into his mouth the brownie went. It wasn't long before he realized his mistake.

Charlotte wiggles a finger at the waiter, and he plods over. Jack watches with amusement as she orders, marveling at the changes made to each item for her preference. She'll have the chef's selection of cheeses, but no blue. The mushrooms sound lovely, but they would be lovelier cooked with truffle oil. Do they serve side orders of bread? And finally, poached doesn't mean over-cooked. After, Jack is quite surprised when she turns to him and asks what he will have. He thought she had ordered for him as well.

"Café." He smiles at their waiter as he passes the menus back.

"I'm curious about something," says Charlotte once the waiter walks away.

"Yes?"

"Why are you helping me? I don't know you. I meet you at the police station and here we are in…" Charlotte's words trail into a whisper, her brows furrow to indicate her thoughts catching up. "Oh," she says finally. "I understand now. You're a reporter, aren't you?"

"No, I'm a professor at Oxford. I'll show you." Jack pulls out his wallet and opens it to perfectly lined plastic – credit cards, driver's license, and an assortment of rewards cards. "I have my identification somewhere. Ah, this should do," he says and holds up his library card.

She snatches the card and flips it front to back and front again, studies it. "Anyone can get a library card from their local university," she says and returns it.

"Actually, not anyone can. I teach Art History and I have a special interest in following this case… um, for myself."

Charlotte removes her cell phone from her purse. Staring at it, color fades from her face.

"What is it?" says Jack.

"I can't access my social media accounts. Or my work email, for that matter." Her voice softens. "Pierre already had IT yank my access." Her eyes pounce on Jack, a sudden fire to them that invigorates her. "Do you know what condition the magazine was in when I became its editor-in-chief? It was barely hanging on, draining Papineau Publishing's resources. Pierre tried to sell it, but no one wanted it. I made it what it is today." She slinks in her chair and groans. "My dedication to the magazine meant I spent every waking moment working for or planning or thinking about it, about future articles, themes. I chose integrity instead of giving into the advertisers to do the best job possible for their readers, and he repays me by firing me? He didn't reach out to see if I was all right. He cut the cord just like that." Charlotte snaps her fingers. "He is such a jerk."

"I'm sorry you're going through this," Jack says and his empathy seems to settle her. "I meant it when I said I can help in some small way. I'm well versed in *Capitaine* Favreau's type and know how to deal with him." He reminds himself not to push. After all, it's better to have her believe she needs his help. "But, if you don't need my services, I can return to England…"

"I didn't say that," she says. "Besides, you're all I have. No one's rushing to my defense. Except my parents, but they're so far away."

If there's one thing Jack's learned from his previous forays into the world of stolen works, it's that there's an art to going undercover. Don't stray too far from the truth, it makes lying easier. Humor and a casual approach give criminals a false sense of security and build on the camaraderie that otherwise wouldn't exist between the two. Put your subject at ease, master them, and gain their trust.

The waiter arrives with two freshly brewed coffees; the strength of the smell alone can wake the dead.

"*Merci*," Jack tells him before he stomps off.

Charlotte tosses her sunglasses on the table, then scoops three spoonfuls of sugar into her steaming cup. Later, the waiter returns with food – an assortment of cheese and bread, no blue, bouillabaisse soup, mushrooms cooked in truffle oil, and poached pears in a wine sauce – plates clinking as he lays them down.

Charlotte rips apart her bread and generously butters it. "Mmmm, this is delicious. I like to get a bit of everything. Are you sure you don't want anything?"

"Positive." Jack smiles and sips his black coffee. He watches her tug at a mushroom at the end of her fork. She smears cheese onto buttered bread and pops it into her mouth, then devours the poached pear with such gusto that he's rather entertained. He's used to awkward first dates where women nibble at their food like mice and pass on dessert, which sucks, because he always wants dessert. Not that tonight is anywhere close to a date.

His eyes drift to his jacket she wears flung over her shoulders and then down to the sleeve that now rests on the tabletop, the cuff unraveled. He's neat and orderly and not normally like this, but she has no way of knowing this. Charlotte's gaze creeps up to his hands that caress a coffee cup, bore a hole into his fingers and, if he were to guess, he'd say his wedding finger, in particular. Surely, the marking left behind from the wedding ring he once wore has faded by now. The thought makes him giddy, and his body releases norepinephrine and dopamine, and serotonin. He feels betrayed.

Between bites, Charlotte says, "Sorry for being cruel earlier. There's no excuse."

"You've had a bad day."

"We've all had bad days," she says and pauses to sip her coffee. "Oprah's big on forgiveness. She says without it, we hold ourselves back in our lives."

"Well, who am I to quarrel with Oprah? I forgive you. Shall I do a sign of the cross to finalize it?"

Charlotte smiles and says, "It's partly your fault anyway."

"Absolutely, it is, but would you mind explaining how so?"

"It's disconcerting how similar you are to my eighth-grade science teacher, Mr. Pepperman. He failed me on an assignment for refusing to cut up a dead frog in biology. I'm still harboring negative feelings towards him."

"Careful there. It could lead to some serious PTSD."

"Teachers can do that. They're cruel sometimes," she says, slurping soup.

Jack raises his eyebrows at her. "Really? I like to think I'm cruel *all* the time."

She looks up at him. "Shit. There I go again. Being mean."

"You should consider teaching as a profession," he says with a smile.

"Charlotte."

They both turn to the voice. An enormously tall woman stands by the door with suitcases in hand. Charlotte wipes her hands with the cotton napkin, flings Jack's jacket from her shoulders, and runs to hug the woman. She doesn't hug Charlotte back. Charlotte's eyes light up at the sight of a valise that sits on top of the larger suitcase. "Oh, my shoes, how I missed you so. I've been stuck with these water-damaged Jimmy Choos all day." She lifts a foot to show the woman, who merely sneers. "Sit down," Charlotte says warmly, slides into her chair and indicates the seat next to her. The woman, upon seeing Jack, changes her demeanor and sits next to him instead.

"Harriet Higginbottom," she says with a smile, extends her hand to him, and leans in rather close.

"Professor Jack Carey. Always a pleasure to meet a fellow Brit."

"Yes, it is." Harriet's smile widens. "Where do you teach?"

"Oxford." This seems to impress Harriet to no end.

"Oh, really!" Harriet squeals. "Charlotte, you never told me you're friends with an academic."

"We just met," says Charlotte, but Harriet seems too engrossed with him to have heard Charlotte.

Harriet says, "And what do you teach?"

"Art History."

"How wonderful. You must be very popular among your students."

Jack blushes, shakes his head.

"You've got to be kidding me?" says Charlotte in disbelief. "My life is in shambles and you two find the time to flirt?"

"You'll have to excuse Charlotte, Professor. She's had a terrible day."

"Of course," says Jack, "we should be thinking about...well about..."

"Chaaaar-lotte." She draws out the letters of her name as a reminder.

"The "C" in Charlotte is silent, dear," Harriet says without taking her eyes off Jack. "I've packed your two suitcases so you're good to go back to New York. Oh, and Pierre says you're fired."

"Thank you. That message has already been relayed to me, by Anne of all people. Not as happily as you did just now, to her credit. Anyway, once I speak with Pierre, I'm sure–"

"–Stupid idea," says Harriet, finally looking at her.

"You don't even know what I was going to say."

"That Pierre will reconsider having fired you. You've known Pierre a long time to know that once he makes a decision, he never reverses it, even if he's wrong."

"You think firing me was the wrong decision?"

Harriet shrugs, her eyes skirt around the room. She lifts a finger to the waiter and says, "Cafe." Turning to Charlotte, she says, "And under no circumstances are you to Google yourself right now."

"What? Why?" Immediately, Charlotte reaches for her phone and types. Even upside down, Jack can view her screen. Up pops CNN's lead story with an unflattering video of Charlotte falling from the helicopter into the Seine, her multi-colored raincoat ballooning, underpants fully exposed. While Jack saw the video earlier that evening, he didn't have time to read the article. He twists his head to get a better view of the headline that reads "Unladylike Guest of Honor Steals Mistress In A Red Dress."

Charlotte groans.

"Soon, New York will wake up with their Starbucks and bagels while looking up your skirt." Harriet's laughter slips out.

"Thank you," Charlotte says in a facetious tone.

"Don't mention it." Then as an afterthought, Harriet says, "Are those Spanx?" She angles Charlotte's phone in her direction to stare more intently.

Charlotte blushes, mumbling, "They're bike shorts."

"If you say so." Harriet wipes a joyful tear. "Also, don't look up #TheDevilWearsOrange. Trust me. Social media has pitchforks and they're looking to skewer you."

Jack recognizes it as the hashtag the police officer mentioned at the station.

Charlotte punches at more keys, then sits there dumbfounded, stares at her phone, and mutters that she regrets charging it. Her thumb scrolls down the page. "These people act as though they know me. What's on social media isn't the real me." She continues frantically searching. "Oh, no. *Catwalk* publicly fired me. Social media has destroyed my reputation in less than a day and shamed me out of a career that took my entire adult life to build. There's a meme of me, too!"

Quickly, she flashes the phone to Jack but all he catches is an image of her hanging from the helicopter.

"I've replaced the 'Just Hang in There' cat except it says 'Don't Hang in There.' This can't be happening." Her hands fly up to cover her mouth as a tiny gasp escapes and she looks up at Harriet, eyes tear-filled and narrowing. "You created a drinking game on social media?"

"Someone was going to. I merely beat them to it. Besides, what kind of best friend would I be if I didn't partake in a little fun at your expense."

Charlotte shakes her head, squints her eyes at Harriet, and says, "Define best friend."

"Best friend: Someone willing to bury a dead body," Harriet answers in a questionable tone.

"You should reconsider some of your friendships. Define frenemy."

"Frenemy: Someone you're friendly with despite a rivalry." Harriet goes quiet. "Oh, I see. Yes, that's more appropriate for us."

Charlotte's shoulders slump and her face crinkles in contemplation. "Nobody would help me bury a body. Oh God, my frenemy is my best friend. My frenemy?"

"Told you," Harriet says.

Charlotte groans. "Just where did all the other friends go? Melted away by a career that took over every aspect of my life, I suppose."

Harriet sighs. "Don't be so dramatic."

"And are these fashion colleagues really my friends now that I've been kicked out of the circle? Hmmm," says Charlotte, "a piece on the levels of friendship could make for an interesting article, prefaced with an "Is She Really Your BFF? Quiz."

Returning to her phone, Charlotte continues to scroll and read, harrumphs and gasps until Jack places his hand gently on her phone. "Put it down, Charlotte," he tells her in a quiet tone. "This is needless torture." She looks bewildered by what she's seen on the news, but Jack sees how scared she is. Whatever these thieves had promised her, it seems she now realizes it wasn't worth her career, or her reputation.

Charlotte puts her phone away and says, "Aren't you going to ask me, Harriet?"

"Ask you what?"

"If I'm guilty?"

"Oh, Charlotte, don't be ridiculous. You don't have an adventurous bone in your body to pull something like this."

"Thank you, I think."

"Where will you go now? The crazed paparazzi will find you no matter which hotel you check yourself into," says Harriet.

"I'm not sure," Charlotte answers quietly. She pushes her plate of food away. "Everyone I know is in fashion and I'm sure my termination at the magazine will lend fuel to this fire, this social media frenzy that has painted me a thief."

Harriet snorts. "I see what you did there."

"I'm done on so many fronts. I have no job. No prospects. I'm going to lose my apartment. I have no place to go."

"I know of a place where we can stay."

Both women turn to Jack. His statement surprises even him.

"It's a vineyard, *Chateau Emilie*, near *Ville de Loire*. It also operates as a B&B during the spring and summer months, so I can book us rooms. How 'bout it, Charlotte? Get away from all this nonsense." The smile is frozen to his face. He has no clue where this idea came from. It's a good idea, he reasons with himself. It will keep him close to her and perhaps she'll open up. So why is he holding his breath waiting for her to answer, heart thumping like a teenager?

"Charlotte," says Harriet, cackling, "won't go anywhere with a stranger. She has men fill out application forms for one-night stands."

"Not true," mutters Charlotte.

Harriet places a hand on Jack's shoulder. "When it comes to sex, Americans aren't progressive like us Europeans."

"Harriet, enough." Charlotte points to the suitcases Harriet brought. "I have all I need to go wherever."

Harriet rests her hand on Charlotte's, her crinkled forehead displays concern. "Poor darling. One would hope you don't have that hideous raincoat tucked away somewhere. Wearing it began this travesty."

A sudden laugh bursts from Jack, which is met with consternation from Charlotte and he smothers his laughter with a cough. Granted, he knows nothing about fashion, but he's glad someone pointed to the ridiculousness of the outfit.

After Jack settles the bill, Charlotte, Harriet, and Jack awkwardly stare at one another next to his car. Silence fills up the space between them though it's time for good-byes. He notices Harriet's demure smile, and the tilt of her head that indicates she can handle the standoff. He hauls Charlotte's luggage into the boot of the car to speed things along.

"Thank you, Harriet, for your help," Charlotte says. Again, she hugs her and, this time, Harriet hugs back with a tight squeeze.

Harriet then breaks free and turns to Jack, arms outstretched. "Don't hesitate to call me," she tells him and wraps her arms around his neck.

"We won't," Jack responds, and he's so uncomfortable with the attention that he breaks away from Harriet's embrace.

Harriet says, "I'm thinking of popping over to England from here, maybe we can get together..."

"Thank you," Jack cuts her off, "that would be wonderful." Then, he plops himself into the driver's seat before they can firm up any plans. After a final goodbye wave from Charlotte, the Peugeot drives away; the image in the passenger's mirror of Harriet waving grows smaller.

A few raindrops hit the windshield.

"Why don't you close your eyes for a while and rest? I'll wake you as soon..." Heavy breathing interrupts him. He turns to see she's slouched in the seat, eyes closed, mouth open.

He's thankful the caffeine will keep him awake for the long drive ahead and wonders what he has gotten himself into; he's an academic and while, yes, he is called from time to time as an expert to help Interpol, he has never been left alone to infiltrate the ring, not counting Switzerland, yet even that was meant to be temporary. This is a first for Jack. He only wishes he wasn't so intrigued by Charlotte and wonders how she got caught up in all of this.

The rain pounds the windshield and Jack turns the wipers to full blast. Headlights of a car behind them bounce off his rearview mirror, high beams temporarily blinding him. It seems that with every turn, the car follows. Paranoia gets the better of him, but, given the circumstances, he can't be too careful and takes random turns. Still, the car continues to follow from a distance.

It can't be Favreau's men because he made it clear he doesn't have the resources. Jack skirts his eyes toward a sleeping Charlotte. It's possible her crew wants her back. His hands tighten on the steering wheel. Jack accelerates, makes a turn onto Quai Henri IV, then a left onto Voie Mazas, before hitting Quai de Bercy. When he drives onto the ramp heading to A6 and merges onto the A10/E50, he realizes he hasn't shaken the vehicle.

Chapter 11

J ACK INSPECTS THE REARVIEW mirror, occasionally twists his body around to ensure no one follows. It was a good half-hour into his journey that the car finally stopped trailing them. Or perhaps he merely lost sight of the vehicle, and it's still lurking at a distance, waiting patiently for Jack to let his guard down. In the hours since he last saw them, Jack has remained on alert.

This country road he's driving on is endless. Beside him, Charlotte shifts, agitated, Jack's jacket strewn over her for a blanket. She mumbles nonsense in her sleep, a sporadic mix of whispers and bawling.

"Charlotte," he whispers, "where's *Mistress In A Red Dress*?"

Charlotte sucks in a breath. "Red's out this season. Floral's in."

He shakes his head. It's a dumb thing to attempt, but people with guilty consciences have been known to talk in their sleep. Or perhaps only in films. "Who are your people?"

No response.

"Charlotte, who are your friends?"

"No friends." Suddenly disturbed, Charlotte shakes her head, and her eyes fly open. She bolts upright, twists her neck to peek out the window behind her, then returns her gaze straight ahead. She grimaces, clasps her hand to the back of her neck, and stretches in slow movements. "Where am I?"

"France," he says in a deadpan voice.

"Very funny," she groans. "Besides, that cow we passed wearing a beret and scarf and singing *La Vie en Rose* gave it away."

He chuckles. "We're almost there."

At a hand-painted sign that reads *Chateau Emilie*, Jack turns onto a dirt road and through an open iron gate, then down a long avenue of trees, lavender planted by their feet. A floral scent fills the car. Finally, an 18th-century home, tucked behind a walled garden of oleanders and English roses, appears.

Charlotte sits up in her seat. "What is this place?"

"A vineyard I stayed at last year. The owners, Philippe and Marianna, are quite friendly."

"It's beautiful," she says before a look of unease clouds her face. "Do they know about me?"

"Philippe is a Luddite, if I remember correctly. You're safe. The village is ten minutes away, and I doubt they care what happens in Paris. They keep a different pace here." He parks at an angle near the villa's grand wooden door.

Climbing out of the car, Charlotte stares at the home until a French bulldog's bark breaks her gaze and she looks down.

"That's Marcel," Jack says. Pointing to chickens scratching about in gravel, he continues, "and that's Chicken. One next to it is also Chicken. Hard to tell the little buggers apart. Here comes Duck."

"You mean *Poulet, Poulet* and *Confit de Canard.*"

"With a nice red."

"Bordeaux."

"*Naturellement.*"

Jack smiles at this little exchange. Turning, he looks out to the swathe of pruned vines he knows are picked by hand for the estate. "If it was a little later in the summer, we'd breathe in the bouquet of the vineyard."

"I've drunk enough wine in my life to smell that bouquet."

The front door flies open, both Jack and Charlotte spin around. Philippe, short and seemingly pudgier since Jack's last stay here, rushes over.

"Professor Jack! We were thrilled to learn you were coming. The room is nearly ready," says Philippe.

"I hope the late booking didn't put you out?" asks Jack.

Philippe shakes his head. "We're not officially open for the season until next week, but it's always a pleasure to have a repeat guest. Ah, and this time you brought a lady friend," Philippe says happily and gives Jack a wink which Jack finds odd.

"Pleased to meet you." Charlotte extends her hand. "Did you say 'room' as in singular?"

"Jean!" Philippe yells without answering Charlotte's question. Jack would also like clarification on this matter.

It takes a moment before Jean appears by the front door, hunched over, toothless, yet, surprisingly, he looks younger than the last time Jack saw him.

"*Prendre leurs biens*," Philippe says to Jean.

Jean shuffles his way to the trunk of the vehicle.

"I can manage," offers Jack.

"No, Professor Jack. Jean can handle it."

When the shuffling and mumbling Jean passes close to him, Jack swears he was the recipient of a dirty look. And all because the last time he was here, Jack took it upon himself to shine his own shoes, offending Jean in the process.

"Really, I can..."

"No, I insist. We will take care of everything during your two-day stay."

Charlotte turns to Jack. "Two days?"

"Let's get you inside," says Philippe.

Passing through a stone-walled corridor, Jack, Charlotte, and Philippe arrive at a living room with exposed oak beams. A well-stocked library – that Jack has lost himself in many times – spans the length of one wall.

Philippe announces, "Marianna! Professor Jack is here! And this time he brought his lover."

Jack smirks, shakes his head, and is about to speak when a joyful scream from elsewhere in the house interrupts him. Marianna rushes in from the kitchen and wipes her hands against her apron, her dark, long hair tied back in a loose ponytail.

"I'm always excited to greet our first guests of the season. Welcome," she says, her Spanish accent heavy. "Jean, take them upstairs to the guest room. Freshen up and we'll prepare a breakfast out on the terrace."

Lugging a suitcase, Jean leads the way upstairs. A fat, white cat, perched in the middle on the last step, refuses to move. After a staring match between Jean and the cat, they slink past the cat.

Jack issues Charlotte a warning. "Stay away from this one. I've worn the scratches of defeat against this feline."

Jean opens a set of double doors to one of the rooms, drops the suitcase near the king-sized bed, a hand-embroidered cover folded back. Fine antiques and cheap imitation art decorate the room. Jean flings open the shuttered window to views of the vineyard slopes below. Speaking French, he points to the sky and kisses his fingers in a fervent expression. Then, Jean leaves to get the next suitcase.

"What did he say?" Charlotte asks. "He spoke too quickly for me to follow."

"He said the moon from this window is the most spectacular in all the house. Its beams creep into this room, spills its aura of lovemaking to the inhabitants while they sleep." As Jack translates, he looks to the king-sized bed. Charlotte's eyes follow his gaze.

"Clearly, they've misunderstood," says Jack.

"Clearly."

"Honestly, I booked two rooms," he says, then wonders if his tone appears too strained as though trying hard to convince her. "I'll get another room."

Charlotte throws herself onto the bed, hugs pillows, then caresses the coverlet. Given the past 24-hours, this must feel luxurious to her. And Jack himself is exhausted, having stayed awake since yesterday morning. He'd like to lay himself down next to her.

"I never want to leave." Charlotte closes her eyes and kicks off her shoes, wiggling her toes.

He stares at her well-manicured toes, up along her legs, past her skirt and up to her face. He studies the strength in her jawbone and the vulnerability of her chin. Charlotte most certainly has a kissable neck.

The sound of Jean shuffling into the bedroom pierces Jack's reverie, and he's embarrassed by the thoughts he's having about Charlotte, but can he really be held responsible for his emotions? Indeed, as long as he doesn't act, he's fine to dwell on them and wonder *what if?* Like *what if,* instead of all this trouble, he met Charlotte at an art gallery, both admiring *Mistress In A Red Dress? What if* she wasn't a criminal and they struck up a conversation? Would she even talk to him? Perhaps if he wore Prada.

The old man drags Jack's overnight bag (that he had packed "just in case") into the room.

"*Non,*" Jack says. Speaking French, he tells Jean to put the suitcase in another available guest room, but the old man puts up a fight, repeating *pourquoi?* several times. He's getting on Jack's nerves like a heckler at a standup show.

After the brief argument, Jean hauls his luggage away.

"You gave in too soon."

Jack turns to Charlotte resting on her elbows, staring at him with a smirk on her face.

"I would have agreed to a clothesline and an extra blanket and played Clara Bow to your Clark Gable."

Jack stuffs his hands in his pockets and leans back on the balls of his feet. "It was actually Claudette Colbert in It Happened

One Night, and you do know they fall in love in the end, don't you?"

"That won't be us," she says in a quiet voice then makes a face and holds her hands in the shape of a heart. "Still nursing a broken heart."

"Someone let you get away? What an idiot," says Jack, and he's surprised to realize it's not a lie.

There's something in the lingering way Charlotte looks at him that draws him in, and he realizes he's a little smitten with the person he's been charged to spy on.

Chapter 12

"HOW DID YOU TWO meet?" asks Marianna, once Jack and I settle down to breakfast on the terrace. She pours us each a cup of coffee. Before us are mounds of jams and croissants and brie.

We turn to one another, stumbling through our answers, neither of us answering the question. Avoidance is key.

Probing, Marianna asks, "And how long have you been together?"

"Marianna, Charlotte and I are friends."

"Acquaintances," I say.

With a slight smirk, Jack says, "We discovered we both have a fondness for art."

My eyes pounce on him. *Don't you dare.* The last thing I need is to be kicked out of the vineyard. This is the kind of place that can make me forget my problems.

"We met over a painting," Jack continues.

His easy laughter relaxes me, and I know he won't betray me.

Marianna beams. "How lovely."

After breakfast, Jack offers a tour of the vineyard. We walk among the pruned vines. A slight chill in the early morning air gives me a momentary shiver. Jack pulls at a vine and twists it to show me.

"They've been lucky in these parts. It's warmer than normal, and you can see it's beginning to flower. They'll have a good quality vintage."

"How do you know?"

"The calmer and warmer the weather, the better the grape...plus they gave a tour last year. In a few weeks, the berries will grow. In mid-summer, the grapes soften and swell significantly. This passage we're on narrows between the spiral of the grape branches."

Memories of my childhood Brooklyn home flood my mind. My grandfather had planted grapes and tied them to an arbor around our back patio. In full bloom, they offered shade as my family sat outside enjoying homemade meals. I miss those summer nights under the stars.

Following Jack on the guided tour, I look down at his loafers, then up to his shirt, sleeves rolled up over a brown cardigan, and neatly tucked into his belted khaki pants. A classic panama hat in tan tops his head. All very British-y, I think. He's maybe a bit over six feet tall, with a medium build and strong jawline. His glasses are a bit goofy-looking. I could do something about his attire. After all, the only thing a woman can change about a man is his wardrobe. But from what little I know about Jack, he has the most crucial characteristic in a man – intelligence. And then there's kindness. Humor. The list quickly grows in my head.

"So, you're single?" The words escape my mouth, mortifying me.

Smiling, Jack asks, "What gave it away?"

"Good odds. I have a fifty percent chance of being right."

"Hmmm. I hope you didn't detect the pathetic loneliness of a single man because that most certainly isn't me. Though, the strange truth is I was at my loneliest during my marriage."

The sincerity of his tone sparks a memory of my last relationship.

"Surely, I'll do better with wife number five."

My eyes dart to him.

Laughing, he says, "There's one ex-wife, I swear. "And what about you?" he changes the subject casually.

I want to press, but suspect it isn't what he wants.

What about me? I recall the time I visited Los Angeles and had Turkish coffee, to which they added pistachio grains. The owner of the cafe, an old woman, made me leave behind the thick layer of sludgy sediment, where it settled at the bottom then turned it upside-down and studied the grounds. Her skin was hard and wrinkled and she simpered when she muttered her prediction. "It's bad. You must work hard for love."

"Single, thirty-three, and living in New York City." I notice Jack's steps tend to slow, shortening the gap between us. "And yes, my parents are very proud." Jack tilts his head back towards me, and I discern a slight smile.

"What will you do when you return home? Look for another job in fashion? I admit I haven't a clue what your line of work entails."

"Some people say I persuaded women to buy expensive bags as a long-term investment."

"You cad," he slips out in a light-hearted tone. "And what do you say?"

"I say too bad for them if that's all they see. Fashion can be a powerful tool for self-expression and representation, to show the world who you are because you've found that item that syncs your internal with your external. Billy Porter said he felt the most masculine in heels. Heels don't make men any less masculine just like pants don't make women any less feminine. Oscar de la Renta once said his clothes are love letters to those who wore them. My work is a love letter to my readers. They mean a great deal to me."

My enthusiasm rises and I bring it down a notch. "Besides, we also sell women on being financially independent with stocks and bonds and real estate. We cover stories on voter suppression, the growing inequities in our healthcare system, and remind our readers that women's rights still aren't recognized in our Constitution. But *Catwalk* didn't used to cover all this. I had to convince them it was important." I exhale. "Sorry, I'm babbling."

"It's alright. I asked."

At the end of the path, the land opens to a small patch designated for farm animals. Jack holds a gate ajar for me to step through, then closes it behind him. Chickens chatter among us, seemingly annoyed by the disturbance. A fat rooster sits under the shade of a large, wooden shed. I tiptoe my way through, careful not to step on any animal droppings.

Jack's phone rings and he pulls it from his pocket. Glancing at it, his demeanor changes, and he stares at the ground for a moment as though contemplating the call.

I say, "Do you need to answer that?"

Jack looks up at me, smiles, and slides the phone back into his pocket. "Telemarketer. Let's continue the tour, shall we?"

We walk in silence, and I'm unable to keep my mind from running wild. I revisit the last twenty-four hours. "How valuable is this painting they stole?"

"Very. Some of Foligari's paintings were destroyed in a massive fire in Copenhagen, where his work was housed. The museum should have taken better care of *Mistress*."

"Yes, the lack of security does seem careless."

"It happens often. Once, a painting was stolen out of a university in America, and it took weeks before anyone noticed. That was a hard case to crack because so much time had passed, and the FBI couldn't narrow down when it was stolen. Eventually, the thieves were caught trying to sell it."

"Is that what these thieves will do?"

"I suspect so. It could even be in New York by now," he says.

"Why New York, and won't it be recognized?"

"The smart ones get it out of their possession as quickly as possible. There are many hubs around the world perfect for reselling stolen art at auction. New York is one of them. Besides, customs officials aren't trained to recognize stolen art and antiquities."

"So, the auction houses and buyers are duped into buying stolen art?"

"Not necessarily. The auction house can do its due diligence – scan the Art Loss Register and both the FBI's and Interpol's websites noting stolen artwork. Many choose not to, though this is a high-profile case."

I stop. There is too much to wrap my mind around. I should start with the basics. "It starts with the thief."

Staring, Jack moves towards me. He has broad shoulders perfect to wrap my arms around. Honestly, I can't understand why I find him sexy all of a sudden. All this clean, open-air living is having an impact on my libido. I get a whiff of Jack's cologne and visualize his hands on my breasts. *Damn it.*

"It starts with the buyer," says Jack, interrupting the porn story now unspooling in my head. "As for the thief, there are those who consider themselves to be a Thomas Crown figure, but they fall short. The golden rule is to stay hidden, fly under the radar. Others are connected to the criminal underworld, so..."

I note that the ending of his sentence hangs as though Jack's trying to figure out which group I fall into. Staring at him, my eyes narrow, and I push aside any lustful, romantic notion I may have had. "I'm not involved in this."

"I didn't say you were."

"You've no idea what I'm going through."

"I didn't mean to offend."

"But you did," I say in a biting tone. I shouldn't blame him. It's not like anyone believes me. Except Harriet, who had no faith in me to begin with. "You have your Ph.D. And you're published periodically."

Jack flinches in surprise.

"I know how the world of academia works, obviously. Well, imagine after spending all those years working to get to this place in your life, someone suddenly accuses you of plagiarism. Now, you didn't do it, but it doesn't matter because you're guilty until proven otherwise. And you can kiss that professorship goodbye. All those people whom you believed were your friends and loyal colleagues? They don't want to be seen with you. You're nothing more than a pariah, and you're contagious. If they associate with you, they'll be cancelled, too." I pause for emphasis. "We need to be clear about this if we're to move forward with whatever it is you're trying to do here."

"I assure you, I want *Mistress* found. Nothing else."

I nod, then wonder if his "nothing else" comment refers to me. I want the painting found, too, but I'm surprised to realize it bothers me that when this ends, we do, too.

Wait, is there even a *we*? Now, I'm back to picturing Jack's hands on my breasts. *Damn it.* This is what France and Jack's accent are doing to me. I shake my head as though the image of me with Jack pressed against a wall, hands tearing at clothes, can fall out. "Tell me how the criminal underworld works it?"

"Different ways. The auction house sells the painting unknowingly to another criminal buyer. The house gets a nice commission. And the criminal organization has managed to launder millions right under their noses."

"Brilliant."

"It really is, especially in a business where everyone's self-proclaimed ignorance helps to fuel the thefts. They used to steal in the middle of the night with less risk, but nowadays, art thieves are becoming dangerous with these daytime heists. Bravado at play."

"Breaking the number one rule of staying out of the spotlight."

"Exactly. The French police are likely questioning museum staff right now. There have been many inside jobs."

"Someone from the Louvre? That would make sense. Tell me more about the anatomy of an art thief."

"Some aren't very bright. They can steal the artwork easily enough, but moving it is a different story. The Hollywood thief persona doesn't exist, not an ounce of truth to it, although it makes for one damn entertaining story. The deception behind Thomas Crown is that he hides in plain sight, so transparent that he's not even considered a suspect."

By now, I'm lost in thought, mulling over Jack's talk of Thomas Crown. Almost to myself and repeating Jack's words, I say, "He hides in plain sight. Pierce Brosnan was at the museum during the theft."

"I saw the McQueen version."

I stare into Jack's brown eyes as if held in a trance, then flash to the exact moment that sent me into a free-fall toward the River Seine. I saw my captor's eyes. My heart races and my fingers tremble at the memory.

Jack continues. "Thomas Crown was a multi-millionaire and could afford to buy it, but he enjoyed the thrill. He enjoyed out-smarting everyone. No one suspected him."

I can't get the image of my captor's eyes out of my mind, and my brain works through yesterday's travesty and, as Jack prattles on, his words pierce into my thoughts.

"...and that's the brilliance of this persona. But Crown is a figment of Hollywood."

"But what if he's not?" I say in a hurried tone and immediately regret it. It's a thought too bizarre to share with Jack or the French police, yet my mind has brought me to a very dark place as I realize the thief's identity.

Chapter 13

B Y MIDNIGHT, A THREE-COURSE meal and three bottles of wine are gone. Each time I finish a glass, it's miraculously topped up again. The wine consumption is a blur, and the thrill of running away from my problems has left me giddy. By the time we move onto Scotch, a bad idea that stops neither of us from partaking, I have no inhibitions left.

Jack slurs, "It will grow hair on our chests," and downs his Scotch.

In an even tone, I say, "I already have hair on mine," and burst into raucous laughter. I would never say that on a date, my God, yet I feel so completely at ease with him that my behavior seems innocuous.

We reach the point in the evening when whatever either of us says induces laughter. Finally, I – or perhaps it was Jack - yell "Bedtime," and we head up to our rooms with Jack supposedly helping me up the stairs. His grip is tight on the railing, and he stomps his foot down on each step with determination, looks down at his foot, and back to me. He tells me, "I've never been one to drink a lot, but being around a vineyard makes drinking wine seem more like drinking water."

At least that's what I think he said. I have trouble concentrating, and it takes him a while to get the words out.

"Here, let me be your guide," I say, swaying into him, and end up splayed across the staircase on all fours. Jack pulls at my arm. "Leave me here," I plead.

"Come on," he tells me and looks up the stairs. "There's light at the end of the tunnel." Jack scoops his arm around my waist, picks me up, and guides me upstairs.

The cat returns, slinking across the upper corridor, and sits down one step from the top.

"Not again," Jack mutters.

"Here, kitty, kitty, pussy catto, kitty," I slur and stretch my hand out to pet the creature.

Jack snaps back my hand. "Don't touch her," he yells. "She'll destroy you."

His tone is so severe that even in my drunken stupor, it terrifies me.

The cat eases its way past us, our breaths held, our bodies motionless, playing dead.

Once the beast reaches the bottom step, Jack whisper-shouts, "Run."

Twice, we blunder our way up and trip. Finally, at the top, I break away and stumble towards my bedroom door. Jack follows, but I swing an arm out to guard my door, preventing him from worming his way in.

"Professor Jack," I garble, "your door is next room." Something about that doesn't seem right, and I think about it before correcting myself. "Your door is next room." *Better.*

"So, it is." He remains, his torso pitches forward unsteadily, and he stares into my eyes.

"Your eyes are very dark," I say.

He places an elbow against my doorframe and leans his head into the palm of his hand. "Helps with the brooding. Apparently, women like brooding characters."

"That's only for vampires." I hesitate and tilt my head forward, conspiratorially, until I'm mere inches from Jack. "It was his eyes, you know, that gave it away."

"Whose?"

"Thomas."

"Thomas who?"

I giggle, and take a step back, leaning against my door for support. Jack's face lights up, and he laughs along with me.

"Thomas Crown," I tell him between laughter. "I saw his eyes when I fell from the helicopter," I say, gesticulating with my hands how I fell.

"Splat!" says Jack.

This elicits a short burst of laughter from me, and I reiterate his "*Splat!*" then slam the palm of one hand against the other. I'm not sure why I find this so funny. "I convinced myself I was wrong. But I'm not. I know the thief's identity."

"Who is it?" Jack says, muting his laughter.

In a deep whisper, I say, "The Prince."

"William?"

"No," I say in a quickened, hushed tone.

"Not Harry? I quite like Harry." Jack's lips curl up in a scowl.

"British royals aren't the only royals out there. The Prince is transparent."

"He's invisible?"

"No," I say in a frustrated tone, then reconsider. "Yes? I think so? What'd you say earlier about...about..." I lose my train of thought, and briefly close my eyes. My head feels heavy and a short snort quickly brings me back. "Uhm, about hiding in plain sight."

He stares at me, and an eyebrow shoots up. "Ah, I understand now."

"You believe me about the Prince?" I'm thrilled it doesn't sound far-fetched after all, but perhaps neither of us are thinking straight with all that alcohol we consumed.

Jack shrugs. "Charlotte, my Charlotte." He leans into me, presses me against my door then taps at his forehead. "You're trying to get in my head."

I like the way he's looking at me right now, as though he's ready to devour me like in those romance novels I used to read in my 20s. "Are you smitten with me, Professor?" I tug at the front of his pants, slip my fingers into his belt, more to steady myself than anything seductive, but I'm pleased when Jack responds. He presses himself into me, his lips hard on mine, his hands reach under my top until they find skin. I wrap one leg around his waist, and reach behind me in search of the doorknob to fling my bedroom door open. My hand slides up and down before I remember it's in the middle of the double doors. When I raise my other leg, while simultaneously reaching across for the knob, Jack stumbles with the full weight of me and we crash to the floor. I bang my elbow. "Ow." What's wrong with me? I'm usually better at impromptu sex. I once did it under the stage during a rock concert, and it was difficult maneuvering ourselves around with all those cables.

"Are you hurt?"

"I'm okay," I say, and roll on top of him. With a smile, I pin him beneath me, legs straddled on either side of him, my hips grinding against him. "What's happening here?"

"Anything you want," he says, garbling the words. His hands slide out from under mine, and he grabs my face, lowering me to him until he's close enough to push his tongue into my mouth.

Moaning, I grind harder against him with three months' worth of pent-up sexual frustration. Hot sex with a guy I just met is exactly what I need. "When you get the painting back, and that little Bonaparte gets his thieving Prince, then...we're uhm...what exactly?" Between kisses, I feel Jack withdraw and I pull back to see a smile on his face. "What's so funny?"

"Is Favreau Bonaparte?"

I nod.

Jack's smile disappears and, with a serious note in his voice, says, "We'll keep it casual because I know the truth."

"The truth?"

Jack places his index finger against his lips.

"What secret are you harboring?" I poke him in a playful manner.

Jack pulls me closer. "Charlotte, you're drunk."

I tilt my head towards him, a demure smile on my face. "Professor, so are you."

"That may be, but in the morning, I will be sober, and you will still be a liar and quite possibly, a thief," he says in a tone of insufferable smugness. "Prince William. Really." He follows with a bellowing laugh.

I push myself off Jack just as his lips brush against mine, and I stumble against my door. It is evident by the expression on his face that he seems unaware he has said something that should not have been uttered. An insult is an insult, and no amount of alcohol can soften the blow for me. Besides, I missed my last bikini wax appointment, so who knows what unkempt forest is growing down there.

"I never said Prince William. It's Prince Rashid Mohammed Salah al-Zayed," I say sternly and slam the door in his face. "Unbelievable," I mutter in my room as I struggle with the buttons of my blouse that won't unclasp. I kick off my Manolo mules one by one, and they manage to land on the floor near one another. As I angrily push the buttons through the eyehole, I catch something in my peripheral. Yes. There it is. The blackest, the biggest, the hairiest spider I have ever seen. I let out a shrill scream and jump on the bed.

The door bursts open. Jack charges through in his bare feet, disheveled and bewildered, eyes wide, then his gaze follows my shaking index finger to the corner of my room. A low whistle blows from Jack's lips. "That's the blackest, the biggest, and the hairiest spider I've ever seen." Unsteadily, he glances down at his bare feet in contemplation. Then he turns to the pair of shoes on the floor near him and seizes one, raising it above him.

"No, wait," I shout. "Manolos don't kill spiders."

Jack hesitates for a moment, but when the spider scurries away, he continues with that forward swing and flattens it. "Splat!" He grins in admiration for his handiwork and tosses the shoe to the floor where he found it.

"There you have it," he announces. Jack sways in his drunken stupor and rambles out with a bit of swagger in his steps as though he just hit a grand slam to bring his team home.

"Idiot," I shout after him. I pick up my injured Manolo and inspect the smear at the bottom. I hold it at a distance as I would a smelly diaper and drop it into the garbage basket.

Chapter 14

WHILE IN FRANCE, ESPECIALLY in the countryside, Jack drives like all respectable Europeans – like a madman. The little Peugeot races over the dirt road past the yellowed greenery of several farms toward a small village situated along the river in the Loire Valley. An excess amount of wine the previous evening led to a late start into town, and, judging by the number of aspirin they each popped, neither of them, it seems, can hold their liquor.

"Slow down, please," Charlotte whispers and holds the side of her head.

"Roll down your window. Fresh air will do you some good." Saying that, Jack fights bile trying to flee and rolls down his own window.

Charlotte lowers hers too, tilts her head out, and leans against the frame.

Jack would love to undo the previous night's events, which didn't go as planned. In fact, he fears he may have made them worse. He wants to agree on an emotional level (a hopeful thought, really) that she's not responsible for the theft and was merely a pawn. During their tour of the vineyard, he said as much, agreeing aloud but secretly harboring the belief that he may have his guilty party. He ruminated on her indignation when he voiced his dirty little secret last night, certainly not something he would have expressed sober. Truth be told, and despite the image some may believe of British men, they, too, think with the wrong head sometimes. Jack was all too willing to jump into that giant bed with her.

When Jack awoke that morning and the fog from the hangover lifted, he reconsidered everything Charlotte said. It wasn't difficult to work out whom she alluded to the night before, and he spent the better part of the morning Googling Prince Rashid Mohammed Salah al-Zayed, learning about his businesses, partnerships, and personal life. Prince Rashid did not steal Jack's *Mistress*. Perhaps he's the intended buyer. How clever Charlotte is, Jack reasons, to ask how the criminal network operates, leading him to consider the painting has already made its way out of France. Indeed, if Prince Rashid is the buyer, he wouldn't travel with the stolen art. No, someone in his standing would ensure he's safely out of the country first, then the painting would follow. According to a tabloid Jack discovered during his internet sleuthing, the Prince plans to attend a charity casino event in Monaco a few days from now.

Brrrring. Brrrring.

Jack's pant pocket rings, an old-fashioned telephone tone he set expressly for *Capitaine* Favreau. He's grateful it isn't set to vibrate. He fumbles to grab the phone, all while trying to keep the car steady on the road. In his peripheral, Charlotte sits up. Speaking to Favreau with Charlotte sitting next to him is high risk, and he lets it ring. Jack gets a surprising jolt when Charlotte's hand thrusts deep into his front pant pocket.

"Relax, Big Boy. I'm only going for your phone," Charlotte says in a near-perfect Mae West impression.

He takes the phone from her and maneuvers the car back to the road. "Thank you," he says sheepishly and answers in a gruff, "Hello."

"You were to call me last night, Professor. I tried you several times. Where are you?" Favreau sounds frustrated on the other end of the line.

Jack glances at Charlotte, worried she can hear the conversation, and discern Favreau's voice. "One moment. Charlotte, in the glove compartment is a map to the *Ville de Loire*. Can you please pull it out?"

Charlotte opens the compartment and pulls out various pieces of paper, flips them over in her hands. "There's no map. I thought you've been to the village countless times?"

"It's the hangover. I just wanted to be sure," he offers as an excuse. The little diversion is all Jack needs to get their whereabouts across to Favreau.

"*Ville de Loire*. Have you learned anything, Professor?" The million-dollar question with a million-dollar answer. He's learned plenty, Jack wants to tell Favreau. Besides, without concrete evidence, would Favreau believe him about the Prince? Can he admit that, maybe, Prince Rashid is a buyer for the stolen painting on a hunch and nothing more? Absolutely not. It was Favreau who insisted Jack keep Charlotte close to gain her trust and, now that he has accepted that challenge, he's determined to see how this will play out. And he needs to see his *Mistress* again, whatever it takes.

"*Comme ci, comme ça*." Jack glances towards Charlotte, her squinted eyes staring at him. "Always ready for a new learning opportunity."

"*Très bien*. And the tracking device?"

At the station, Favreau had given Jack a device as a backup in case Charlotte threw away her phone, something the police expect her to do, destroying the electronic trace on her through the GPS.

"In place," Jack says.

"One more thing, Professor Carey. Next time I call, I expect you to answer."

"Understood. I will have the Assistant Professor take care of that until I return." Jack hangs up and places the phone in his front shirt pocket.

"I know what you're up to," Charlotte says, fixing a deep stare at him.

"I'm not up to anything." The words tumble out in a hurry.

"Were you speaking to the media?"

"I most certainly was not. It's the University. I do have obligations that I have put aside to help you sort through this mess." It isn't a lie. Yesterday, before his much-needed nap, he reached out to his teaching assistant and provided him with lecture notes and, when he offered to grade the tests, Jack took him up on it.

"Help me? You made it clear last night you believe I'm a thief. Your only interest is in the painting," she says in a sharp hiss.

His eye twitches. "I was intoxicated. I didn't mean it."

"It's been my experience that alcohol merely eliminates a filter."

Jack searches for what to say next, something that will satisfy her, an answer so definite that she wouldn't dare question it. "You're absolutely correct. Favreau has influenced my judgment of you, and I'll admit, I'm greatly torn. No doubt you helped them steal the painting. It's possible it happened as you say, and that you were merely a pawn in their heist and a victim in all this."

Charlotte faces forward, and in a quiet voice, says, "That's right, I am a victim."

Saved.

"I want the painting found, but I'd also like to help clear your name."

"Why?"

"Why? Well, if you didn't do it, you deserve justice." Right answer, he thinks, honest, yet non-committal about her guilt or innocence. "Besides, that was a magnificent Mae West impression." Jack catches her blush, and she veers her head to look out the window, her lips turn up in a smile.

Chapter 15

AHEAD OF US, THE village spreads out over a two-mile radius a short distance away, and by the time Jack turns the car into a narrow gravel road, my headache vanishes. Jack parks under a tree near vehicles sporting a selection of European license plates. I climb out of the car and gulp fresh country air. Jack is right – this is what I need. The sudden urge to shop smacks me as though losing myself in the act can return chaos to normalcy.

The village is pedestrian-friendly, with a labyrinth of tiny cobblestone walkways. Tourists outnumber the villagers two to one and, from where I stand, I spot a florist shop, cafe, bookstore, and aha! – *pâtisserie*. I read once only a bakery that employs a licensed master pastry chef can legally use the word *pâtisserie*. The French are serious about their baked goods.

Beside me, Jack says, "Let me know what is of interest to you, and I can..."

I step away before he finishes, still angry with him. Then again, why do I expect more from him than my own friends? I've reached out to several people since leaving the police station, and not one has responded – save Harriet. Not only had Pierre snubbed me, but his assistant did, too. And my conversation with Anne at the station had been so bizarre and demoralizing that I didn't leave a message after dialing her number.

Inside the *pâtisserie*, I drown in delicious smells of butter, lemon, and vanilla. It takes mere moments to choose what will satisfy my sweet tooth and, with my finger pressed against glass,

I point. The handsome baker wraps the delectable item in wax paper and slides it into a white paper bag. By the time I exit the *patisserie*, I'm biting into a strawberry custard tart.

"Do Americans usually eat dessert for breakfast?" Jack says, materializing like a magician after a disappearing act.

"You're British. Do you want to discuss gastronomy with *your* palate? I keep hearing about this cheese and pickle sandwich and don't understand how toppings can be a sandwich?"

"Correct me if I'm wrong, but don't Americans smother street meat in chili?"

"Hmmm. Point made," I mumble. "So, what's on the agenda for today?"

"How about a picnic? We'll pick up bread, some cheese, olives, maybe some *Pâté de Foie Gras.*"

I wrinkle my nose at the mention of *foie gras*.

"Or not," says Jack.

Inside the cheese shop, we order brie made along the nearby river banks, and another soft cheese with small dried grapes added for flavor.

"We mustn't forget the camembert," says Jack.

The shopkeeper offers me a taste of blue cheese, but I can't put something that smells like dirty socks in my mouth. Jack and I finish up with baguettes and wine, having convinced ourselves more wine is necessary "obviously," and "11AM is close enough to noon," and "when in France..."

"We seem to have everything," Jack says and lifts a fabric shopping bag overflowing with food.

I slip my hand through his proffered arm, memories from last night diminishing, but can't prevent myself from saying, "Don't read anything into this. You're not entirely forgiven."

We stroll to a quiet area and locate a bench near the small stream that runs along the outskirts of the village, the parking lot to our backs. Jack rests the grocery bag between us, then digs his hands in, fetches a napkin for my lap and a small paper cup. I take it from him in anticipation of wine.

"We don't have a corkscrew for the wine," I say.

"Screwcap." Jack twists the top off and pours us each a glass. He proceeds to lay the cheeses on a sheet of wax paper and slices them with his Swiss Army knife.

In silence, I nibble on some cheese and tear into the baguette. "It's so pretty here. This reminds me of Central Park."

"It reminds me of the grounds at Oxford. The garden here is very well planned. Those there are peonies from China. The scent it will give off when in full bloom is incredible."

"You know your flowers."

"I work in my garden during my spare time. I'm a closeted horticulturist."

Quietly, we chew our food. A bird flutters down and lands a few feet away in probable anticipation of crumbs.

Jack says, "Be wary of that bird. It looks ominous."

I shift my body to look at the animal behind me. "She's sweet-looking. Birds love me."

"Yes, I heard them singing as they dressed you this morning."

I turn to him, a smile winding its way on my mouth. "Speaking of dress, I noticed your stylish outfit today." When he knocked on my door that morning, I was surprised by how well he looked in aubergine-colored pants that perfectly matched one of the multiple stripes of the Paul Smith shirt he was wearing. His hair looked different, too, as though he had added product to give it style. I have a habit of being attracted not to the man himself, but to the man attached to the accent or attached to the Armani suit. Yes, I'm a byproduct of what I have created in my articles — *don't become who you want to be, become who you are wearing.* I actually sold that idea.

"They're Philipe's old clothes. Marianna insisted I do better. I had forgotten how meddlesome those two are, and I think she has Jean burning my clothes as we speak."

"If he's not, I certainly will."

"They're only clothes."

My back stiffens. "Only clothes? You do realize fashion is my livelihood? Don't be a snob."

Jack shrugs it off.

"There's a correlation between art and fashion. There are some pieces done at an atelier shop that is an absolute work of art. One time, Hermès sent a craftsman to their store in New York, and every day for one solid week, I visited him, witnessed the progression he made on a Birkin, working the leather in his hands, smoothing it, stitching. It's an art form. I've visited the ateliers in Paris, where artists worked on couture pieces with hand-embroidered fabric. That's art. But you don't see it, don't recognize it because it doesn't fall into your idea of what constitutes art. It's wearable art. You assume art can only hang on a wall."

"I stand corrected."

"Damn, right." I laugh, but it dies down too soon. I play with the bread in my hand, a heavy sigh escapes me.

"What's on your mind, Charlotte?"

"Just thinking about New York. I think it's time I go home and try to salvage whatever's left of my career. I'm emotionally spent. I'm on edge here."

"But we haven't accomplished anything."

I turn to him. "Were we supposed to accomplish something? I don't know where the painting is, Jack."

"Last night, you announced a big reveal about the Prince, and now you expect me to forget it?"

I wince. "I hoped you wouldn't remember. If Favreau knew whom I suspected, he'd laugh at me. He already thinks I'm guilty. Imagine what he would say if he thought I was trying to frame someone like the Prince. You know I'm not talking about William, right?"

"Understood."

"Prince Rashid."

"Got it."

"It sounds so ridiculous to hear it out loud." I bury my face in my hands. "Just forget I said anything."

"If you want to clear your name, then you can't leave now before we even get started," says Jack. There's no mistaking the desperation in his voice.

My eyes flick to him, but I remain silent.

"Well, do you? Remember what they're saying about you? Not just in the mainstream media, but social media where trolls can post anything they wish with no regard for truth. You were trending number one on that platform with the ridiculous rebrand. And that meme of you is grotesque."

My mouth falls open.

Jack carries on. "I admit I had to look up what trending and memes are and, I'd have to say, in your particular case, it isn't good."

As of late, I've avoided browsing through social media. It's my reputation, my career, my life on the line, affected by a tabloid story based on a misunderstanding. Captain Favreau must know I'm innocent, but with no other person of interest and no arrests, media attention — not to mention social media gossip — will remain focused on me. *Price of Fame* = *Price of Shame*.

Jack pops a bit of bread into his mouth and before he finishes chewing, says, "We simply can't let them get away with this."

Jack gets me riled up, and I nod along as he lambasts the faceless trolls.

"Let's get to work then."

"You going all Danny Ocean on me?" I say with a smile and a wink.

"Not the first time I've been compared to Clooney." He winks back.

My sudden laughter startles him. "All right, Danny, who's the target?"

After a pause, Jack says, "The Prince."

"This is insane. To what purpose?"

"To keep your enemy close. Consider it's what you have to do to clear your name."

"What do you get out of it?"

"The *Mistress*. This morning, I did some research, and we have an opportunity to confront the Prince. We have a few days to devise a plan. It's not that insane," he says.

"Professor, take a picture of me, will you?" I say and shift a bit, posing with my elbow against the back of the bench. The request seems to catch Jack off-guard, but he acquiesces, pulls his phone from his shirt pocket, and snaps a picture. He looks at it.

"Nice," he says, then flips the phone my way.

I barely look at it and shrug my shoulders. "Do it again, but this time get the black sedan that's been following us since we left the vineyard."

Looking nonplussed, Jack lifts the phone and clicks a few times, then shows me the images. I place my fingers on the photo, enlarge it to ensure the license plate is legible. "In case you're still wondering, they're not with me. Am I making myself understood?"

His eyes flicker past me, rest for a bit, then return to me. "I'd be an imbecile to think otherwise."

"Good," I say, though I'm not wholly convinced he means it. "Favreau should take a look at that plate because if the occupants in that car work for Prince Rashid, and should any-thing happen to us, at least we can leave some breadcrumbs for Favreau to follow. That is if they don't belong to Favreau. I know you're feeding him information about me."

"I most certainly am not," says Jack in a pitchy voice.

"Jack, don't lie to me. If we're going to do this, you have to promise you'll run things by me first before you share them. We're either working together or you're working against me."

He stares at me. "I promise."

I look away to the small shops ahead of us, at the tourists traipsing in and out of storefronts, not one with an expression of solemn contemplation like the one, I suspect, is on my face.

Turning to Jack, I say, "You said we have to devise a plan. What do you have in mind?"

Chapter 16

T HE PLAN WAS SIMPLE. Get in. Make contact. Get out.

It was a team effort. Jack reached out to a former student named Baldie, the son of the hotel owner where the event is taking place. When nothing came of it, I reached out to Harriet, who contacted a publicist she knew, and expeditiously provided Jack and I with access to the charity casino event. At some point, Harriet will ask for something in return, which is worse than owing the mob. Jack used his credit card points to secure train tickets and a hotel room, mumbling about forfeiting the points for his vacation.

We went over the plan ad nauseam, considered different scenarios that could play out, none of which ended badly. There was always the possibility that it wouldn't go smoothly or that, unlike a well-crafted screenplay, the dialogue wouldn't flow as we had rehearsed. Still, we were confident our plan would prove infallible, and we'd infiltrate our target's shield.

Get in. Make contact. Get out.

Imbued with its original spirit of the Belle Epoque, the Casino de Monte Carlo perches on the Mediterranean Sea in a principality known for its luxurious lifestyle. Monaco smells differently here by the salty, ocean air. I hear the crashing waves in the distance, and elsewhere, the squeals of party-goers, and the monotonous tones of cars on the roadway. Before reaching the red-carpeted steps, I sweep past parked Ferraris, Bentleys, and two Aston Martins; a man exits from one, a cigarette dangles from his lips, and his eyes seem to examine me.

Inside the casino, sculptures, frescoes, and mirrors swirl around me in the cavernous setting. I stride through the lobby past guests milling about between columns while, in a corner, a man in a tuxedo, shouts into a cell phone. Those near the caller ogle him, exhibiting their disdain at his apparent lack of civility. The slot machines ping and the rattling of balls at the roulette wheels swell around me in a cacophony of excitement. I can still smell the cigarette smoke from the Aston Martin driver and feel his eyes on me though he's long gone.

A sign on a gilded tripod points me to the gaming room, transformed into a private charity event. The gambling tables are lined in green felt, the chairs in burgundy, and overhead, numerous chandeliers sparkle. I slip my invitation to a slender man standing near the entrance and dip a hand into my purse to fetch my passport. He looks briefly at my photo before admitting me.

The people here are glamorous and ostentatious, yet all eyes, I believe, are on me. Dressed in a barely-there Versace, I had spent more than an hour stuffing myself while I zipped, strapped, taped, and dabbed sweat from the exertion. And when I exited the bathroom of the hotel we had checked into, Jack's eyes grazed me up and down. "Wow. You... look like a Bond girl," he said, his voice deep.

I spot Prince Rashid at a center casino table. *Damn*, his beauty stuns me just as he had done the first time he walked out on stage. He looks up from his playing cards and spots me, surprise morphing into a mischievous smile.

A Bond girl? Jack got it wrong. I'm no Bond girl. I *am* Bond.

Rashid has just won a poker hand, and the losing player abandons his seat across from him. I slide in without a moment's hesitation.

"*Bonsoir*," I say to Rashid. He quickly masks his surprise.

"*Mademoiselle* Milton, it is both a pleasure and a surprise to see you here." I recognize the accent and soft intonations as that of the thief from the Lumière show. The memory of his scent, his touch on the small of my back, pound against me with the brute force of a hurricane.

"You speak English," I say a little too quick to prevent the girlish swoon from overtaking me.

With a smile, he says, "I speak many languages."

"You had me fooled," I say, and pause for effect, then add, "that you spoke no English."

"I do not recall being asked."

From my purse, I pull out chips. I tried to get Jack to give me more money, but he was far too nervous about the amount he had already given me, hemming and hawing until, exasperated, I gave up and walked away with the piddling amount. I place the stack of chips before me, unnerved by the mounds resting in front of Rashid. Poker, I told Jack, is my game. "How do you think I paid for university?" I said to him coolly and left out the part about the partial scholarships and the nights I lost big.

"It's a 3,000 Euro minimum table," the dealer informs me.

"What?" I say, distracted. I look to the dealer, a short woman with blonde hair pulled back in a tiny ball.

"It's a 3,000 Euro minimum table."

Flustered, I peer at the others seated at the table, at their chips stacked before them, and I'm embarrassed by the way they stare at me, seemingly harassed by the delay.

"I was assured each table had a 500 Euro minimum."

"This table was added at the last minute to accommodate higher stakes players."

"Oh, I see," I say and stand. "I see," I repeat, unsure what to do next. Getting thrown off the table so early wasn't written into our script, but what else can I do? I have no more money, and Jack, who assured me 2,500 Euros would be sufficient for a charity event, isn't due to show up just yet.

Rashid waves his index finger to a man behind him and whispers into his ear. The man, dressed in a black shirt and suit, takes a mound of Rashid's chips and walks them over to me, placing the stack before me.

"I couldn't," I tell Rashid.

"Please," he insists. "After all, it's for charity."

Humiliated by the encounter, I wonder if he's referring to me rather than the event. The episode knocks me back to Bond girl status. I sit.

"Aces high," the dealer says, repeating the same in French and hands out one card to each of the four players, then a second one.

I peek at the Queen and 10, both clubs, in my hands. They'll do as a starting point, but they don't put me in the best position. The player, to Rashid's right, thumps his index finger, a possible tell. To Rashid's left and my right, the other player stares at the pot in the middle, boring holes into the chips. He's trying too hard to keep a blank face. He'll be easy to decipher.

"Anybody know where Josephine Baker is buried?" Finger Thumper says. "I promised my wife we'd scope out the cemetery. We did the same thing back in LA with Marilyn, spent her birthday drinking coffee and eating croissants by her graveside."

Without breaking stride, Rashid tosses in chips and says, "3,000."

The others, including me, toss in our chips. I note Finger Thumper (though The Chatterbox now seems a more appropriate nickname) is the last in.

"You must got good cards," The Chatterbox says to Rashid and it has me wondering if playing the annoying guy at the card table is his shtick.

"Call. 3,000," the silent one says.

The house shuffles out cards and displays the 10 and 2 deuces in a rectangle on the table, then reveals a 10 of diamonds, 2 of clubs, and 2 of spade. The Chatterbox checks his cards and taps his hand on the table; meanwhile, I scoop up some of my chips and shuffle them around in my fingers to distract the other players. Rashid bets 10,000. Raising his eyes to mine, he holds them on me, piercing through me. I can't get a read on him, but I'm sure he can see how his stare affects me. A little part of me just melted. *Focus!*

"Twenty," I say, flinching. Oh no, I've been so cool up to this point.

"Hugh Hefner, may he rest in peace, bought the plot next to Marilyn decades ago. Imagine spending eternity next to the most beautiful woman in the world? My wife says 'but honey you are.'" He laughs.

It's not a shtick, I determine.

"I'm out," The Chatterbox says and tosses his cards face down towards the dealer, who places them back into the muck with the other folded cards. Rashid and the silent player call, accepting my 20,000 and toss in their chips.

The dealer displays another card, 7 of diamonds. There is hesitation in the silent man's movement, and then he checks his cards a second time. Keeping my eyes steady on Rashid, I toss in another 25,000. The silent player rests and then throws his cards down in a huff, unable to play along with me.

I notice Rashid's eyes on my hands as I play with the chips, clanging them against one another. Now that I've pulled myself together again, I'm confident he can't read me. When his eyes move up towards mine, they blink ever so slowly. He folds and reveals his hand – Aces of Heart and Aces of Clubs—a quiet *"oh"* echoes from the onlookers around us.

"Ms. Milton," he says, "will you do me the honor of showing your cards?"

"Your Highness, I believe revealing one's cards is optional. If I may be so bold, I decline your request."

The corner of his mouth twitches. It's exposed him, giving me some insight into his behavior with a hand most certainly better than my own. I played him and won.

Cue Jack.

If this were a Bond film, the camera would pan from the smug look on my face to the entrance awaiting Jack's arrival. Casually, I look toward the entrance, and Jack is standing near the slender man who had greeted me earlier. Beside Jack stands another man. While I wholeheartedly threw myself into the part by dressing in a knockout designer gown, I remain a little perplexed by what role Jack is supposedly playing. Where, I wonder, did he pull that sweater vest? Apparently, he was joking when he said Jean burnt his clothes, but I had hoped it was true. Before I left him, I had laid out an outfit for him to wear which included a borrowed jacket procured by the concierge. Had I been with Jack when he dressed, I would have begged he wear the horrid tweed jacket instead of this monstrosity.

"Three players," the dealer says, bringing my attention back to the table and Rashid, but his eyes are where mine had been. Did he catch me staring at Jack? Finally, he looks away from the front entrance to me.

Bets are made. Cards are handed out. Peeking at my cards, I hold my hands over them, then keep them face down. The house reveals its cards – Ace of Hearts, 9 of Clubs, and Queen of Diamonds. Again, I play with my chips in an attempt to mask my hand, fumbling them as I did before. I toss in 20,000, and the silent one meets my raise. Light flicks off Rashid's diamond and gold watch as he reaches out to meet my bet.

Another casual look to the entrance reveals a strange pantomime with Jack handing over his sweater vest to one man while the slender man helps him into a black jacket. Jack should have known there'd be a dress code for the charity event, and I wonder why he didn't consider it, but based on what I've seen of his wardrobe over the last few days, I know the answer. For Jack, clothing is only meant to prevent people from being naked.

The house reveals its next card, a 10 of Diamonds.

I raise another 40,000. The silent player folds, mumbling he "won't go through that again."

"And then there were two," I say. "Or maybe just one."

"Two is a perfect number," says Rashid, meeting my 40,000.

The house reveals an ace of diamonds next. I want to focus on the game but strain to peek at Jack, who searches his pant pockets, then the pockets of the borrowed jacket. *Oh God*, I want to moan. His passport must be in the pocket of his sweater vest. Jack gestures wildly, hands flailing in response to something the other man said, his body language registering somewhere between oafish and cross. He's supposed to join in for the next game and introduce himself to both Rashid and me, but at this pace, I worry he won't get here on time. But my current winning hand, I suspect, will entice Rashid to keep playing until he wins.

"All in," I say and push forward my entire winnings.

Chapter 17

T HE PLAN IS SIMPLE. Get in. Make contact. Get out.

Jack frets that if the plan falls apart, it will be at the hands of Charlotte, for she seemed to pay attention only half of the time over the last few days while he plotted and drew diagrams of the casino's layout. She nodded – he thought to validate his plan – but then, holding up two bottles of nail polish, she asked which he preferred. Charlotte was quite perturbed when he said, "the red one" and she answered, "but *which* red?" then rolled her eyes and disappeared into the hotel bathroom before he understood he'd said something wrong. When she emerged two hours later, Jack was blown away by Charlotte wearing what she referred to as a *barely-there* Versace dress.

"You look like a Bond girl," he said, the words escaped him before his brain had an opportunity to shut him up. He had expected to zip her up, but, much to his chagrin, she hadn't asked. What must she think of him ogling her the way that he did? If she slapped him, he'd deserve it. He's not entirely certain his mouth had been closed, and, most likely than not, it wasn't.

He spies an outfit Charlotte had laid on the bed for him and slips on the jacket. It's a good fit, but he doesn't like how the fabric restrains his arms and shoulders, so he tears it off, and dismisses it outright. It's only clothes. Besides, given what he's about to walk into, he'd like to feel relaxed in his own clothes.

Jack waits the required fifteen minutes after Charlotte's departure, then travels to the casino by a different path. From the charity event entrance, he spots Charlotte at the Prince's table, and, for several minutes, he watches, mesmerized by the way she commands the table. No, by the way she commands the men at the table. He suspects Prince Rashid is intrigued by Charlotte, and how could he not be? Jack has difficulty concentrating with her around, too.

Get in. Make contact. Stop daydreaming about helping Charlotte out of that barely-there dress and get out.

"Excuse me, Sir," says a slender man with a French accent, "we have a dress code for the event. Gentlemen must wear a suit jacket."

"Be careful who you call a gentleman," Jack jokes. The slender man stares at him without expression, and immediately Jack feels like a buffoon. This is precisely the kind of corny joke his grandfather used to tell.

"I'm afraid we must insist. If I may, I'll take your…your sweater vest, and Gerard will supply you with a jacket."

Jack turns to a man, presumably Gerard, who holds three black blazers of varying sizes across his arm. Mulling them over, Jack points to one and proceeds to remove his sweater vest. Everything, Jack realizes, had been planned, contemplated, and reconsidered, yet he dismissed the wardrobe Charlotte had laid out for him. In retrospect, he should have listened, but in his defense, he does think the sweater vest makes him look quite spiffy.

"Invitation and passport, please, sir."

"Of course," says Jack, and searches his jacket pocket, then his pant pocket. "I'm afraid I left them in my vest along with my phone." He turns to where Gerard had stood to find him gone along with his vest. "Where did he go?"

"Follow me, please, sir," the slender man tells Jack.

Following him out, Jack takes another panicked look at Charlotte sitting at the table while cards are distributed. He should be there by now. This simple plan is beginning to fray, and as they search for Gerard, Jack realizes he is running out of time.

Jack pleads that they admit him into the event while they search for the vest that *they* misplaced, but they insist it would be against the rules to do so. Flummoxed, Jack raises his voice and says, "Do you know who I am? Baldie won't be pleased to learn how you mistreated his cousin. I insist you get him on the phone immediately."

He stares hard at the manager, hoping he won't call his bluff. Archibald E. Lambert, III, 'Baldie' to his friends, won't be happy about his former professor pretending to be a relative.

The manager apologizes profusely and just as they're about to let him in, they find his sweater vest, along with the invitation and passport. Finally, he's let in and approaches the casino table. But Charlotte is gone.

Flustered and agitated, Jack's unsure how much time passes before he recognizes a gentleman who had been at the same table as Charlotte.

"Excuse me, sir, I'm looking for a woman who was at your table. Dark hair, blush-colored dress with these metallic...I suppose metallic isn't quite the accurate description, though they do shine."

"The Versace," the man says.

Jack barely registers his statement. He would never have pegged this guy as a labels man.

"My wife wouldn't stop talking about that Versace dress, and now she wants to go shopping tomorrow instead of visiting Josephine Baker's grave. Can you believe that?"

Jack satisfies him with a "wow" and shakes his head in solidarity. With the New Jersey accent and overcompensation of gold jewelry, this man exudes a lack of finesse. New money, Jack determines. "Do you know where she is?"

"Josephine Baker?"

"The Versace woman."

"Last time I saw her, she was looking pretty intimate with His Royal Highness at the bar."

"How—what?" says Jack in a high-pitched voice, and swallows this inexplicable lump in his throat. He sounds like Hugh Grant playing the Bumbling Idiot in just about all Hugh Grant romantic comedies.

The man winks. "Let's just say it looks like they were getting to know one another. They left together." The stranger pats him on his back before leaving.

The room spins uncontrollably, and it takes a few seconds for Jack to realize it's him that's whirling, glancing at every table, his ears pricked by the shrill laughter of a woman at the bar, his eyes inspecting hidden corners looking for Charlotte. The Josephine Baker man has to be wrong. Once their plan began to unravel, surely she would have remained until Jack showed. He would have thought of something in the spur of the moment to introduce himself to them, and they could pick up from their plan to infiltrate Rashid's circle. Jack is perfectly capable of spontaneity, and he'd love an opportunity to show Charlotte that side of him. And what was it about Charlotte with the Prince that looked intimate? Jack is perfectly capable of intimacy, too.

Finally, Jack pulls out his phone. *Missed call* pings at him on the screen. He hadn't bothered checking it earlier when they found his sweater vest because all he thought about was getting into that room. Dialing into his voicemail, Jack listens to Charlotte's somewhat anxious, somewhat accusatory message. He rubs his eyes, listening further to the disheartening – for having let her down – message until he arrives at the end, which he replays, having convinced himself he misunderstood the context.

"I'm in with Prince Rashid and leaving you–"

There is no mistaking Charlotte's jarring message. Jack agonizes over the tone of her voice, which sounds *happy? Relieved? Triumphant?* That's it. Charlotte Milton is triumphant for putting one over him. He'd applaud her if he wasn't so stunned by her betrayal. Jack admits he hadn't been forthright about why he is helping her or that he's there on behalf of Favreau. Up until now, he thought her a pawn in this game. Now, he realizes he may have been the pawn all along.

Overwrought by this newfound realization, Jack sprints towards their hotel, still wearing the casino's blazer. Running down the hotel's long drive, he doesn't get far before he's out of breath and hails a taxi. Did he really think he could run all the way to the hotel? Exiting the cab, he catches a glimpse of Charlotte stepping into a black limousine with tinted windows.

"Charlotte!"

She hesitates for a moment, then proceeds into the limo. He'd like to give her the benefit of the doubt and believe that she hadn't heard him before the limousine sped off. Jack even chases after them down the street, dodging oncoming traffic, and calls out to her. Exhausted and out of breath, he stops, hunches over, hands on his knees, and his breath comes in hard. He groans in frustration. He's a fool to let her out of his sight and a bigger fool for liking her. Damn that barely-there Versace.

***

Not long after Charlotte disappears into the limousine, Jack commits his own act of treason – the sign of a desperate man – and notifies Favreau. Leaning against the doorway of Charlotte's hotel room four hours later, he finds himself an outcast from a plan he put into action. He wonders how he could have been so blind, then remembers he let his guard down the night they spent at the vineyard. It felt good to have Charlotte there, and he liked how she got on with him as though they have a long history together. Jack pushes the thought from his mind.

Around him, Capitaine Favreau and the local police survey the scene, search the closet, turn drawers out and upside down, and strip the bedsheets, simultaneously displaying signs of disappointment towards Jack, their eyes continually flick towards him, their lips pursed. Favreau, Jack assumes, must have told them plenty about the British fellow who fancies himself a spy, omitting how Favreau left him with no choice.

The uniformed unit manages to attract the attention of a small band of tourists, some with the audacity to approach the scene, peek inside and ask, "what happened?"

"*Américains*," mutters one of the officers before pushing Jack out of the way to close the door on the tourists. Jack's been asked to step aside by four different officers, all of whom expressed their disdain as though he's contaminating their investigation. Yes, he's in the way. He gets it. Yes, he was supposed to keep an eye on Charlotte and lost her. He gets that, too. No one is more disappointed in Jack than he is, yet Favreau's presence has a way of magnifying his failure.

"You can search which limousine service had a pick-up here at the hotel, can't you?" Jack says to no one in particular. Silence. "Have you checked the train station?" More silence. "The airport?"

Favreau looks at him with haggard eyes, beneath which are dark circles, and grey stubble sprouts from his weary face. He, too, appears to be keeping himself out of the way of the local police, having no jurisdiction, though, out of respect, they seem to accommodate him. "You watch too much American television. Professor, what exactly are you and *Mademoiselle* Milton doing in Monaco?" says Favreau in a gravelly voice.

Jack knew that by calling Favreau, he'd have a great deal of explaining to do, but being forthcoming isn't an option. If Favreau knew the truth, he'd accuse Jack of obstruction and send him back to England. It's impossible to abandon his *Mistress*, not now, when he still has much to prove. Besides, Favreau would think Jack has lost his mind if he knew they were suspicious of Prince Rashid. The diplomatic fallout of an accusation would terrify Favreau.

"Keeping an eye on her, as you suggested, Captain." Good answer, Jack thinks to himself, but Favreau apparently feels otherwise and rolls his eyes.

"And why did she come here? Surely, she must have said something to you."

Jack racks his brain for an answer. "Well, uhm, it became quite urgent that we leave France...because... there was a car following us in Ville de Loire, and it had her all worried, and she wanted to hide out..." *In Monaco?* "...with plenty of people around. I sent you the plate number of that car. Did you determine who it belonged to?"

"Yes, but Professor, I mustn't tell you everything about this case. You are *my* informant."

"Well, of course, but I should be informed in order... to inform you... better. It could be a clue that means nothing to you, but to me, why it could break the whole case open." Jack extends his arms wide to exaggerate his point.

Favreau sighs. "The car was rented by an Omani national, quite possibly a tourist."

Jack goes quiet, contemplates the number of Omani tourists in France. While Oman is a neighbor to the UAE, the close geography does not necessarily make Jack confident that Rashid is behind the tail. Charlotte hinted she believed the men following them in Ville de Loire could be on the Prince's payroll, but why, if she had been part of it all along, suggest any links to Prince Rashid? Could it be a ruse on her part to think of something so extraordinary that only a fool would believe her story? Jack certainly feels like Charlotte's fool.

"No idea what the connection is to Oman," says Jack.

"She's a smoker?" asks Favreau.

Jack shakes his head, then follows Favreau's gaze to a lipstick-smeared cigarette resting on a teacup saucer by the bed. That looks like Charlotte's lipstick. He really doesn't know her at all.

"*Capitaine*," says one of the officers exiting the bathroom and carries a plastic bag with a mobile phone in it. He tells Favreau it had been dumped in the toilet.

"As expected. We have a back-up." Favreau shrugs his shoulders and, turning to Jack, says, "You set the tracking device we gave you?"

Unclear if it's a question or a statement, Jack doesn't respond.

"Please, tell me you put it in place," says Favreau.

"Yes," Jack answers tentatively. "I did."

"Good, we can track her that way."

Favreau motions to a female officer, a streak of blonde runs through her hair, a diamond stud glistens on her nose. She picks up a briefcase near her, places it on the bed, and snaps it open. Inside the case is a laptop, she flicks on, waits a few moments, and then nods towards Favreau.

"*Prêt*," she says.

Favreau says, "*Bon*." He motions for Jack to stand next to him so they can all view the laptop. Pointing to the monitor, Favreau explains, "This little red star represents *Mademoiselle* Milton. We can follow her whereabouts as she moves."

The red star flashes in place, and for a moment, they believe there is movement; excitement mounts until they realize the indicator hasn't moved at all. They've been staring at the monitor for too long that their eyes played tricks on them. Favreau looks at the computer, eyes furrowed. He bangs on the side of the laptop, and before he can do it again, the female officer pushes his hand away.

Favreau leans on the bed, drums his fingers on the mauve bedspread, haphazardly tossed back on after the stripping, and stares at the red star as though willing it to move. "Why is she standing still? Where is she standing still?"

The female officer types in some keystrokes and, turning to Favreau, says, "Here in this hotel."

Enunciating every word, Favreau says, "Professor, where did you place the device?"

Jack pulls a kerchief from his jacket, dabs at the perspiration building on his forehead, aware that both Favreau and the female officer are staring at him.

"Well, here's the thing. I thought the best place for it would be her shoes." Jack's voice is so weak that he doesn't even convince himself.

"How did you place the tracker on her shoe?" says Favreau.

"Well, I didn't place it *on* her shoe as much as *with* her shoes...in her suitcase."

"Her suitcase?" he sneers. "You thought it was more valuable to place it in her suitcase than on her physically?"

The female officer glances to the floor then kicks something underneath the bed. Kneeling by the edge of the bed, she pulls out a small brown suitcase with LV logos. Tossing it on the bed, she searches inside until she locates the small tracker Jack had placed in there. Everyone in the room stares at him.

"How was I going to get it on her?" he asks them, looking from one officer to another. "She changes her clothes often."

"Does *Mademoiselle* Milton carry a handbag?" says Favreau.

"Chanel," Jack answers. Favreau raises a wry eyebrow at him. Beside him, a droopy-eyed officer scoffs. "Oh," says Jack, finally understanding his mistake, "hide it in her purse. I see. But you don't understand. She loves her shoes! She wouldn't go any-where without them."

Favreau turns to the unit and twirls his hand in the air to indicate they speed things up. He calls for the female officer to put the case away and follow him out. As a member of the team, Jack follows them into the hotel corridor where curious onlookers remain. Favreau spins around and places his hand on Jack's chest to stop him.

"Not you, Professor. We are done here," says Favreau crisply before he leads the female officer down the corridor towards the elevators. Favreau and the female officer disappear into the lift. Jack looks back into the hotel room at the team of uniformed officers collecting evidence. He had thought he was in control, felt guilty about pressuring Charlotte to partake in his scheme, yet, and he can say this with certainty, it was Charlotte who made a fool out of him. Now he's more determined to find her and the painting. Somehow he must persuade Favreau he's worth another chance. He may have been imperfect in the way he has helped Interpol in the past to retrieve stolen pieces, but he has never been incompetent. This time, he thought with the wrong head.

How could he have got it so wrong? And just what happened to Charlotte?

Chapter 18

Hours earlier...

"**A**LL IN," I SAY and push forward my entire winnings with a gesture meant to display my confidence in my hand. Perhaps my cockiness is unnerving Rashid, knocking him down to a mid-level Bond arch-nemesis. I'm stunned when he mimics me by pushing all his winnings forward. I had expected him to fold.

"Show your cards," the dealer instructs.

I'm the first to reveal my Quad Aces of spades and clubs. A gasp circulates throughout the crowd. I've won the second hand, too, and can barely restrain myself from jumping up on the table.

Rashid clasps his hands together, leans forward, and rests his chin on the peak of his fingers. No doubt, my hand surprises him, yet there's something odd in the way he looks at me. He shifts in his chair; his back straightens, and he flips his cards.

The crowd explodes in dismay.

My mouth drops open.

A perfect and inconceivable Royal Flush beats a nearly perfect and unbelievable hand of Quad Aces.

Rashid's cards eviscerate me. They chop me down to a fraction of the forceful persona I envisioned earlier in the evening and suck me into a vortex where the gasps and applause from on-lookers sound muffled and distant. Each detail is recalled; collected into a part of my brain to take things into account, dissect every move. No matter the numerous times I scrutinize the scenario, there's no way I could have anticipated a hand like the one Rashid had. My only mistake was to believe that I, Charlotte Milton, is capable of deceiving a presumed art thief. I imagined myself as James Bond when Austin Powers aptly describes me.

"I've lost everything," I whisper. I had promised Jack his 2,500 Euros were safe in my hands, but I let foolishness and arrogance drive me. I forgot all about our plan, all because I needed a win.

Eyes hard on Rashid, I say, "The least you can do is buy me a drink, Your Highness."

Anguished, I cut through the crowd to the bar, and order a Scotch, holding up three fingers. The bartender pours a triple. I look back at the table where Rashid remains. *Damn,* I thought he'd follow me to the bar. *Now what?* I should see if Jack has finally made his way into the charity event, but at this point, I wonder why bother? If I do see Jack, embarrassment will prevent me from speaking. What would I say to him, anyway? *"Hi, there, Jack. Hope you weren't expecting that money back because it's gone! Ha ha! Just like my career and reputation."*

I itch to glance over. Surely, Rashid has abandoned the table and he's approaching right now, isn't he? I spin a bowl of nuts on the bar, pretending it has my attention then I take a quick peek. Rashid is no longer at the table or anywhere I can see. I bite down on my lower lip. Should I rush the entrance in case he tries to escape? Peering over my shoulder, I don't see him at the front door either. It was bad enough that Jack didn't show, but now I've lost Rashid.

I was hopeful in Ville de Loire when Jack first relayed his plans, but it wasn't until we were on the train that I felt bullish about getting my life back. I envisioned a reunion with friends, a restored reputation, and a promotion at Papineau Publishing, making my already unhealthy attachment to work more detrimental. Now, I feel like a divorcee whose ex got the fabulous

New York apartment, investments, and all the cool friends, while I end up with the debt.

"I could offer an apology though I don't think it's warranted."

I turn. Rashid is at my side, his bodyguard behind him. He took longer to follow me than I anticipated. "Have you come to gloat or buy me that drink?" I say and point to the barstool next to me.

Sitting, he says, "I don't relish in what transpired."

Gulping back a mouthful of Scotch, I wince and say, "Another please."

"Perrier," Rashid tells the bartender, who nods and turns away. "I play to win, Ms. Milton but took no pleasure in beating you. If it's any consolation, I donated all my winnings to the charity."

"Of course, you did," I mumble and swig down the remainder of my drink. I can't escape the intensity of his gaze on me.

"Astonishing," he says.

Me?

"Very astonishing that you should be here."

"It's not a coincidence."

"Really? Well, I certainly look forward to hearing more," he says. Casually leaning one arm on the bar, he swivels his chair towards me, so his knees graze my leg. His hand creeps to his knee, rests so close to my thigh that I wonder if this insouciant gesture is his signature move.

God how I want him to touch me. His eyes captivate me, and he has me feel like I'm the only one in the room. It's a trick many celebrities use when they're in promotion mode, and I'm immune to it. At least I was. I pull back when the bartender interrupts with Rashid's drink and frees me from the hypnotic state.

With the bartender now gone, I turn to Rashid and allow the Bond persona to take over. "The society pages announced you would be attending tonight's event. I cashed in a favor for this, even borrowed money so I could play at your table. It sounds so silly now when I say it aloud but all this," I point to the poker table, "was about impressing you." My chair slowly turns toward Rashid as if he has an invisible string pulling me to him. "Back in Paris, I missed our meeting. It couldn't be avoided." I pause to see if there's an inkling of remorse from him. "I recalled hearing a rumor of a start-up magazine. There were no details other than some very wealthy players were behind it."

"And you would like me to introduce you to these wealthy players?"

"We've already been introduced, Player." Without meaning to, it comes across in a sexy tone. Oh God, what is wrong with me?

Rashid's lips turn into a quick uptick. "The magazine world isn't very good at keeping secrets."

"Afraid not."

"The meeting with Pierre was preliminary but enough to determine we're not compatible. Pierre wants a silent financial partner. I want to build something of my own."

"I'm certainly glad to hear that. I've come a long way to pitch myself as your new editor-in-chief. I understand your focus is more on lifestyle, less on fashion?"

Rashid nods.

I continue, my confidence building. "Your ideal reader should be as interested in the economy and politics and philanthropy as they are fashion."

Rashid furrows his brows. "How is it that you've come to know these details?"

"I'm connected, Your Highness." (Good ole Harriet, again!) "Even in my *current* situation." There's no doubt he's cognizant of the public fallout surrounding my involvement with the heist, so why pretend otherwise? Besides, this plan won't work unless a part of him, no matter how small, feels guilty about the pain and upheaval he's caused. Continuing, I say, "There's this young woman who does TikTok tutorials on how to curl eyelashes or plump lips using gloss, all the while talking about human rights violations and ghost nets that kill fish and the melting ice caps in the Arctic. It's not a bait-and-switch because she's delivering exactly as promised while adding the extra. I know how to add the extra to your magazine."

"I'm impressed. Ms. Milton, after our brief encounter the night of *Catwalk Style Magazine*'s party, Pierre spoke highly of you. I must say, I was quite impressed with the changes you made – your innovative shoots, the direction you brought the magazine. It shouldn't come as a surprise to you that I had already considered you for the editor-in-chief position."

Now I feel as though I'm the one with the invisible string pulling him towards me. "That explains why you gave me the rose," I say, a little flirtatious.

Rashid tilts his head and stares at me in befuddlement.

"At the fashion show," I say to jog his memory, and in a quieter, dubious voice, I add, "when you handed me the rose from stage."

"That was *you*?"

Embarrassed, I wave my hand to the bartender for another drink. "Yes, well, with all the lights blinding you, how could you recognize me?" I clear my throat.

He smiles at my blunder as though amused. "I'm teasing, Ms. Milton. I gave the rose to the most attractive woman there."

"What you're doing is sweet, but it's okay if you don't remember me."

"You wore all black and sat in the front row."

Black is a staple in the fashion world. It doesn't prove a thing, but still I'd like to believe that he chose me because I was the most beautiful.

"And you were fanning yourself."

My eyes widen. He's telling the truth. Oh no, he must have seen my mouth gaped open, too. "So, we were discussing the magazine..." I say to steer the conversation back on track.

"If I may, I'd like to tell you my vision for the magazine, though it seems you understand. *Extreme Lifestyle* is all of us. Travel destinations, home decor, more art, and less entertainment, the culinary arts. It won't focus on luxury but rather life and living it to the maximum, for pure fulfillment and enjoyment. There's a group of men in their sixties I've come to know that toss themselves off mountain cliffs in wingsuits for the exhilaration. I've indeed eaten at the finest restaurants in the world, but I must confess when in New York, I track a particular food truck where they make the best Salvadoran pupusas."

"Latin Cowboy?" My eyes widen at this detail that has him come across as grounded. Perhaps I've bumped into him looking unrecognizable in jeans and a T-shirt over muscled biceps decorated in tattoos. No, a prince wouldn't have tattoos, would he? Maybe he should saddle up for an inspection, strip down to his underwear.

"You've been?" he asks appreciatively.

I nod my head.

"What I need," says Rashid, "is the right person at the helm, a visionary who will understand what I hope to accomplish, which is why your name appears on the shortlist."

Shortlist? Wait. What just happened? Wasn't I in control a minute ago?

"Though I don't mind confessing to you—"

—Yes! Here comes the admission that you ruined my life!—

"—that you are at the top of that list. Let me offer you something I won't offer the others. I'll be traveling a great deal over the next two weeks. I'd like you to come with me; let me introduce you to a few people, and I can observe what you bring to the magazine."

"Observe? Will you have time for brainstorming sessions? I'd like to bounce a few ideas off you." *And off your abs, too.* "And you'll be accessible to me?"

"In close proximity." He never takes his eyes off me, burrowing a hole to my inner core.

Concentrate on spinning that web around the mark, I practically yell at myself. I turn my head slightly, but not enough to break my gaze.

"You will be generously compensated for your time, but make no mistake, this will be a long, arduous interview," says Rashid. "I can be hard sometimes."

I bet you can be, I think, failing at all attempts to concentrate on The Plan.

Something catches his eye behind me, and he glances at his watch, breaking the spell.

"Unfortunately, I must depart for Cote D'Azur Airport for an important meeting in Dubai. You must decide now if you'll join me."

My back stiffens. "*Now* now?" I say as though there are different meanings for the word. I bet he travels by private jet and there's a chance *Mistress* is on that plane. If she is, then I have to be as well, but would James Bond get on a plane with his arch-nemesis? I pluck a memory from the time Bond was pushed out a plane without a parachute. "But it's so sudden," I blurt.

"Yes." He pauses, a stern look of contemplation on his face. "As you said, you've come a long way to pitch yourself to me which illustrates drive and ambition. I like that. I must leave now, so if you plan to accept my offer, my driver will accompany you to your hotel to pack for Dubai." With that, Rashid stands and places more than enough Euros on the bar to cover our drinks.

Get in. Make contact. Get out. I've accomplished two out of three. The initial plan was for Jack and me to infiltrate Rashid's world. I can't go it alone. Besides, Jack is the experienced one – he's told me more than once – regaling me with stories about his work with Interpol. Rashid's suggestion that I accompany him moves too quickly for me, and I search the room for Jack. *Cue Jack! Cue Jack!*

"I could meet you in Dubai?" I propose, fear, and pressure mounting.

In a quiet tone, Rashid says, "Ms. Milton, I demand people who work for me be available at all times, and, as I said, you'll be well compensated for this enormous strain. If this is too taxing for you, then please let me know, and we can part here."

I open my mouth, but nothing comes out. Jack is nowhere to be seen. What if this is a trap? What if he means to kill me? *Oh, that's idiotic. Give one good reason why he would want you dead?* The schizophrenic dialogue in my head should scare me.

"Good evening, Ms. Milton. I wish you well." Rashid makes the decision for me, probably reading into my hesitation. I can breathe again, my shoulders relax, and I step back from that ledge. Rashid offers his hand, a gentle shake, and his thumb grazes my fingers. I inhale a whiff of his cologne while his eyes hold on mine. Then, I picture *Mistress* loaded on his plane.

"I'm in," I blurt. Desperation has me ignore all my instincts, and I walk back out on that ledge.

Chapter 19

I T IS A TRUTH universally acknowledged that a man in possession of stolen art must be in want of a taciturn witness. Following that logic, Rashid's driver must be a spy. Why else would he be in my room watching me pack? I try to persuade him I don't need help, but he merely smiles and hefts my luggage off the bed, placing it by the door and waits for the next one. Perhaps he really is there to help. So, I have nothing to worry about, right? I'll simply board that private plane and fly out to Dubai with an art thief no one suspects. Even Jack, my partner in this madness, regards Rashid as the intended buyer only. No matter how often I shouted, "He has eyes like the thief!" Jack shook his head and muttered something about my excellent detective skills. For me, this isn't a game or a film or a story in a heist novel. This is *my* life, and I'm terrified of going to jail if this plan backfires.

The driver's phone beeps and he checks it, two fat thumbs typing away. Who am I fooling? He's obviously there to spy on me.

"Cigarettes," I shout.

The driver looks at me quizzically.

"I could use a pack of cigarettes. Would you be a doll and get–"

A pack is in his hand before I can finish the sentence. Of course, he'd be prepared. I take the proffered cigarette and lean toward the lighter in his other hand. I can't remember the last time I smoked. "Thank you," I say, before a hacking cough follows. "This is stronger than my usual brand." I inhale another quick puff before placing it on a teacup saucer on the nightstand.

With another suitcase open on the bed, I toss in clothes, rush back and forth between the closet and bed, haphazardly throwing in my bras and panties. I examine the mess. Jack would be the type to carefully fold each piece, perhaps color coordinate them, then organize by fabric. I wouldn't be surprised if he irons his boxers.

Jack. I have to tell him what's happened. If I don't try him now, when can I possibly make that call? Reaching for the cigarette, I inhale again and stare at my belongings. The next pull on the cigarette is longer, and I blow it out through the side of my mouth like I've seen actresses do in '60s films. The act allows me to press pause, slow things down and give me time to think.

"I'd like to change my clothes, please, if you'd just wait outside."

The driver is motionless. Finally, he acquiesces and heads out the door.

I've bought myself five minutes.

Cell phone in hand, I dial Jack's number; the European ringtone sounds like an alarm in my ear. I head to the bathroom, closing the door behind me. Surely, the driver won't be able to hear my conversation through two closed doors.

"Hello. This is Professor Jack Carey."

"Jack! Thank God! I thought our plan was blown—"

His voice interrupts me. "If you would care to have your message returned, please speak clearly and leave your name, telephone number, the date and time you called."

I open my mouth to speak, but the message proceeds after a short pause in which I thought he had been finished. I roll my eyes and mumble, "Come on," then peek out the bathroom door to check I'm still alone. Satisfied, I shut the door.

"If you wish, please identify the purpose of the telephone call. Thank you."

"Jack!" I breathe a half-whisper into the phone. "I thought our plan was blown when you didn't make it inside the event, and then I lost sight of you and...and, wait where are you, anyway? And why aren't you answering your phone? I feel like I'm doing this alone. Is that what's happened? Have you abandoned me?" I pace the small space of the bathroom, my body agitated, my voice rising at the possible abandonment. "This is *your* idea. You pass yourself off as some Interpol James Bond-type spy saving the art world, then you let me go in it alone. There are spies everywhere and I'm terrified so I want you to know that I'm in with Prince Rashid and leaving you–"

A hard knock at the door jolts me, and the phone slips from my trembling hand. By the time I realize what has happened, my mobile sinks into toilet water.

"No, no, no, no!" I plunge my hand into the toilet to retrieve it, shake the excess water. A second knock startles me, and I drop the phone again. The screen cracks as it hits against porcelain.

"Shit!"

The thumping at the door continues, harder and more pronounced.

I throw the door open.

Rashid's driver stands in the hotel hallway. "You didn't change," he says, looking me up and down.

My eyes are drawn to the gun strapped in his waistband holster, something I hadn't seen when he was inside my room moments ago. Terrified, I don't take a last sweep through my room to ensure I've collected everything.

Chapter 20

C HARLOTTE MILTON WASN'T PART of Rashid's plan. At least not initially. But when they arrived at the Lumière show, an opportunity presented itself and it was easier to use someone who was already on the inside, which allowed Rashid and his men to hide in the shadows. However, it meant the involvement of an innocent woman. Charlotte's entanglement was to end at the tent but, with adrenaline pumping through their veins from the heist and the heated exchange with Charlotte by the roadside, one of his men made the incalculable decision to grab her. Afterward, when they managed to escape through Paris's streets to their hideaway, and once the helicopter lifted from the roof, Rashid was awarded the briefest of moments to consider *what now?* What was he expected to do with Charlotte?

Then he lost her.

It was sudden and horrifying, and he was wracked with guilt when she plummeted from the sky. And later, when he learned she had been plucked out of the River Seine, relief consumed him.

Rashid believed no one would consider Charlotte as anything other than a victim, made to commit a crime under duress with the threat of life directed at her friend and the museum guard, so he was aghast to learn the police thought her a suspect. Suspect? Surely, they'd figure it out soon enough, wouldn't they? Terrible as he felt, he couldn't barge into the police station with the best lawyer in tow and draw attention to himself. Besides, he was fifteen minutes late for his scheduled meeting with Pierre and Charlotte, enough time to start chipping away at his alibi. The feeling of shame overcomes him when he recalls his exasperated behavior with Pierre when Charlotte hadn't shown for the meeting. Meanwhile, *he*'s the miscreant.

At first glance, it appeared fate brought Charlotte to him in that casino. She pitched herself for his magazine, and he saw a chance to make things right; he could save her reputation, and, if the police continue with their idiocy, he'd be in a position to hire a lawyer for his employee.

And suspicion would not fall on him. Not that it ever does, despite all his escapades.

As the eldest son, a life awaits him that drives him mad, and there are expectations made of him. He's spent a lifetime obeying his father, performing, concealing the sheer boredom and resentment within him. Every so often, he pushes the limit and does something that, if caught, will offend his father, though it's never his intention. He simply wants to break free from the constraints of his birthright. And the money the thefts bring may be enough to set him up financially, and he can escape his father's control.

During the infancy of his chosen profession – before the partners, the negotiations, and the elaborate plans – there was Copenhagen. During an aimless stroll through the bustling city, the air chilled from the dreary, rainy day, Rashid was smacked with a sense of discontentment about his rigid life that had reached its pinnacle. He picked up his pace, skirted around a taxi, attempting a right turn. Above him, scaffolding surrounded a museum. It had not been up very long; in fact, work began only two days earlier. When he first arrived in the city and passed the museum on his way to the hotel, they were just in the process of erecting it. He paid little attention to it, his focus planted on the paper he was reading in the backseat of the car.

Rashid returned the next day for a tour. The guide was young and knowledgeable enough about the artifacts in the museum. Nothing amused him in the first room. Nothing delighted him in the second. The third was the largest on that first floor, and off to the left was one casing that captured his attention. Inside sat Perseus, on one side of a golden salt cellar, legs entwined with Medusa's, his head turned away, sword in hand ready to strike.

Rashid was appalled that the museum had not given the small statue the deference it was owed, for indeed it was the most beautiful and extraordinary artifact there. As the only surviving gold piece by the great Renaissance master, Polluci, it's a rare find. Did they not know how significant the work was?

Rashid returned at 4AM, stood on the first step of the covered scaffolding, two feet above the sidewalk. Wearing rubber-soled shoes, he quietly sped across the 38 mm thick wooden board; a dark blue plastic cover shielded him from view to the outside world. Within moments, he reached the small first-floor window, barely large enough for him to slide into. Rashid took a circle-cutter from his bag and held its pivot to the glass with a suction cup. The glass cut with such patience and precision, his steadiness equal to a doctor saving a life on the operating table.

Unlatching its lock, he hoisted himself one foot to the frame and pulled himself through headfirst. The knapsack snagged, and he tugged, accidentally unfastening it. The circle-cutter fell. Swiftly, he reached out and grabbed the flying tool before it hit the ground. His body tingled at the thought of a near disaster, and the excitement lifted him from his earlier ennui. He pulled at the bag again until it gave way, releasing him, and he landed on the museum floor with a quiet elegance.

He waltzed with the beams connected to the alarm – slid on his belly and dragged his knapsack behind him. He kept his heart rate at a steady pace, his sweat to a minimum, his breath controlled. Finally upright, he searched his knapsack for the hefty circle-cutter that had fallen to the bottom, then placed the tool on the display case and cut the glass. Rashid peered beyond the small hole to the artifact. He reached in and deliberately picked up the salt-cellar, amazed that such a small piece weighed so much. His fingers caressed the smoothness of Medusa's arm like a lover admiring her beauty and craftsmanship. Holding it gave him an intense sense of pleasure, and something stirred within him.

A hacking cough sounded in the next room. A guard must be on his rounds.

Quickly, Rashid escaped. Once on the street, he rambled away. Having Perseus and Medusa safely tucked away in his bag was an adrenaline rush.

There was a period when he thought they'd be enough, but time left Rashid insatiable, and the money was never enough. He needed more to flee the life he was born into, so the thefts became grander, the payments astronomical. Over the years, he perfected his ways, improved his tools, learned to work with trusted teams for bigger jobs. Payments awaited him, though it wasn't only about the money, despite the autonomy it gave from his father's fortune. It was during these heists that he finally felt in control.

He realized that disposing of the stolen art quickly lessened the chance of capture. But for a time, however brief, the art is his. And right now, it appears he has both *Mistress in a Red Dress* and Charlotte Milton to contend with, though he must rid himself of the first before it becomes too hot. As long as the painting remains in his possession, the *Mistress* could be his downfall. Or perhaps Ms. Milton will hold that honor. She shares an uncanny resemblance to his *Mistress*.

For the moment, he possesses Lady Sheffield, but it's Lady Milton he'd like to spend more time with. And Monaco would have made for a perfect backdrop until Professor Jack Carey appeared at the casino that night.

Ten years had passed, but Rashid recognized Jack – hairstyle and spectacles unchanged – from a newspaper clipping of him presenting the retrieved painting to the Queen of England. Rashid doesn't believe in coincidences. This heist, being significantly flawed, has led Professor Carey to his front door—unless he had been following Charlotte instead. He fled Monaco that night, but in hindsight, he wonders if he would have been better off not pushing Charlotte to Dubai. Besides, he can't shake that niggling question – what if Charlotte is working with the Professor? There's no basis for it except...except...except of all the casinos in all the towns in all the world, Charlotte Milton walked into the very room where he sat with a hand of cards. Well, he considers, if she is working with Professor Jack Carey, it's best he keeps Charlotte close to maintain an eye on her. And if she's innocent of any spying, well, keeping Charlotte intimately close to him is an added bonus.

Chapter 21

@BitchinDiva8901

OMG some tourist dude in Monaco snapped pic of #EditorInThief #CharlotteMilton at a casino. Must be nice to be a rich bitch.

@FashionSmasher4367

Ha ha she thinks she's a Bond girl. Look at that pose. #TheDevilWearsOrange

@CovetThis6889

Is that Versace? I'd kill for that dress. #TheDevilWearsOrange

@HarrietCatwalkStyleMag
Replying to **@CovetThis6889**
She got that Versace for a steal!

@HowToWearIt3434
HOW IS SHE NOT IN JAIL?

@ImThatDude$$$
Hey I played a couple of hands with her. Nice lady. Didn't know a damn thing about Josephine Baker tho. Never knew she was that #EditorInThief til my wife tole me

@HowToWearIt3434
Replying to @ImThatDude$$$
Is it true she lost big to #PrinceRashid? He's hot!!

@ImThatDude$$$
Replying to @HowToWearIt3434
She lost big but didn't seem too heartbroken. They looked pretty cozy at the bar if you know what I mean.

@HarrietCatwalkStyleMag
Replying to @ImThatDude$$$ and @HowToWearIt3434
WHAAAAAAAAAAT! Charlotte was with Prince Rashid? WTF!!!

Chapter 22

HEAT SEIZES MY NOSTRILS, occupies the space around me, suffocating me as I descend the steps of Rashid's private jet. When Rashid turns to smile at me, I catch my reflection in his aviator glasses and like what I see. If I had a photo of myself descending onto the tarmac, I'd splash it all over social media and hashtag the hell out of it. *I'm back, be-atches!* it would scream. But I'm not Harriet with her kick-ass attitude. Besides, I'm hesitant to return to social media. Strangers are trying to destroy me and, from my vantage point, they're succeeding.

A driver, who looks to be in his mid-50s, his face thin and clean-shaven, holds open the door to a white limousine.

"Omar will be your private driver while in Dubai," Rashid tells me, and briefly speaks to Omar in his foreign tongue in what sounds like an exchange of pleasantries.

Inside the car, the navy-blue interior is retrofitted with leather seats, plush pillows lean into corners, and there's a bar filled with juice and water bottles. As the highway gives way to the city, with buildings so tall they catch light in the sunshine like diamonds, the car pulls into a private bridge that leads to a hotel situated on its own island. I read about this 7-star hotel a Sheik designed. The building curves like a sail, and beyond it, the ocean is clear blue.

The white noise of a fountain greets me as it spurts water upwards. By the front entrance, staff wait for us. A female staffer steps out from the line to offer a few drops of a scented liquid to cleanse my hands. I bring my fingertips to my nose. Rosehip. A man offers a traditional tea poured from an Arabic teapot, black and green in color with a tall spout. The warm cup in my hands is whisked away after a few sips of the hot liquid. I'm sure I look very much like the Wicked Witch of the West melting right before them. I need something cold to drink.

Rashid heads to an escalator inside the hotel and, hand outstretched, motions for me. I sprint across the carpet and climb onboard ahead of him. Above me, the atrium's blue and white colors swirl, and I nearly trip from the dizzying effect when the escalator arrives at the top. Several people trail behind, while others run ahead to greet us at the elevator.

"I have a standing reservation here," Rashid explains.

I nod, half-listening, half enthralled by the opulent ceiling stories above me. He beckons me into an elevator, and we swoosh up to a corridor on the 44th floor. The door to the suite is already open, and we waltz into a marbled entranceway that houses an iron-railing staircase. The scent of orchids wafts to my nose. While I'm lost in wonderment, Rashid strides past.

"This is enormous," I say. When he said he has a standing reservation, does it mean he lives here? I've always fantasized about being Eloise but have never actually met one.

Rashid glances around, and a small look of wonder catches on his face as though cognizant of my reaction. "I suppose. I was afraid you'd be disappointed that we aren't in the penthouse. That's usually reserved for my father. The bedrooms are up the stairs."

Bedrooms? Plural?

"Would you care for room service?"

"Don't you mean mansion service?" I chuckle. Rashid smiles politely, and I wipe away the awkward smile. "No, it's been a long day. If you don't mind, I'd like to take a long bath and a nap."

He stares at me, a look of intrigue on his face, and I contemplate what has him so mesmerized.

Finally, he says, "Very well," and moves toward me in measured steps.

I scurry backward until I'm pressed flat against the wall. Is he going to carry me up the steps? Draw a bath for me? Bathe me?

"Excuse me," he says and raises his hand above me to push a small button on the wall.

Within moments, a young man arrives.

Rashid says, "Hamed, draw a bath for Ms. Milton, please."

"Yes, Your Highness."

Hamed is young enough for me to draw him a bath and wrap in a burrito towel. As he quietly ascends, with Rashid and I following, I examine Hamed's thinness, his jacket too big for his small frame, his hands tiny, dark, and delicate.

Outside a room, Rashid says, "I'll leave you, then," and carries on down the corridor.

I stare after him, hoping to get a glimpse into his world, but I can discern very little in the split second it takes for him to open and close the door.

The guest bedroom is the size of my New York apartment. My luggage has already arrived, and neatly placed by the closet but my valise holding my shoes is missing. *Crap!* I was in such a hurry and terrorized by the image of the driver's gun that I didn't do my compulsory sweep of the hotel room.

A noise draws my attention elsewhere and, with the bathroom door ajar, I study Hamed as he marches back and forth in preparation, laying down towels and running water in a tub. Scented oils, floral with strong notes of lavender, drift into the bedroom. Next to the bed is a telephone, silver and modern in design, and so sleek it barely looks like a phone. Another consequence from me being so flustered when Rashid's man, a gun strapped to his waist, banged at my hotel room in Monaco is that I immediately forgot I had dropped my phone in the toilet.

I have no way to reach Jack or the authorities if needed. At the private airfield, I made a show of speaking to everyone, ensuring I'd be remembered just in case. The thought of *in case* makes me shudder, and I contemplate the sequence of events I didn't want to dwell on earlier – *in case* they kill me on the plane and dump my body somewhere it can never be found. *In case* they strip me of my identity and imprison me in a foreign land. All the scenarios are equally dark, but by the time the plane touched down in Dubai, I believed I had nothing to worry about. If Rashid was onto me, he would have done something already.

I lift the receiver and dial "0" for the hotel operator. A male voice comes on the line and says in a soft tone, "Hello."

"Uh, hello?" I say and wonder how it is that I recognize the voice. "I'd like to place a long-distance call to 44 for Britain and the number—" I halt, recognizing the background noise behind the operator that eerily sounds very much like mine. "Hamed?" I say finally into the phone, then turn to the direction of the bathroom.

"Yes," Hamed says from the bathroom doorway and looks at me with a phone clutched to his ear. "Do you have the number?"

All outgoing calls are being monitored. I slam the phone down. How much would I have given away on a phone call to Jack? *Everything.* "I just remembered my parents are on a plane. I'll try again later."

"Yes, Ms. Milton," he says with a smile, unperturbed by the encounter.

From the doorway, I survey how Hamed meticulously rolls towels and places them strategically about the tub. "Have you worked for the Prince long?" I ask Hamed and eye him to gauge what his facial expression will reveal.

He nods. "His Highness employs me in-between the school years."

Hmmm, that came out relatively easy.

"Where do you go to school?"

"London Business School."

"You travel far for a summer job."

Hamed smiles. "It's more than a summer job. Prince Rashid pays for my schooling, and when I graduate, he will help find a placement for me at one of his family businesses. If you need anything else, please let me know."

After Hamed leaves, I soak deep in the tub and mull over the brief conversation I had with him. Rashid may not be a bad boss, but he damn well stole that painting and framed me for it. At some point, I'll search the suite, but for what exactly? Will I find *Mistress in a Red Dress* hanging on a wall above the mantel? *Doubt it.* I tilt my head back against a padded pillow suctioned to the tub, and close my eyes. Jack. I have to get my hands on a new phone.

Pounding startles me, and I thrash about in the tub. Regaining my equilibrium, I catch my breath and listen to the bangs against a door downstairs. Someone, most likely Hamed, answers. A door squeaks open down the corridor from my room, and footsteps hurry along, then strike the marble staircase. Raised voices are muffled by the time they reach me; the sound echoes in my cavernous bathroom. I emerge from the tub and, still wet, slip into the hotel's robe. Outside my room, I press myself against the wall and will my legs forward to view the floor below. My heart races and pumps fear through my veins as I edge closer. Within seconds, I spot Rashid with his arms wrapped around another man, half holding him, half carrying him into a room below, and closes the door. On his hands and knees, Hamed mops what appears to be blood on the white and gray marble floor.

***

The next day, my fingers work the fabric. Cashmere. Expensive. I unclasp the topcoat button, slide my hand in, and scrutinize the stitching on the inside. The male model stares straight ahead, avoids eye contact with me as I continue with my inspection.

"The stitching on the inside is poor," I tell the young designer, Anton. He nods from a few feet away, his hand cups his chin, blue eyeglass frames set against dyed blond hair.

I step back to take in the whole ensemble, my head cocked, lips pursed in concentration. "Who's your customer?"

Anton clears his throat. "The young professional in his twenties, thirties. He works hard and enjoys the finer things in life. He wants to stand out as a hipper version from his father's generation."

I turn to Rashid, settled on the sofa of a private office in the hotel suite, his mobile phone in his hand. I raise an eyebrow his way. Earlier, he encouraged me to speak the truth to this young designer, but I worry just how strong a reality check Rashid will be comfortable with.

"What's your price point?"

Anton is too quick to answer. "In American dollars, nine ninety-five."

"Really?"

Anton's eyes skitter to Rashid, then he returns his attention to me. I can tell he's getting nervous and defensive. There was a time when my opinion mattered, when I could lift a designer from obscurity, and people hung on my every word. God, I miss it.

"It's the right price point," Anton says, watchful of my examining hands. "We feel we're targeting the below a thousand market which is accessible."

"Not to twenty-something males. They can't afford it. It's a fantastic fit, clean, but bland. If you're targeting a hipper crowd, then they'll want to stand out. Have you considered doing a color block version?"

Anton stammers, "N-no, but we're open."

"Good. Now take off the coat, and let's have a look at that blazer."

The young model, whose name escapes me, hands the coat to Anton. He hangs the outer coat on the clothing rack he had rolled into the suite earlier. I quietly inspect the stitching and fit, periodically motion to the model to turn around. Having him face me again, I shake my head.

"This is fine work, but it's missing something. How about a little fun pocket square?"

"No," Anton says, "that's something his father would wear."

"Pocket squares come in many fun colors and patterns. A man can never have too many. Yes, a pocket square with a custom-made shirt. You don't make shirts do you?"

Anton shakes his head.

"Once you go custom, you never go back, and cashmere socks – the ultimate orgasmic high." I turn to see both Rashid and Anton stare at me. "So, I've heard. All right, Anton, a buyer at Nordstrom's wants this jacket. How many units can you give them?"

"What?" says Anton, his mouth gaping.

"Hypothetically speaking," I elucidate, "a buyer at Nordstrom's wants to purchase them. How many units can you deliver?"

"When?"

"Now. Buyers are purchasing ahead of time. You need to know how many units you can provide, what price point makes sense, you need to know what your customer is wearing now. Three months from now. Six months from now. Be a risk-taker. And color block."

Later, after Anton hauls his line back down the elevator, Rashid pours me a drink. I take it and, lifting the glass to my nose, sniff the scotch. One sublime sip tells me it's not just any old scotch. It's sweet and smoky with notes of orange and rose.

I consider taking the bottle to bed with me. It's the best I've ever had.

"I was too harsh," I say, before Rashid has a chance to admonish me.

"He needs to hear the truth. Besides, I promised his father I would finance him if you believed in him."

"So, this is on me?"

Returning to the bar, Rashid fills half his glass with ice, then pours carbonated water into it. He sits opposite me, one leg crossed over the other, a cashmere sock exposed. I force myself to look away and take another swig. My eyes dart to the bottle on the shelf, and I decide that yes, I will definitely take it to bed. That bottle, plus the hotel's 1,000 thread count of Egyptian cotton, equals heaven. I once dated a man, a boy really, who slept in black satin sheets, a throwback to the '80s, and I always found myself sliding off the bed during sex. No wonder I always thought sex with him was mediocre. Does the quality of the bedsheets improve the orgasm? Now there's an idea for the magazine to sex it up a little.

"Did you manage to nap after your bath," he says, eyeing me before adding, "no disturbances to keep you up?"

"Well," I say, hesitate, then elect to show my hand, "someone was banging on the door with what seemed to be a pressing matter." I neglect to mention the blood on the floor. Everything about Rashid – from his appearance, to his near-perfect English, to his manner – is controlled. He's confident, assured, and moves with intent, unlike Jack, who seems to move through life unselfconsciously. So, it astonishes me to see Rashid's cheek twitch.

Finally, he says, "It was a business associate with an urgent issue."

Is that what happens to business associates? Am I technically one? An image of my blood staining the marble floor pierces my thoughts. *Damn*, I need Jack. Pushing that image aside and changing the subject, I say, "Do you know where I can buy a cell phone? Mine was accidentally destroyed."

Rashid strides to a mirrored credenza and opens a drawer, pulls out a box wrapped in cellophane. "A company phone," he says and extends the package to me.

"Wonderful. Well, I'll get this all sorted out," I say, referring to the new phone. Glancing at the computer on the desk, I say, "In the meantime, do you mind if I use your computer to access my email?"

"Of course," Rashid says. "I'll see to it you're not disturbed."

Before the door closes behind him, I hear Rashid laugh, saying, "Ultimate orgasmic high."

"It's true," I call after him. "I know you're feeling it right now."

I kill the laughter once the sound of his footsteps recede. Time to get down to business. I pull out a flash drive from my pant pocket and insert it into Rashid's laptop, my finger on the mouse dancing through files and copying them quickly. I've done this before. After breaking up with an old boyfriend, I realized I left some articles I had been writing on his computer and snuck into his apartment when I was supposed to be meeting him to return his key. I was in and out before he knew what was happening (much like our sex life, as I remember it). At the coffee shop, I handed him the key, gave him a peck on the cheek, and wished him well. He told me to drop dead.

Light footsteps sound on the other side of the door, and I suspect they belong to Hamed. Still, to be safe, I open my personal email account and work on that screen while downloading. As expected, my inbox has received an influx of emails. Sifting through a few nasty messages, I skip ahead and scan subject lines that seem to shout: *We Want Your Story* and *Thief!* and *Rot in Hell.* Those I eliminate straight away, press the delete button as quick as I can, then wonder why leave room for more irascible emails?

One subject line stops me.

Where are you? from Jack Carey. I select the message and skim through – *worried about you. Please call…* and, fortunately for me, he leaves a contact number. I jump as the office door swishes open, and Rashid stands in the doorway, staring at me.

"I didn't mean to scare you," he says.

"You didn't." I shrug and give him one of my big, toothy smiles I would often give men when I was younger. Glancing at the computer, I note the copying is nearly done.

"We've been invited to attend the races this evening." He takes a few measured steps towards me. "There are some people I'd like you to meet."

"Absolutely," I say, detecting a slight strain in my voice. The bar, indicating the copying status, moves forward on the computer.

"I'll leave you to your emails," he says and closes the door behind him. This time, I don't hear his footsteps. Is he there, eavesdropping, or is it that I can't hear anything beyond my heart pounding in my chest?

The computer beeps. All downloads are completed. I sign out of my email, erase the file history, and pull the flash drive from Rashid's laptop. Holding it between my thumb and index finger, I kiss it for good luck and say, "Let there be proof." My reputation is counting on it.

Chapter 23

F OLLOWING A DAY OF meetings (and after leaving two anxious messages on Jack's phone), I sit in the limousine next to Rashid. He's dressed in a gleaming white *dishdasha*; front buttons hidden behind a fly front for a sleeker look, a flowing black cloak edged with gold braid. On his head is a white *shemagh*, the scarf secured by an *egal* in black. For myself, I chose a masculine pantsuit in white, a bright orange tie at the neck, but wonder if a hat or fascinator for this outing to the races is required. We're not in England, so perhaps not.

I wipe my sweaty palms on my pant legs and then tighten them into a ball. Telling myself I have nothing to be nervous about, I lean over to lower the window. "Do you mind?" I say, turning to Rashid.

"No."

Palm trees fly past as we make our way to a large hotel and racecourse entrance, the diamond-shaped green glass luminous in its wave-like design. It resembles something out of *The Jetsons*. When the car stops under the canopy, a greeter is there to open the door.

"Welcome to the Meydan," the man says, then guides us into the lobby.

The tiled floor has the glossy smoothness of an ice rink, the vastness of its impeccable architecture reflected in its surface. I look up at the triangular formation of the ceiling, the exposed glass elevator, and my head swirls, wondering if it's possible to suffer from vertigo from the ground looking up.

We are led down a corridor, through a few doorways opened only by keycards, and out a back way to the racetrack. The thunder of the crowd smacks me. The chaos of it all – men in white *thobes*, others in western business attire, the women in a multitude of colors and, yes, hats – is like looking into a kaleidoscope. Some of the outfits are literally hot off the Paris runway. It seems everyone in the city is at the track tonight – Emirati, ex-pats, laborers.

Cameras flash. When the white flash disappears from my sight, I note we are now in a diamond formation of bodyguards who lead us through the crowd, down a set of stairs, and, finally, into a private area overlooking the race track. From this vantage point, I can see all below us and across the track. I turn down offers of food and refreshments, afraid I'm too nervous to keep anything down.

"This is totally fire," I shout over the crowd to Rashid and wonder when I began to use the vernacular of a sixteen-year-old girl circa 2015.

"Members of the Royal family own the racehorses," Rashid explains, "and while gambling isn't allowed, there is a prize given to the owner of the winning horse."

"But, won't that always be a member of the Royal family?" I ask.

"Yes," he responds, seemingly unaware of the absurdity of the question and the situation – the Royal family, it seems, will never lose a race because they are the only owners.

A camel race entertains the audience before the official start of the horse race. Rashid points out to me twice that the jockeys are adults, and I understand his concern. The UAE has been known to bring children from places like India and Pakistan to jockey the camels. The animals and jockeys are released from the lineup. A handler gets bustled in-between the camels but appears to be okay.

"This is hilarious," I say as I watch the camels move at a slower pace than racehorses. Looking about, I spot quite a bit of commotion below; a crowd surrounds an older man and a beautiful young woman, whom I suspect is his daughter.

"Who are they?" I say, pointing.

Rashid's face stiffens. "My father."

Shit. Why didn't he mention his father would be in attendance? I swallow hard, trying to contain my nerves. "Is that your sister?"

"My father's fourth wife."

It's not the answer that stuns me; it's the untroubled manner in which Rashid says it.

"Oh."

For a moment, Rashid seems unsure of himself. He steps towards me and then hesitates, looks down, and twists a ring on his finger. I realize he, too, gets nervous, which surprises me.

His eyes turn to me. "Charlotte," he says in a quiet voice, "my father is from a different era, a different place. I am not my father. I will never be like him."

I can't bring myself to turn away. Nor can I come up with anything to say. An announcement breaks the moment.

Appearing dismayed by the interruption, Rashid says, "My horse is in this race."

"Which one?" I say and eye the starting plate.

Rashid leans in close. "Third from the right. *The Girl.*"

"Couldn't come up with a name?"

Rashid smiles. "It's the name of the role Marilyn Monroe played in *The Seven Year Itch.*"

"My first apartment in New York had a set of stairs that led nowhere. At the time, I thought it was funky but now I see it as a metaphor of my life."

"They led you here."

I lean into him and, with a small smile on my lips, I say in a sultry voice, "Quite true. *The Girl* it is, then."

"I'm afraid you may be the only one cheering her on. She's not very fast."

"It's very American to root for the underdog."

The race underway, I scream for *The Girl*, who gets off to a good start but falters as the race progresses. A horse comes up from behind, passes *The Girl*, falls back some, then sprints. Up ahead, a tight race takes place between the two favorites, but my thoughts are on *The Girl*. She gains a little, bypasses the horse that overtook her.

"Our horse is gaining," says Rashid.

When did it become our horse? I wonder, and I like the idea of it. *Our* horse passes, and I lean over the railing, pump my fists in the air. "Come on!" One by one, other horses pass *The Girl*, each slowly comes up alongside her, and then passes, leaving her behind. The distance between her and the one closest to her grows. It seems Rashid and I are the poor horse's only cheerleaders as it huffs into last place.

"Well," Rashid says, appearing unbothered by the outcome, "horses aren't my passion."

"What is?"

Looking directly at me, he says, "Beauty."

My face flushes, surprised by the flirtation and by how deeply he looks at me. It's so easy to lose focus, which may be his intention. I force myself to look away, say something about nothing, and hope Rashid doesn't notice my unintelligible musings. Plus, I can't believe I let a line like that sink me. Maybe I am sixteen, after all.

"My cousin owns the winning horse. Come, we should congratulate him."

Rashid leads the way towards a group of men wearing the traditional *dishdasha* and introduces me to several of them. We nod and shake hands before moving through the crowd, swept up in the sea of patrons in a celebratory mood.

With Rashid by my side, I find myself in a line to meet the Sheikh. I turn to escape but get jostled by those behind me. It would be too awkward if I step out of line now. How does a foreigner greet his... *Holiness? Oh no, that's the Pope.* Do I refer to him as *His Highness?* Do I kiss his hand? His ring? Or is that the Pope again?

The Sheikh appears older than the mid-sixties I suspected from afar. His eyebrows are dark and bushy, his mustache and beard trimmed on a pudgy face. Rashid has nothing in common with his father except for those mesmerizing eyes. In Arabic, Rashid says something to his father, who furrows his brow, nods, then turns to me. When presented, I do the only thing that seems logical – I curtsy. The expressions on the faces of those around me indicate this is the wrong thing to do. Finally, the Sheikh smiles; more words are spoken in Arabic, and then Rashid places his hand on my shoulder and leads me away.

A middle-aged woman near the Sheik stares at me. I turn away, and when I bring my gaze back, there are now three middle-aged women staring at me.

"Why are those women giving me the evil eye?"

Rashid follows my gaze. "They each have daughters they wish me to marry."

"You're engaged?" I exclaim. The news shocks and upsets me. Though I'm not supposed to care about his personal life, I couldn't help notice his interactions with me have been quite flirtatious this evening.

"Not yet. I had hoped your presence would stave off my father's intentions for the evening. He's quite perturbed I brought you."

"Doesn't he know I work for you?"

Rashid says, "He's under the impression you're my betrothed."

"How did he get that impression?"

His hand touches the small of my back. "From me. The older I get, the more intolerant and contemptuous I am of his plans for my future and for one night, I'd like a reprieve from all his nonsense. I apologize. I shouldn't use you as a pawn in this game with my father."

I lean into him ever so slightly. Two can play at this flirtatious game. Besides, I wouldn't mind a reprieve, too, from this spy game I'm playing. "That's fine, though I suppose those mothers may put a hit on me. I'll need protection," I say, my eyes drift along his body.

I look back to the women who are now surrounded by what must be their daughters. They are all stunning. I whistle. "Wow. I would not turn them down."

My comment has Rashid take a second look. What am I doing putting ideas into his head?

"Not for me. Besides," he continues, "these rigid, old-fashioned ideas end with my father's generation. Certainly, my children won't be subjected to the same upbringing I endured." When he says this, he turns back to his father, and I detect a note of resentment in his tone.

"Was it that bad?"

"When you're on the outside looking in, all you see are the homes and jewelry and private planes, and it becomes hard for people to see how we're trapped within a gilded cage, or to understand our loss of freedom."

"Can't you make a royal exit?"

"Working on it," he mumbles.

"You mentioned children. You want them?"

Of my last six boyfriends, not one wanted a family. I was beginning to believe men no longer wanted what I did.

"A strong want," he says, his eyes look at me intensely. *Damn*, everything about him is intense. "With an equal partner, not a girl who thinks she must obey me."

"I had a boyfriend once who couldn't make a decision on his own. I suppose he was my submissive."

"And how was the relationship?"

"Hmmm. It's the only one where I had control of the TV remote. I suppose I should have married him."

"Is that your standard for spending a lifetime with someone?" he says, smiling at me. I read it as teasing.

There's definitely some flirtation on his part. And I've probably batted my eyes at him a million times, so I'm giving as much as I'm receiving. But *playing* the game and getting *trapped* in my own game are very different. Yet, there's something in Rashid's gaze and in the softness of his voice that gives my heartbeat a little thump, and I have to remind myself I'm only playing a part. Still, I don't look away as we stare longingly into one another's eyes. Damn Rashid and his symmetrical face.

Rashid draws in closer. His eyes scan my lips. By all accounts, it is a perfect moment for a first kiss, but someone behind Rashid captivates me, and I break our gaze.

"Don't turn around, but there's a man staring at us. He's wearing a navy suit, and his hair is pulled back in a ponytail, and two very muscular men flank him. They look like bodybuilders. Are you supposed to marry his daughters, too?"

Rashid catches the eye of someone moving past, greets him, and turns to glance at the man I pointed out. Rashid's jaw tightens.

Chapter 24

WHEN RASHID'S EYES MEET Levan's, he's unable to hide his surprise and anger. The other night when his man, Raheem, arrived, bloodied with three fingers and two ribs broken, he knew that Levan would pose a problem. And now he dares to show himself at Rashid's family's event. The look on Levan's face seems to mock, a threat written in the lines of his smile: "I can get to you anywhere."

Rashid can't say he hadn't been warned about getting involved with him.

Immediately, he excuses himself from Charlotte, mutters something about a business meeting, and walks past the uninvited guest. Levan follows, and together they escape to a private room overlooking the races, with Levan's men close.

Rashid sits, his eyes scan the crowd for spies, contemplating if others recognize Levan enough to report to his father. Levan takes the chair next to him, a cigar in one hand, scotch in the other. He puffs at the disgusting cigar, the smell wafts to Rashid, and he wrinkles his nose instinctively.

A smile jumps to Levan's face; he shrugs and rests the cigar on the edge of a plate on the table between them, the nasty odor lingering. Rashid wants to hurry, cut this meeting short but he spots Levan stir his drink in a slow motion with an index finger, like a man who believes the world waits for him. Finally, he takes a swig.

"Did I ever tell you the meaning behind my name?" says Levan.

Rashid doesn't respond.

"Lion," he says and follows with the sound of a lion's roar. "King of the Jungle. My parents named me well. I am my namesake." Levan casually crosses his legs. "Certainly, there was a time when I had failed them. Yes, when I think back a few decades to the moment I hid in the hull of a ship, a stowaway on a boat run by bandits, I feel shame."

"Why are you here?" Rashid can't bring himself to look at him and keeps his gaze squarely on the crowd below. There, he sees Charlotte, who has a perfect view of the private box, stare in their direction.

Levan ignores the question and continues with his story. "I should go back a little to explain why I was on the boat. I was a small thing, skinny, but strong and smart. My parents sent me to the best school in Georgia; they had the money to do that until that little coup happened. My father was a writer who wrote favorably about the government, and my mother a homemaker, but she inherited a large sum from her father. When they heard the rumblings—"

Facing him, Rashid interrupts "—Levan, why..."

Levan holds up his hand to silence Rashid. Continuing, he says, "... the rumblings of civil war, my father wrote in support of our President. I attended university at the time, and sometimes I was in class, sometimes I joined rallies. Education no longer mattered because the university supported the opposition. Things changed, power was exchanged, and eventually, my father disappeared. My mother searched for him, hearing a rumor he had been picked up in a sweep. She never returned. It was how do they say 'Tit for Tat'? Our President kept political prisoners, so now the Zviadists, his loyalists, were imprisoned. I was too involved myself, a young student who thought he understood everything. They'd look for me eventually, so I ran.

I paid what little money I had to stow away on a ship I thought was heading for Europe. I trusted the wrong smuggler. Instead, the ship sailed for Oman.

"So, I'm on the boat. Three others hid with me, crouching, quiet. But they didn't hide as well as I did. One snuck out for food, and I heard the commotion when they captured him. Then I heard his screams when they chopped off his hands and tossed him over the side into shark-infested water. I heard everything. The crew was thrilled to watch the sharks circle him then—" Levan chomps down on air, laughing. "Even after what they heard, the other foolish men snuck out, thinking they'd never get caught. But they were. They caught me, too. Dragged me out from the darkness. I was so frightened I pissed my pants. One of them came at me with a machete, but I ducked out of the way. Remember, I was lithe and quick, quick, quick. Oh, he was mad, but the other men laughed, delighted with the entertainment. He grew angrier. Each time he swung, I managed to slip past his machete until it became lodged into a wooden pole, and while he busied himself yanking it out, I grabbed a machete from another and hacked his fighting arm off."

Rashid turns away, grimacing. Down below, he can see Charlotte straining for a better view at them.

"The men were riled up, so I chopped the other arm off. I threw him overboard and proved I was just like them. Everyone has a story about how they were made. I was made there on that boat." Levan swirls the glass in his hand. "Now, we have some business between us that's unsettled. I trust your man, Raheem, explained matters to you? Yes?"

Silence fills the space between them as Rashid fights to control his anger at Levan for what he did to Raheem, for renegotiating their deal, for showing up here of all places with his men. There is nothing they can do to one another in public, though Rashid envisions retaliation for putting Raheem in the hospital.

"The new lower price stands. Understand it is the cost of doing shoddy business. How can I unload that painting now? You promised it would be practically unnoticeable. Do you call a police chase through the streets of Paris unnoticeable? Do you consider their capture of one of your team unnoticeable? It's only a matter of time before Miss Milton talks."

Rashid jumps up from his chair, fists clenched. Levan's bodyguards step forward, but Levan waves them off.

"Sit down," Levan says in a calm voice. "Please, there is no need for theatrics. We don't wish to give onlookers the wrong impression."

Rashid looks to Levan's men. If they tried anything, his family's men would arrive in mere seconds to protect him, but it would bring questions from his father, and he can't risk that. Begrudgingly, he takes his seat next to Levan.

"She knows nothing." Rashid eyes Charlotte as she moves through the crowd below. It's bad enough that the French police suspect her, but now that he's brought her to Dubai in a weak attempt to make amends, it appears that there's more to her involvement as far as Levan is concerned. Rashid should have considered this. "She's nothing but a scapegoat. I brought her here to determine what she knows, and I guarantee you, it is absolutely nothing."

"She will lead them to you, and then you to me," says Levan. "I can't draw attention to myself, have the police knock down doors, draw the ire of other criminal organizations my way. Law enforcement has the resources to bear down on me, and my business, and that woman will sing to them. She's not like us. This isn't personal. It's just facts. Next time, you'll be more careful, yes?"

"I said she knows nothing. I promise you that. Now, I will agree to the lower price as a sign of good faith for the problem that I caused."

Levan downs the remainder of his drink and grows quiet for a moment. Then he says, "I'll need something else as a sign of good faith. This Milton woman knows more than you're saying and needs to be disposed of. Do it, or I will. I trust you'd be swift like those sharks." He leans closer, and whispers, "Me? I enjoy taking my time."

<h1 style="text-align:center">Chapter 25</h1>

A FAMILIAR SONG PRICKS my mind and interrupts my snores. I sleepily hum along to the repetition, doing backup to Blondie's "Call Me." But there's strangeness in my landscape, and I bolt upward from a lipstick-smeared pillow, my thoughts disoriented. It's my new cell phone. Jumping out of bed, I race to my purse I had thrown onto a chair last night and dig inside.

"Hello. Hello?" Dead silence greets me. Checking the clock on my phone, I realize it's the middle of the night. Through sheer curtains, a sliver of moonlight peeps into the room. I'm startled by a woman staring at me in the semi-darkness. The woman's smudged raccoon eyes and the greasy, flattened hair, I discover, belong to me! My image reflects in the mirror before me. Disgusted, I plop back into my bed and place my cell on the nightstand.

I try to fall back to sleep, but have something on my mind. On the drive back from the races, I had gently asked Rashid about the man at the racecourse. There was something in the way the stranger stared at me that unnerved me. Paranoia had settled in, and I wondered if Rashid knew I copied his computer files. But Rashid insisted he was a casual acquaintance. Still, I remember the indignant look on Rashid's face when he first saw the man, a cold, hard stare that grew deathly serious during their meeting. It was enough to persuade me to snap a picture on the sly. Rashid wasn't his usual charming self during the car ride, then, when he changed the topic by announcing plans for a boat ride this evening, I sensed something was amiss.

"No, he doesn't know," I say aloud, then stand and pace, my body a bundle of nerves not willing to believe in the lie. How could he possibly suspect anything? I was careful, yet I've seen enough cop procedurals to know nothing is ever truly erased from a computer's history. After all, I was frazzled sneaking through his computer files. My palms begin to sweat; I'm agitating myself unnecessarily. Rashid knows nothing. Rashid suspects nothing. Still, I'd feel better if Jack was by my side; I need someone I can trust. After all, this is his plan, though, technically, his plan fell apart rather quickly, which begs the question, whose plan is this? *Oh God*, did I just throw myself into a ridiculous situation with no plan? And can I still expect Jack to support me after he failed the first time back in Monaco?

Still unable to sleep, I sit on the edge of the bed, reach for the TV remote, and am pleasantly surprised to find many English programs. While channel surfing, one unfamiliar image morphs into another until I flip to *On The Runway TV*. The host, Marlene Baker, is reporting outside the Dior fashion house during Paris Fashion Week only two weeks earlier. To me, it seems like a lifetime ago.

My mobile rings on the nightstand, and I answer it absent-mindedly. "Hello."

"Charlotte, finally. Where are you?"

"Oh, Jack! I left you messages, and I worried when I didn't hear from you, but then Rashid had me turn my phone off last night at the races."

"Races? Charlotte," he says, "it's important you tell me where you are. Do you understand? I need to know..."

"I'm in Dubai," I say, and think back to my countless messages. Did I not tell him where I was in any of them? "I'm sure I told you."

"No! I've been frantic this entire time!"

"Hmmm," I mumble, distracted by the captions on the TV show. The camera pulls back, and standing beside Marlene is a somewhat nervous Jane whose exaggerated smile displays Osmond family-style teeth. "Jane?"

"Who's Jane?"

"My former assistant."

"Are you with her now?"

"Why would I be with my former assistant?" In a low whisper, I add, "Listen, Jack, I copied all sorts of documents from Rashid's computer onto a flash drive."

After a moment of silence, he asks, "You're still on board with the plan?"

"What!" I mutter, stupefied by his question. "Of course, I'm on board. When did I get off-board?"

"I thought, given everything that happened, you had changed your mind."

"I went to the casino because of our plan and have no idea what happened to you. I came here to Dubai because of our plan, constantly watching my back, worried that Rashid will suspect I have ulterior motives. But, hey, I got this. You stay safe in Monaco or Paris or London or wherever you are."

This silences Jack, and I want to ask if he's still on the line when he finally speaks.

"I'm sorry. I couldn't reach you and thought our plan failed. Then your voicemail messages had me all confused, and I thought you had bailed on me."

Curious about why Jane is being interviewed, I try to tune into the show and listen to Jack.

"Well," says Jane on TV, "orders are coming in from all over, the largest from Saks Fifth Avenue in New York and, Selfridges in London, everywhere."

To Jack, I say, "Before I forget, I snapped a picture of a man at the races. There was something odd about him, about the way he looked at me, that scared me, but I couldn't get a good photo, well, it's a little blurry. The other night, an associate of Rashid's arrived at the hotel suite, all bloodied. I'm scared here on my own, Jack."

It's difficult to be simultaneously speaking with Jack and concentrating on the TV screen. Marlene's voice narrates over images of several fashion shows, but it's not until the third shot that I realize I'm in all of them. "How opportune that this success came from that infamous day during Paris Fashion Week when all eyes were upon this scene."

The episode cuts to an amateur video of me dangling from the helicopter, then falling, with my colorful coat-turned-parachute, into the Seine. The amateur cameraman had zoomed up my skirt. He must have been on a nearby boat to get a shot like that. *Damn the tourists and their cameras.* This, I determine, is what happens when you wear color. I'll remember this the next time I stray from my usual uniform of black.

"I've named it *The Charlotte*, after my great friend, Charlotte Milton. I'm thinking of you, Charlotte," Jane says to the camera. Onscreen, the program flashes various social media comments – most incredibly nasty, with only one in support of me – which Marlene Baker reads aloud. Each post verbalized smacks me with shame.

"They're opinions from nobodies," I mumble to myself.

"I didn't mean to offend you, Charlotte," says Jack.

Then the camera cuts to a nervous Anne. She mumbles in a monotone whisper as though reading off a teleprompter. "Charlotte Milton has not been charged because they've found no evidence against her, yet."

Yet?

Harriet suddenly appears on screen. "Of course, she's innocent," she practically screams.

A swell of gratitude blooms in my chest. "This heist required clever planning that only a megalomaniac could have pulled off, and you'd be truly impressed with how depressingly bland Charlotte Milton is."

"Oh, no, I'm doomed." I moan, shaken by the *depressingly bland* label, and throw myself backward on the bed.

"Charlotte," Jack shouts, "where are you?"

"Dubai."

"Yes, but where in Dubai? I'll see how quickly I can get there."

For each day that has passed since the theft in Paris, I have fooled myself into believing my reputation can be restored, but social media, and now mainstream media, have made me realize that rescuing my name is impossible. I have been utterly destroyed. Of course, I can always change my name and live in a small town where no one knows me, but what good will any of that do if my history is forever plastered on the world-wide-web?

"Charlotte, where in Dubai?"

I give a desperate laugh. "I should change my name."

"What? Charlotte, are you traveling under a pseudonym?"

I don't understand why; maybe it's the shock of my situation, but Jack's question has me erupt in laughter. "Yes, Professor, I am. I'm an extremely connected woman. Russian mob. Arms dealers. That painting is nothing compared to what I'm involved in now." I succeed in silencing him again, so much so that I sit up on one elbow, wondering if we've been disconnected. "Jack? ...Jack, are you there?"

Finally, I hear his voice, low and quiet.

"Please, tell me where you are."

I sigh. What am I doing? He's the only one who hasn't judged me.

After I provide him with the hotel details and arrange a rendezvous, I say, "Look, Jack, I'll see you later when your plane gets in but I've got to go now. I just received some devastating news and need to bury my head somewhere." I disconnect then hug the phone to my chest, contemplating if this latest PR catastrophe will deem me unemployable in Rashid's eyes. If he fires me (though he hasn't officially hired me yet), then I'll never be able to prove my innocence.

Quickly, I key "Charlotte Milton" into YouTube's search function. The first video displayed is the one of me dangling from the helicopter. It's received three million views.

Chapter 26

Both men speak in tandem, picking up where the other left off. One of the men holds a laptop, his fingers flip through slides of their real estate endeavor complete with near lifelike computer drawings. The building is too tall and fantastical, and expensive. It's something Rashid has heard before, and he can't understand why these developers aren't better informed about where his interests lie, but of course, this is the result of continuing to live under his father's shadow.

"Gentlemen, I apologize for the interruption, but you must understand I am not my father. This is too grandiose a venture for me, and I absolutely did not buy that land to build something more elaborate than the last one built in this city. People need affordable homes."

Briefly, the men fall silent. "Of course, we understand. This project is tailored specifically with you in mind," says the one with the laptop. "The next slide will show you the projections with numbers that have been vetted. We can slip in a couple of affordable–" (Rashid swears he hears contempt in his voice at the word *affordable*) "studios. We expect to sell the minimum number of units in a short period after launch. In fact, we're working on a waitlist for this is luxurious living at its best."

Rashid laughs. These two, he determines, can't read the room. The other man jumps in, his words quick and desperate to close the deal. But as he drones on, Rashid scans the hotel restaurant. Nearly half, he assumes, are wealthy tourists – lawyers and executives, the unemployed children of the rich, and a celebrity that one of the developers pointed out as a YouTube sensation. The other man sitting with the YouTuber is either a Los Angeles director or a Silicon Valley tech guy. Those are the only professions that can explain the white sneakers, baseball hat and hoodie, as well as the casualness in which he slumps back in his chair, one foot resting on his knee like he's in the comfort of his own home. Then, a recognizable face enters the restaurant.

"Will you excuse me, gentlemen," says Rashid, and quickly approaches Omar by the entrance. He sweeps Omar away from the hostess. "Where is Ms. Milton? You're not to leave her alone."

Omar glances to the floor, his voice quiet. "I don't know where she is."

"It's your job to know," says Rashid, keeping the volume of his voice low.

"She didn't tell anyone she was leaving. I checked her room, and she's gone."

"Was she taken?" he says in a hurried tone. If Levan has her, how long will he keep her alive? He had warned Rashid last night that if he doesn't take care of her, Levan would. Rashid had thought he'd have more time to deal with his Charlotte problem, and give her the one thing Levan wouldn't – mercy.

"No." Omar shakes his head profusely. "I reviewed the security video at the hotel. She left on her own volition, but…"

"But what?" says Rashid angrily.

"It could be nothing but there were two men in the lobby who were watching her. They both had baseball hats and sunglasses that obscured their faces. Then security cameras outside picked up a taxi she took. Alone. She could be anywhere."

Rashid echoes the same thought. *Charlotte Milton could be anywhere in Dubai.* He dials her number but it automatically transfers to voicemail. His tone is casual as he leaves a message though it doesn't reflect the anxiety he's feeling.

"I called her several times, but her phone must be turned off and..." Omar trails off.

"And what?" Rashid says in a clipped tone.

"And I didn't have time to place that GPS tracker on her phone like you asked."

Rashid sucks in a breath and tries to control his anger. Baffled that she slipped away, Rashid tries to anticipate places she'd go. He considers when he last spoke with her, and there was nothing to indicate something was amiss. So what exactly is she up to, and was it planned?

Rashid glances at his Rolex for the time. "Have Khalid track her. He'll know what to do with her. And have that security footage viewed again. If those men stayed at the hotel, I want to know who they are and what their interest is in Ms. Milton."

Rashid has another meeting in an hour, and while he'd love to cancel, his father will be in attendance, and his absence is the very thing his father will no longer tolerate. Rashid will sit there, his mind elsewhere until Charlotte is located. He'll have Hamed alert him if she returns to the hotel. No, not *if,* but *when*. His mind shouldn't go to dark places, but it's impossible not to after his conversation with Levan.

Chapter 27

J ETLAGGED, JACK HAS BEEN waiting at this cafe by the water's edge for more than an hour now with no word from Charlotte. Connecting the previous evening, they planned to meet so he could retrieve the flash drive. He double-checked the name of the café. He triple-checked the arranged time. There's no doubt he's in the right location at the correct time, so where is she? He'd like to call her, but what if she's not alone, and it somehow gives her away? No, everything's fine, and Charlotte is merely being Charlotte and has probably become distracted by something.

Jack finishes his second iced hibiscus tea, a variety of berries float in the drink. Crossing his legs like a little boy unable to control his bladder, he contemplates how much longer he can wait before heading to the toilet. He glances at his watch and crosses his legs the other way. This is absurd. He can't possibly miss Charlotte in the few minutes it will take him. Stepping up to the bar, he asks for directions and finds the bathroom situated at the end of a paneled corridor. The urinal is right there, and although alone, he can't bring himself to use it and enters a middle stall. It's public urination, he's tried to convince his closest friends, but even they, who have known him all his life, believe him odd when it comes to this.

The bathroom door swooshes open, a lock slides in place, and shoes clank slowly against the tiled floor. Jack tilts his ear to listen, then, persuading himself that he's paranoid, finishes and zips up, simultaneously flushing. It's only when he's about to unlock the stall that he realizes the footsteps have stopped on the other side of his door. Was he followed? But by whom? No one knew about his travel plans except for...Charlotte! Her lateness hasn't been explained away by a text from her. Were her intuitions correct, and did Rashid suspect her? If Rashid questioned her, did she tell him everything? Jack wouldn't blame her if they threatened violence. When Charlotte mentioned the man at the races and the bloodied business associate of Rashid's, Jack should have contacted Favreau straight away, or he should have found a way to extricate her from this dangerous situation.

If someone is on the other side of the stall door, then surely they're waiting for him to open it to get the jump on him. He'll be ready for them. Slowly, he turns the lock and waits. The door is thrust open, and without thinking, Jack head butts the person trying to gain entry. A terrible scream follows, and the assailant falls back against the stall, holding the tip of a bloody nose.

"Charlotte?" Jack gasps, pulling her towards him while she tilts her head back.

"I'm getting blood on my pashmina."

"Sorry, yes, of course," he says and grabs at a wad of toilet paper. He guides her to the washbasin, pressing the toilet paper to her nose.

Tears well up her eyes. "My nose stings. Oh, this is painful. Why would you head butt me?" she says through a plugged nose.

"I thought I was being followed."

"You were," she shouts. "By me. I couldn't approach you out in public in case someone saw us together. When I saw no one else was in here, I locked the bathroom door behind me."

"I feel terrible," says Jack. "Absolutely terrible."

With her head still tilted back, she looks down at him through slits. She appears to soften. "It was an accident."

"Is it broken?"

"No." Charlotte pulls the tissue away from her nose. "Looks like it stopped bleeding." She turns on the tap to wash the blood from her face. Turning to her purse she had dropped on the floor, she says, "Can you pass me my Judith?"

"Judas?"

"Careful there. I may interpret a Freudian slip. My Judith Leiber. You really don't know fashion, do you?" Once he hands her the purse, she pulls something out from it. "Here's the drive. I was incredibly nervous having this on me. There was a moment I thought it had been stolen and I panicked. Turns out it had slipped to the bottom of an inside pouch. I swear, it gave me a heart attack right there in the middle of the street. Then, I caught sight of two men in baseball hats and I recognized one in a Manchester United jersey from my hotel lobby because I practically crashed into him. I had convinced myself they were following me when one hurriedly tapped his friend on the shoulder, and they scurried away. I spent the rest of the afternoon looking over my shoulder, but I never saw them again. I think paranoia is getting the better of us. By the way, I emailed you the photo of the man from the races. I can't stay long. I'm late meeting Rashid." She hesitates and stares at him. "Something hasn't felt right ever since Rashid met with that man. We're going on a boat ride tonight, and I'd feel a lot safer knowing you were out there somewhere."

He nearly broke her nose, and *he* makes her feel safe? Life just became progressively more dangerous for Charlotte.

Chapter 28

Dressed in a flowing chiffon dress paired with a wide-brimmed hat and a pair of stilettos, I skip from one stone step to another towards the marina. Flats would be more appropriate, but considering the bathing suit under my dress, I judge the heel will do wonders for my calves, and I need all the help I can get. Omar had dropped me off and he seemed upset that I had disappeared on him the way I did. Though he didn't say much, his responses to me were curt. I had to wonder, was I in trouble with Rashid? I'm certainly glad I had asked Jack to be here as I didn't want to be alone with Rashid at the moment. Something was definitely off with him.

Taxis fly in and out of the parking lot, cyclists zip past along the boardwalk, and a couple with a bright pink selfie stick pose with boats to their background. A group of tourists embarks on a ship, slipping their arms through orange life jackets. I stroll past a small crowd of people mingling on the boardwalk.

"Charlotte."

I turn. With all the distractions, I had walked past Rashid standing a mere twenty feet away and next to a boat called *She Is Mine.* I hope the reference is to the boat; still, I can't ignore the misogyny of it all. I hurry along to him.

"Be very careful when stepping onboard," he says, gets into the boat, and turns to extend a hand.

The boat, I realize, is not the yacht I had pictured. There will be no lounging on the deck in my bathing suit and no servants serving us supper. No, this monstrosity is a speedboat. *Ugh*, how I hate the way they smash against waves while racing, and worse still are the men with the need to drive them. Yet, Rashid doesn't strike me as one of *those* men. After all, he has real power, so why bother with imitation? I step onto the boat and sit in the bucket seat next to the driver.

"Are you driving this thing?" I ask.

"Yes, unless you would like to."

I shake my head. "All yours."

Looking back at the marina, I notice Omar at the pier some thirty feet away, his eyes on us. I thought he had left when he dropped me off. Then, a second man joins him, and together they both stare out to the boat. I am about to comment when I catch Rashid's eyes flick towards this other man, and there, almost imperceptibly that I nearly miss it, is a nod. The unspoken glances between them arouse my suspicion.

"You know we don't have to leave the pier? It looks pretty busy out there."

Rashid looks briefly at the waterway dotted with boats. In a serious tone, he says, "There's a secluded area we'll go to."

"Secluded?" I glance at the busy waterway and wonder where among all that, he will find a secluded area? More importantly, *why* does he want seclusion?

"Ready?" says Rashid, and without waiting for an answer, starts up the engine and pulls away.

Absolutely, I'm not ready! Not now that the presence of this unknown man has filled my mind with a million questions for which I have no answers. Dread consumes me as the boat moves me away from land, from witnesses, and from safety.

"Life vests," I shout above the roar of the engine. "Where do you keep them?"

Finally, past the chaos of boats, Rashid kills the engine, and we bob. It's a strange motion that makes me feel like a duck on water.

Duck.

Sitting duck. That's the expression that best describes my situation.

"They're in the side bench."

I scramble to the bench he points to and pull out a bright orange vest.

Rashid's gaze fixedly on me, he says, "You've been causing trouble."

My body tenses, a rigidity I hope goes undetected. *Get yourself together*. He can't possibly know. No one, I'm certain, followed me when I met Jack, yet, the more Rashid stares at me, the less confident I feel. I make a quick calculation as to how far the closest party boat is. I could swim to it if need be.

"I don't know what you mean," I say, trying to keep my tone even. The life jacket slips from my sweaty fingers.

"Charlotte," he says, sounding more like my father than my own father ever did when he scolded me, "Omar informs me that you disappeared from the hotel without saying a word to anyone."

I breathe a sigh of relief. He doesn't know about my meeting with Jack. "Am I a prisoner?"

Rashid is taken aback. "Of course not. I have a staff to drive you wherever you wish to go. I can't have you running off someplace dangerous."

I lightly scoff. "Someplace dangerous? I'm a grown woman who's well-traveled. I don't need a chaperone."

"You're misconstruing what I'm saying."

His avuncular tone makes me feel a little castigated. Perhaps I should behave like a petulant teenager and sulk and whine, but instead, I say, "Noted. I merely wanted to explore the city on my own. I ate enormous amounts of sweets and drank cardamon coffee," I tell him. Nervousness has set my mouth to babble at full speed.

"Did anything unusual happen?" There's a slight twitch of his cheek.

Again, I worry he's alluding to my meeting with Jack. No. I can't worry and allow paranoia to get a solid footing. Yet, my eyes drift to that party boat, again.

"Everything about Dubai is unusual, from the skyscrapers to the man-made islands."

His face relaxes, and he seems to accept my answer. "Promise me you will never disappear again."

"Mmm," I mumble, acknowledging his concerns, but stop short of actually agreeing to his terms.

He stares at me, his eyebrows knotted. "Did you hurt yourself?" he says and points to my face.

I wrinkle my nose and inspect my face in a small, handheld mirror I pull from my purse. When I checked my face immediately following the incident, there was no bruising. Now, a purple welt marks the bridge of my nose.

"I bashed my face into a store door," I say hesitantly, then in a bright tone continue, "There was an incredible sale at some touristy trap I found myself at."

"Would you like a doctor to look at it?"

I wave my hand in the air. "Oh no, I'm fine."

He continues to stare. The look on his face is as unreadable as it was that night I played poker against him – a look I determine that is somewhere between romantic wedding proposal and murder on this Pick-Your-Own-Adventure I've landed myself on. Fifteen minutes swim, and I'll reach that party boat.

"What's your poison?" Rashid says in a severe tone.

I turn to his voice, frozen and terrified, until I realize he's gesturing to a collection of alcohol in a bin.

"What would you like to drink? Daiquiri? Mojito? Cosmo?" he asks again. "I had my staff prepare several drinks, all tucked away here."

Sweat trickles down my bare arms; my hands twitch with fear. "Your staff? You mean that man with Omar?" I say, pointing to the pier too far away to view.

With hesitation in his voice, he says, "Yes."

"I've never seen him before."

"I have many people who work for my family. I use him for special occasions."

There's an emphasis on the word "special" or perhaps it's my mind playing tricks on me. "No, thank you." I force a smile, but the fakery of it remains frozen on my face for too long. *Where's Jack?* I had asked him to be around, but I can't be sure he's anywhere in the vicinity. "Walking in the heat earlier is making me feel queasy now. The booze might send me overboard."

Rashid tilts his head and eyes me as though contemplating something. "Are you feeling light-headed? Nauseous? Your breathing appears normal. I don't think you're suffering from heatstroke."

That's a good idea, I think and nod like he's on to something. "Heatstroke... I've had it a few times before, and I'd rather not risk it. We should head back to the hotel."

"Of course, but before we return, there's something I believe will make you feel better. May I have your phone?"

I envision him flinging it in the water. I make a show of rifling through my purse and feel my dress though it has no pockets. "It must have slipped out."

"In the car? I'll have Omar retrieve it." Rashid pulls out his phone. "Omar, please search the car for Ms. Milton's phone. I'll place you on hold while I dial."

Rashid punches a second number, and suddenly my phone beeps from within my purse.

"What was that?" says Rashid, voice tinged with suspicion.

"What was what?"

Eyes on me, Rashid gets Omar back on the line to cancel the search. His face appears to soften as he holds out his hand, palms up. "You won't regret it."

I gulp. I regret so much – following the thieves to their car in Paris, sneaking a USB with duplicates of Rashid's computer files to Jack, and boarding this damn boat. With no choice, I dig into my purse to retrieve the phone when an idea hits me.

"Don't move," I tell Rashid. "The background and lighting are simply perfect." I pose for a selfie, lips puckered, Rashid smiles in the background. Then, I email it to my parents and Harriet and even Anne, fingers flying to type out the message "On a yacht in Dubai with Prince Rashid." My parents had left a message earlier, begging me to come home, again, but this photo is intended to calm their nerves. Besides, if I do disappear, here's the proof that Rashid was the last person to see me alive. Trembling, I place my phone in his hand.

He jabs at it, then returns my lifeline. "I've added your social media accounts to your phone."

Puzzled, I stare at him. "What do you mean? I don't have social media accounts anymore."

"My PR staff took care of that. You've been online for more than a week now."

"What?" I swipe between different social media platforms, viewing my new profiles. Already, there are numerous photos – me inspecting one of Anton's jackets, a clothes rack in the background; me at the races, greeting Rashid's father and countless others. I hadn't realized at the time how significant these people were, but now seeing the responses on social media has put everything into perspective. My followers are already in the tens of thousands. The comments are relatively kind, with few alluding to the theft business in Paris.

"You've been taking these when I wasn't looking?"

"My staff has as well. After all, my new editor-in-chief must maintain a social media presence for our brand. I'm..." he starts and abruptly stops. Rashid turns away from me momentarily, as though it's unbearable for him to maintain eye contact when he continues. "I'm so very sorry your life was thrown in turmoil." Bringing his eyes back to me, he says, "You have a new handle, a new life. Isn't it about time you put that other life behind you?"

"I got the job?!" I exclaim, pumping a fist in the air. "You were right. I do feel better." I slip the phone back into my purse and tuck it by my feet. My body slackens; all that tension leaves me, reassured by the fact that Rashid has no idea what I've been up to with Jack. Of course, I'm not in any danger. Rashid wouldn't have spent the last week setting me up within his company if he were planning to kill me. Yet, there's a small part deep inside that's tugging at me and makes me feel guilty about trying to expose Rashid that will have him thrown in prison.

Chapter 29

J ACK, SURROUNDED BY A crowd of tourists, looks across the waterway. Up ahead, he notices a motorboat, white with beige trim, the words *She is Mine* sprawled across the back. Gross.

A woman, wearing an ostentatious wide-brim hat, passes *She is Mine*, stops in mid-stride, and turns so Jack can see her profile. Charlotte. Jack huffs. She told him she'd feel safer knowing that he's nearby, and he can't let her down.

Though Favreau never responded about the blurry photo of the mystery man at the races, Jack had dutifully couriered the USB to him with a short note, indicating there may be something of value among the files that could lead to *Mistress*. Sealing the envelope, he hoped he wasn't making a mistake and purposely left out how he obtained the USB. He couldn't tell Favreau that he had stupidly followed his gut, traipsing after the inscrutable Charlotte Milton from Paris to Monaco to Dubai. The *Capitaine* would consider him a fool.

Charlotte boards the boat *She is Mine,* and a man rushes to her side. Rashid. *Of course, the boat is his!* Once Charlotte joins him on the speedboat, it's not long before they pull away.

Jack shoots a hand up to hail a water taxi. "I'd like a leisurely tour," he tells the driver upon arrival. He climbs on board the small white boat with navy blue trim and takes one of the two seats in the back. The driver revs the motor from the idling position and guides it across the water, and the boat smashes against tiny waves. The traffic reminds Jack of Italy, where anarchy rules the roadways, drivers cut across one another. Among the traffic, he searches for Charlotte.

Jack spots *She Is Mine* and breathes a sigh of relief. He can't lose sight of her again. After all, should anything go wrong, he'll need to do something though judging by the water traffic, it seems highly unlikely Rashid would try something here. Still, Jack will be ready if need be.

"I'm here, Charlotte," he says in a low whisper. "Circle that boat there. Not too close."

The driver looks back at him and nods, steers the water taxi to loop around *She Is Mine*. Charlotte stands next to Rashid as he drives, the pair of them looking like an advertisement for beautiful, rich people in exotic destinations. She appears unscarred after that head-butt he gave her that he felt so guilty about.

His life has been exciting since she came into it, and he dreads returning to the tranquil life he set up for himself after finishing what they'd started. Jack has spent a lifetime marching towards the ordinary. Perhaps it's time Jack chose extraordinary. If he can help capture the people responsible for the theft and retrieve the stolen artwork, it would do wonders for his career and reputation at Oxford. Perhaps there would even be renewed interest in his book proposal on horticulture and the modern man.

A woman's scream slams into Jack's reverie, a cold sweat taking over. Is that Charlotte?

Chapter 30

M Y SCREAM CATCHES ME off-guard as I'm thrown out of my seat. One white-knuckled hand clutches the rail beside me while the other holds my hat down on my head. The boat speeds along, skimming the waves. I imagine the wind sweeping my mind of fear and doubt, while my peals of laughter linger like a trail behind me. I haven't felt this carefree in a long time.

Rashid smiles over at me, then looks up to the setting sun. "You don't need the hat anymore."

"Not one ray will hit this face and wrinkle me like a prune when I'm older." I'm not sure he can hear me over the sound of the motor or the jackhammering of my heart.

Rashid slows, and it's not until the boat sits idle that I discover how far he's taken us. My hand drops from holding my hat. "Why are we stopping here?"

"Turn around," says Rashid.

I twist around, my dress tangles around my legs.

"It has the best view of the city," he continues, gently touching my lower back.

"Beautiful," I say of the skyscrapers.

"It's extraordinary given our humble beginnings as a fishing village. Eventually, the area attracted merchants and traders. Against protestations from Britain, Sheikh Rashid bin Saeed Al Maktoum built up the infrastructure, planned for an airport, a port for trading."

I should be listening, but I'm distracted by the tingles where his thumb caresses me.

"The Sheikh had a vision..." Rashid's voice drifts. Something in the waterway preoccupies him, but he doesn't rest on the distraction for long before continuing with his history lesson. "... a vision after our short-lived endeavor with oil. See there," Rashid says, pulling his hand away and points to the right of us.

I scan the coast while he carries on, disappointed by the absence of his hand at my back.

"The Palm Jumeirah is manmade."

My attention is focused on the artificial archipelago, but in my peripheral, I notice Rashid turn. I follow his gaze to two men on a smaller boat closing the distance behind us. Riding past, the men – wearing a Manchester United jersey and baseball hats – study us. Their familiarity strikes me. Of course, I saw them earlier in the day when I believed they were trailing me from the hotel, but there's something about their clothes that loosely cover bodybuilder shapes, and their arms that appear too short for their upper torso, that remind me of something. I'm close to loosening that memory that will tie it all together.

The races! I shiver even in the soaring heat, experiencing a visceral fear of danger. These two men were the bodyguards of the man whose cold stare intimidated me.

Circling us, the man in the Manchester United jersey locks eyes with the Prince, a lingering look. I gasp. The bodyguards of the man Rashid met with must have been following me all day practically unnoticed by me. I was foolish to think I could spy on Rashid without his knowledge. The surprise boat trip, the Manchester United men, and the man left behind at the marina who carries out "special" work for Rashid all add up to one thing.

"Assassins," I whisper.

The assassins travel full circle again and back our way. My eyes flash to my surroundings. Loud music emanates from the closest ship, partygoers mill about. They'd never hear me scream for help even if I tried. I scan the water, hoping, praying, anticipating a way out of this but the other boats are too far off. I'll drown trying to reach them. I'll die if I stay. My eyes drop to the sea while I work up the courage to dive in when a tinny motor sounds. I look up at a flat-topped water taxi heading for my general area.

"Charlotte, we're going back," Rashid says in a clipped voice, and starts the engine, then turns the boat around. Phone in hand, he quickly presses at numbers with his thumb, speaks Arabic, then slides the phone back in his pocket. "Stay low."

The Manchester United boat follows, picking up speed as Rashid accelerates. His jaw tenses, his hands steady on the wheel. Spray hits me in the face, and the wind steals my breath. Rashid had told me to get down yet I stand, clutching the back of the seat, my body rocking as the boat slams into each wave. My gaze drifts to him. Has he changed his mind about killing me?

Manchester United cuts across our path. The surprise throws Rashid off-balance, and he swerves to miss them. I lose my balance and knock into the side of the boat, and nearly topple over. With one hand still fastened to the back of the chair, Rashid reaches over and pulls me upright.

"I said stay low!"

I don't want to stay low. I want off! The water-taxi continues to make its way to us, and I abandon my spot at the rear bench. Perhaps the people on that water-taxi can help save me unless they're also assassins. My God, just how many people does it take to kill me?

Rashid looks at me over his shoulder. "Get down."

I sink to my knees. Our boat thrusts forward into full throttle, throwing me backward, and I land on my ass with a hard thump. Saltwater shoots up from the side and dumps on me, gets into my mouth, up my nostrils, and whips off my hat. With our boat pounding against waves, I'm pitched a few inches into the air.

Clutching the rail, I examine the growing distance between us and the assassins.

A bullet whizzes past and ricochets off the metal frame of the windshield. Rashid whips the wheel around in a sharp turn, steering us away from danger. Ahead, the water-taxi turns towards the marina and away from the shooting. The driver appears panicked, incessantly turning back to the shooters, and the passenger waves his arms in the air like he's directing a plane on a runway. There's something familiar about the aircraft marshaller – a man in a white linen suit with a tan shirt like the one Jack wore earlier in the day. And the tan hat he wears is also recognizable and British-*y*, much like the one Jack wore at the vineyard. This man doesn't just resemble Jack – he *is* Jack. Emotion swells up to my throat and stops just short of my eyes. I hold back tears. He came, just as I had asked.

"Charlotte, I can't drive and worry about you," Rashid says. "Get down." This time, I throw myself flat on the wet floor, and find my hat wedged beneath the bench. I reach for it, and place it back on my head like a turtle hiding in its shell.

Another shot rings out, and the windshield shatters. Rashid grunts. My head pops up to see if he's hurt, and, seeing the blood, I get up on my knees then unsteadily to my feet.

"Are you hit?" I stare at the blood running down his arm. It seems too risky to shoot at Rashid if he's with them. Is he or isn't he? I can't make up my mind with bullets whirring past.

"Get down!" he says, gritting his teeth. "We're heading back to the marina. They won't follow if we lose ourselves among the other boats."

While I agree that sounds like a good plan, it seems somewhat impossible to do. The Manchester United boat is now between us and the marina. Rashid aims our boat away from them and towards the water-taxi that is trying to escape us. The water-taxi driver hurriedly waves his hands in a shooing gesture. Jack looks at me from the back of the water-taxi.

"He's trying to kill me," I shout, hands cupped around my mouth like a bullhorn.

"We're coming for you," shouts Jack, though his boat is heading in the opposite direction.

"Get down," says Rashid.

"No. No. No," shouts the water-taxi driver as he chugs away.

A siren sounds in the distance. I should feel relieved but I've been in this situation before, and it didn't end well. *She is Mine* gains on the water-taxi. Manchester United speeds alongside us; the passenger's arm extended, a gun aimed directly at me.

"Charlotte, down!" shouts Jack.

Another shot rings out. I stagger forward, then jerk backward when Rashid wrenches the boat into a quick turn. I tumble over the side and hit the water with a splash.

Chapter 31

"TURN THIS AROUND AND go to that boat!" Jack shouts to his driver, but the man continues to drive in the opposite direction. "I will triple what I offered you." Still, the boat doesn't turn. Jack keeps watch on the area where she fell, looking for her to resurface, but it gets harder the farther out the driver takes them. Charlotte could have taken a bullet before she hit the water. He whispers "Come on, come on," wishing for her to appear. "I'll pay you whatever you want. Just do it," he yells, finally bringing his eyes to the driver.

The driver looks to the shooters driving away from an approaching police boat and finally steers towards the spot Charlotte fell.

Frantically leaning over the side of the boat, Rashid calls Charlotte's name and almost falls out as he wildly scans the water. Lining up about thirty feet away from Rashid's speedboat, the water-taxi cuts its engine, idling.

"Charlotte!" Jack shouts, racing from one side of the boat to the other to inspect the water. Looking up to Rashid, he yells, "Do you see her?!" The Prince shakes his head, keeping his eyes on the surrounding water. Finally, Jack points out a hat bobbing in the sea. Rashid leans over the side of his boat to pluck the hat. He rips off his shoes and shirt and jumps in.

"Charlotte!" calls Rashid, resurfacing.

Jack weighs the benefits of diving and trying to find her while in the water versus the wider viewpoint he has from the boat.

But while he's contemplating scenarios, Charlotte is sinking to the depths below. He flings off his shoes, his jacket, tears his shirt from his body, and jumps into the ocean. He takes long, determined strokes until he's in the middle of the two boats, dives down, and continues to search. Popping his head back up, he sucks in a deep breath and dives underwater.

"Jack."

A woman's voice, distorted, calls him by name like a Siren's song to a watery grave.

"Jack."

The voice guides him upward, and he breaks the surface, spins until his eyes focus on his water-taxi. Charlotte clutches the taxi driver's hand as he pulls her in. She tumbles into the boat and disappears from view. Water streams down Jack's face, and laps up to his chin. He swims towards the water taxi where the driver hauls him into the boat as well, and plops down beside Charlotte, his breath coming in hard. Jack clasps his arms around her, her wetness now pressed against his, two dampened bodies.

He draws her head closer, covering her with small kisses, and listens to her quiet sobs. Trembling, she places her head against his chest, her body convulses as her cries grow louder, and she brings her knees up to curl into him. He holds her tight, too tight, a mistake that's giving him away – Jack Carey cares for Charlotte Milton more than he realized.

Chapter 32

"PLEASE, REMOVE YOUR CLOTHING," says the young servant named Hamed.

"Aren't you going to buy me dinner first?" Jack winces at his own joke. He's glad Charlotte isn't around to hear him, though, if she were, she may be too exhausted to roll her eyes at him.

"The hotel has wonderful room service. I can get you a menu if you like."

Jack had obviously been joking, but now that he thinks about it, he's barely eaten all day and drank too many iced hibiscus teas. Thankfully, the police didn't keep them very long after they plucked Rashid from the water and led them all, the water taxi driver included, back to the marina for questioning. Jack felt obligated to pay the driver exponentially more than he had promised.

"Thank you. I am feeling rather peckish." Jack slips into casual slacks and a white shirt that Hamed brings him while his suit is laundered.

"When you are ready, sir, His Highness would like to see you in his office."

Jack can't say he'd like to see Rashid. The way he fawned over Charlotte like she was helpless irritated him. "Are you cold, Charlotte?" he mimics Rashid when he's left alone. Chivalry and grand heroic gestures were overkill on Rashid's part, noted Jack, who quietly seethed watching Rashid play hero. Besides, it was the taxi driver who pulled Charlotte from the water, and it was

Charlotte who managed to get herself to the safety of the water taxi in the first place, so what's Rashid going on about?

When Jack is taken to the office, he finds Rashid and Charlotte sitting close on a settee, looking a little too intimate.

Charlotte pulls away from Rashid immediately and pops up. "Let me get you something to drink." She's changed her clothing and wears her hair, still wet, sleekly pulled back in a ponytail, but the fear she felt on the boat remains with her. He can see it in her eyes. Rashid, Jack notices, glistens and looks even better with the blue of his eyes pronounced, and a black shine to his hair like he's using some expensive product. Jack probably looks like a fuddy-duddy in comparison.

Jack welcomes the glass from Charlotte and spies the bottle in her other hand. He savors the delightful sip of Bunnahabhain. He was 16 the first time he got drunk. His parents returned home to find Jack nursing their bottle of Bunnahabhain and grounded him. So, Jack has a bit of a bad boy streak in him after all, he'd like to convey to Charlotte, if she's into that.

Charlotte pours a glass for herself and downs it. She grimaces. "Oh, that's strong," she says, then pours another.

Charlotte returns to the two-seater with Rashid; Jack sits opposite them, a pillow haphazardly folded over and pressed awkwardly into his back. There's something odd in the way Rashid stares at him, hard and stony-eyed. Jack averts his eyes and scours the room from the desk to the mirrored credenza, and he nearly chokes on his drink when his eyes fall on a Picasso.

"How's your arm?" asks Jack.

"The doctor said amputation isn't necessary," jokes Rashid. "It was a small nick."

"It's nothing to joke about," says Charlotte, gently pressing the palm of her hand on Rashid's arm. She seems genuinely concerned.

Lucky you, Jack wants to say, a little jealous Rashid took a bullet meant for Charlotte. But what does this all mean? Who were those men trying to kill Charlotte?

"We can't thank you enough for your assistance. Most people would have headed in the opposite direction, Professor... Carey, is it?" says Charlotte.

"Please, call me Jack."

"Where do you teach, Professor?" says Rashid.

"Oxford."

"Oh, that must be exciting," says Charlotte, "surrounded by the young intelligentsia. And what do you teach?"

Jack pauses before he goes in for the kill. "Art History." It surprises him when Rashid shows no response. He was sure the answer would have piqued the Prince's interest.

"I must say, I need to get a closer look at that Picasso," says Jack, indicating the piece above the fireplace.

Rashid ignores his comment, and instead asks, "What brings you to Dubai?"

"Vacation," answers Jack. "Normally, my summer vacations are fully planned, but just this once, I decided to leave myself open to whatever life brings. It wasn't until I arrived at the airport that I chose my next destination."

"Do you normally live so dangerously?" says Charlotte.

There's a sexy throatiness in her voice, or perhaps he just imagines it. "Quite the opposite," says Jack. He shakes his head and laughs. "I am enjoying the recklessness of it all."

"Which airport?" says Rashid.

"Pardon?" answers Jack, wondering where this conversation is going.

"You said you arrived at the airport and chose the destination. Which airport did you fly in from?"

"Heathrow."

"From Heathrow straight here?"

"Uh, huh." Legs crossed, Jack shifts uncomfortably at the thought he's being interrogated. "I'm sorry to bring this up again, but I was under the impression by the police at the marina that they want to speak to me further. Shouldn't I head to the police station?"

"No," says Rashid in a steady tone. "They have all the information they need."

"That was scary business back there on the water," says Jack slowly. "Those men–"

"–Kidnappers. I'm embarrassed to say I'm worth an extraordinary amount of money."

Jack furrows his brow. "Forgive me, but why shoot at you if they wish to hold you ransom?"

"Obviously, intelligence plays no part in this," says Rashid in a light tone.

"Hmmm." Jack sips his drink. "It's unfortunate they got away."

"I, for one, am grateful you were there to save my life," says Charlotte.

Jack averts her stare and brings his fingers to his eyebrow to hide his embarrassment. "Anyone would have done the same." When he returns his gaze to them, he notices Rashid coolly study him. What's he playing at? Jack wonders, though he can't help but feel they're behaving like two schoolboys pulling Charlotte's pigtails.

"Not true," Charlotte says.

Jack says, "Technically, it was the water-taxi driver who pulled you out."

"Oh, yes. He was absolutely terrified. I swear, if we hadn't heard the police sirens when we did, he probably would have left me there to fend for myself." She laughs lightly.

"I find it strange," says Rashid in a somewhat serious tone, and he turns from Jack to Charlotte, "back on the boat, you said 'he's trying to kill me.'"

Her eyes widen, her smile stiffens. "They were...us, they were trying to kill us."

"Yet, you said *he* rather than *they*. Curious," says Rashid, "to imply I'd harm you."

Charlotte laughs nervously until it dissolves to silence. Her eyes dart to Jack. "What? Obviously, I said *they*, I mean why...for what possible reason would you want to kill me? That's absurd."

Now Rashid turns to Jack and says, "And Professor, amid all that chaos, you called Charlotte by name. This would lead me to believe you two know one other."

Jack nods his head in agreement, stalling. "That's right...after I heard you scream her name when she went overboard." The lie sounds truthful to his own ears. When he saw Charlotte in danger, all he could think about was saving her and tossed their plan into oblivion.

Rashid remains quiet, contemplative. "Quite correct, Professor," he says at last, "except I thought Charlotte called out your name, too." Rashid keeps his eyes squarely on Jack.

"It's an American thing," Charlotte pipes in, "to call strangers Jack. *You don't know Jack. Jack me up. Jack of All Trades. Jack off.*" Her hand flies to cover her mouth, her eyes wide in seeming embarrassment.

Jack hopes to assuage Rashid's concerns because, at this point, he doesn't appear to be fooled. "I must confess, and I'm embarrassed not mentioning this earlier, but I do recognize you from news reports, Ms. Milton. I'm sorry for what happened to you."

"As an art historian, I'm sure the news story intrigues you," Rashid tells Jack.

"The art world, as you can imagine, is overwrought with such thefts. Frankly, it comes down to greed on the thieves' part and a sense of entitlement for the buyers. The world is the true victim as they don't share in the beauty of the stolen work."

"Professor, you assume that all art thieves do it for the money. Some are merely transfixed by the work," says Rashid.

Jack guffaws, a tone of displeasure to his voice when he speaks. "I assure you greed is behind each theft, and I can think of no other reason than money as an incentive for someone to commit such a horrid crime."

"Horrid?" repeats Rashid. "That's rather strong given you use the word *theft* quite liberally. After all, the painting doesn't belong to colonizing Britain, yet, somehow your countrymen's illegal ownership of it is justified–"

"Illegal ownership? The painting was commissioned by a member of the Royal Family, King Henry VIII, and to suggest that Britain isn't the rightful owner–"

"You misunderstand," says Rashid, a sly smile on his face, "I merely wish to point out that Foligari was never paid for the work; therefore, it rightfully belongs to *his* descendants."

Charlotte's head darts from left to right like an attendant watching a tennis match.

"Yes," says Jack, barely containing his anger, "I'm sure the thieves stole the painting to give it to Foligari's descendants free of charge."

"Have you seen her before?"

Jack's eyes skirt to Charlotte. "As I said, I recognize her from news reports."

"Not Ms. Milton, the *Mistress*." Rashid gazes at Jack intently and his eyes narrow.

Jack's trying to play it cool, but he wonders...*is it possible?* Does Rashid know he retrieved the painting all those years ago? Revealing himself in the spur of the moment can ruin their plan, but hiding his true identity can cause more harm if Rashid recognizes him. Finally, he takes a chance and says, "Yes, at the Victoria and Albert Museum in London."

"Well," Charlotte clears her throat, and inserts herself into the dialogue. "It certainly was an ordeal for me..." she says, "...being kidnapped by those art thieves and then...then," here Charlotte's eyes make their way to Rashid, "falling into the waters below. I nearly died."

Rashid's eyes hold steady on hers when he says, "Thankfully, you're here with us today, Charlotte." There's an unmistakable blush to Charlotte's cheeks, and she looks away in embarrassment. Jack registers her descent into schoolgirl crush territory and rolls his eyes.

"Where are you staying, Professor Carey?" Rashid asks.

"At an Airbnb on the Marina," Jack replies.

"And how long will you be in town? I must thank you with a proper dinner," says Charlotte.

Jack smiles and shakes his head. "That's not necessary."

Rashid's eyes bore into Jack as he says, "I should warn you, Charlotte has a way of getting what she wants. I'll have one of my drivers take you to your Airbnb and have you move into a suite here as my guest."

"Oh, no, that would be too much—"

"The more you protest, the more insistent I get," says Charlotte. "I won't take no for an answer."

"It's agreed then," says Rashid, his gaze intense. "Professor Carey, I look forward to discussing further our love of art and getting to know everything about you."

Chapter 33

F EW SCOTCH CONNOISSEURS CAN afford the Balvenie Cask 191. At a mere $40,000, it isn't the most expensive, either. Rashid's elderly host sloshes the liquid into a thick crystal Baccarat glass; the smell of toffee, marzipan, sweet oak, raisins, and nuts seep into the air. His host offers the glass to him, but he declines and raises a glass of sparkling water to his lips. Rashid watches as his host limps to a chair, places his cane alongside it, and plops down hard. A stroke has hampered his mobility, but Rashid knows better than to let the depiction of a helpless septuagenarian fool him. One thing Rashid knows for sure is that Noam Ehrlich is a dangerous man.

Noam pulls a cigar from his breast pocket, causing one of his men to bolt forward and snap open a gold lighter, flame at the ready. Noam twirls the cigar in his mouth until lit and puffs out a tiny swirl of smoke. He's as eccentric as ever, peering at Rashid from behind round, Ozzy Osbourne-style sunglasses.

"Not your vice, my friend, is it?" he says.

A hint of a smile jumps to Rashid's face. "Come now, we both know about my vice."

"That I do, my friend." Noam laughs, but soon his laughter turns into a harsh cough. His man pours a glass of water, but Noam waves him away and drinks his scotch instead. "Leave us alone," he orders, and the man vacates the room.

Relief consumes Rashid as he never has become accustomed to other people's armed men.

Quietness engulfs the room. Finally, Noam says, "I trust the money transfer went smoothly?"

"Yes," says Rashid, putting the lateness of the payment behind him. Noam has never been prompt, but two months late is unusual.

"Unlike the problem you've encountered with one *Mistress?*" Noam asks with a raised eyebrow.

Rashid keeps his composure, but sucks in a slow breath, waiting for what's next.

"Yes, Rashid, I know about your deal with Levan. It should come as no surprise that if you work on a deal without my protection, it will fall apart. Levan lives by a different set of dangerous rules, not the kind you're used to. Unfortunately, his kind is all too common for me, and so I offer you my services. Say the word, and I will take care of him for you."

Noam has earned a reputation for dealing with problems in a most horrific way, and accepting his help would be signing Levan's death warrant and make Rashid indebted to him. "He's my mess to clean up."

"Very well." After a pause, Noam says. "You must be wondering why I asked you here. There is a family matter I need help with. My mother's father was a German shopkeeper in the 1930s. He did well, not too prosperous, but life was fun for my mother. She and her brother enjoyed skiing and school and music, all provided by that little shop. But then..." Noam stares hard into his glass and swigs. "Like many Jewish families, they suffered greatly. Please, will you retrieve something from the top drawer of that corner chest?"

Rashid pulls open a drawer and, grabbing a folder tucked inside, holds it out to Noam.

Noam lifts his hand in protest. "No, that is for you."

Rashid carries it back to his chair and flips it open to the first page. It's all in German, but Rashid can identify an address, a name, and a birthdate written alongside a photo of a man taken from the 1940s.

"For too many years now, I have been searching for that man: Armin Holger."

Rashid pulls out another photograph of a man taken about two decades earlier and compares it to the older picture. The eyes are the same.

"We believe he made his way to Luxembourg after World War II and changed his name to Andrew Banning to hide his identity as the youngest, mid-level ranking officer of the Third Reich. Holger terrorized people in the Jewish Ghetto. Lives were lost, and many families had valuable items stolen – gold, silver, jewels – and art."

At this, Rashid looks up from his folder, his interest piqued. "Go on," he says.

"So much art was stolen from many families. The Swiss authorities have recovered some, others were illegally sold, and the families are fighting to get back what is rightfully theirs. But not all the works have been recovered."

Rashid continues to flip through the pages in the folder. He doesn't need to read the German detail written alongside the photos to understand what was stolen. One portrait captures his attention, and he scans to the painter's name in the caption below: Karl Sonnenberg. The painting is a self-portrait of the post-impressionist artist, and to have that in his possession, even briefly, fills Rashid with desire.

"Karl Sonnenberg was my great uncle, and that portrait was to remain in my family."

"Are you certain this Holger is now Andrew Banning?"

"Quite certain. He was a self-made multimillionaire."

Rashid's eyebrows arch up. "Was?"

"He's deceased now."

Rashid closes the folder on his lap, unsure about the point of this exercise.

"He is survived by his son. The father made his money in steel, but eventually, the family business turned to banking through his son. The son now holds everything," Noam continues.

Understanding now, Rashid reopens the folder, searches through images of Andrew Banning, and flips through many surveillance photos of a man that must be the son. He holds the photo up in Noam's direction.

"The son, Hector," Noam confirms. "He's highly protected and surrounds himself with those he trusts. It is difficult to break the circle, but not so difficult to become part of the circle. You see, he is infatuated with titles – not the Italian or Greek titles. They mean nothing these days. But something like the British Monarchy, or Monaco, or Dubai. He holds a romantic notion about the whole thing. And I've discovered his one weakness."

"Which is?"

"His love for his wife. Nasty business this thing called love. It'll do us all in."

Rashid's mind flashes to the incident on the water and his failure to protect Charlotte. What if next time Levan succeeds? He has to agree with Noam; love (or perhaps the promise of it) will do Rashid in.

"You'd like my help, but I don't think I've ever been mistaken for Robin Hood," Rashid says, choosing his words carefully. This is a personal matter for Noam, and when emotions interfere, problems arise. Like falling for your pawn in a heist, Rashid reminds himself. He knows better, yet he flew Charlotte to Dubai, offered her a job, and shares a hotel suite with her. Now Jack's arrival has further complicated things, and his story about recognizing Charlotte is obviously a lie. There's no question that Jack is after him, and it's very possible that Charlotte is, too. His misgivings about Charlotte tear him apart, but he knows he can't let his feelings for her blind him. At least with both of them staying at his family's hotel, he'll be able to spy on them to get to the truth.

Noam smiles. "You'll be paid quite handsomely, but the trove of stolen art must be returned to all the families. It's unpleasant for men like us to do good in the world."

Men like us? Rashid's eyes flicker to Noam. He's technically a thief, yes, but not a killer, a torturer. He's nothing like Noam, and to be thought of in such a way makes him cringe.

"The file contains information on Hector's home in Switzerland that was once a grand fort. We believe he keeps the stolen artwork there. I paid a great deal of money for the plans that you hold."

"And how accurate are they?" says Rashid, scanning over blueprints.

"It was quite difficult to piece all the information together, and while we are sure the plans are accurate for the main floor and above, we can't be sure of what lies beneath the home. There is a rumor of secret passageways and hidden dungeons, but who can tell for certain? Take the file and give me your final answer in 24 hours. I trust the temptation of what's hidden there will be too great, and do with it what you will, however, return to me and others what is rightfully ours."

"And you want only the paintings back?" Rashid questions carefully.

"No," Noam says, leaning forward in his chair. "The sins of the father are visited on the son. I want the man dead."

Rashid stares, contemplating a way to refuse without ending up dead himself, when a smile breaks out on Noam's face.

"It's just a joke."

Another thing Rashid knows about Noam Erhlich is that he is a humorless man.

Chapter 34

"Hamed. Hamed."

I stir in bed, roused by Rashid's voice. He must have forgotten he had dismissed Hamed before he slipped out for his late-night business meeting. Creeping out of bed, I open the door a crack, and peek. Rashid stands in his darkened doorway, his white shirt untucked, buttons undone.

"Did I disturb you?" he says.

"It's okay. You sent Hamed home."

"Oh, yes," he says in quiet exasperation.

"Is there something I can help you with?"

"No," he says and remains by the door.

"Rashid, please tell me what you need."

After another moment of hesitation, he sighs and says, "I need help changing the dressing on my arm."

"Be right there," I say and close the door behind me. I slip my arms through a robe and, in the bathroom, swish mouthwash. There's no reason to torture Rashid with bad breath. Sucking in deeply, I'm satisfied with the minty scent. Then, I yank my phone from its charger and, on the way to Rashid's room, search YouTube for how to change a bandage.

I'm disappointed to find Rashid's room lit only by a few weak lamps, and hoped to gain insight into him.

"In there," he says.

I proceed to the bathroom but an open folder on the lit dresser catches my eye. My pace slows, allowing me to linger at the scattered contents – photographs of artwork and a blueprint. Good lord. Is he already planning something so soon after the last fiasco?

"Charlotte?" Rashid rushes over and gathers the papers together, giving me a scolding look. Lifting a painting off the wall, he reveals a safe.

My thumb scrolls across to the camera setting on my phone and, switching on video, zoom and record. Rashid shifts in front of the pad to block me as he keys in a code, but I maneuver my phone into a better position. Fingers spread wide on the pad, he hesitates, tilts his head slightly towards me, and then uses his other hand to cover what he's typing. The safe opens, and he pops in the folder. I stop the recording, hoping I captured enough to determine the pin number.

"What are you doing with your phone?" Rashid barks.

I move my thumb quickly back to the browser where it opens to my last search and flip the screen to him. "YouTube. I'm sure a nurse has posted a how-to." I wander into the fully lit bathroom and spend a few minutes watching the video I found. "Got it," I say, then turn to eye the supplies – gauze pads, clean towel, cotton-tipped applicator, and transparent dressing – laid out on the marble counter. Rashid sits in a chair by me and retrieves a cleaning solution from a drawer.

Hovering over him, I push up his sleeve, but can't reach the wound. "Uhm, I think you should remove your shirt," I say. *And your pants, too, if you're up for some adventure.*

His chest is smooth, arms muscular, abs toned, and I'm reminded of the time not so long ago when I pictured him in his underwear. Yes, he can definitely do a Calvin Klein ad with that body or the cover of a romance novel or a cologne ad wearing nothing but the cologne.

"Charlotte."

"Huh?"

Rashid half-smiles, half-smirks as if to say, *I get it, you're into me.*

Oh God, how long have I been staring? "Right. I need to wash my hands." As I apply the soap, rubbing my hands until it foams, I try not to look at him through the mirror, but my eyes apparently have a mind of their own. And he's peeking right back at me.

"Ready?" I ask him.

"Yes."

Gently, I pull at the old tape and dressing until the wound is fully exposed. "Oh God," I exclaim, taking a step back. "You said it was a little nick."

"The bullet grazed me. It looks worse than it feels, though the pain medication is wearing off."

"Do you want to take another pill now before I do something to hurt you?"

Rashid laughs, low and calming. "You won't hurt me."

Ah, but I would. At least that's my plan, anyway. I wish he'd stop staring at me with those pensive eyes and sanguine smile because guilt has me bursting to come clean. I think back to the theft and how he whispered the *Mistress'* love story into my ear, how he stood close to me and caressed my jaw. My heart flutters at the memory of the first time I saw him on stage and how his presence makes me feel like a schoolgirl in love with the high school quarterback. Teenage me would let Rashid-the-quarterback feel me up during a game of Spin the Bottle. But he'd be part of the cool clique with no time for the dull, smart kids, so in what world would teen me be invited to the same party?

"I wish you had rested instead of running off to your business meeting but I suppose duty called."

Rashid sighs.

I peer at him. "Did I say something wrong?"

"No, it's the mention of duty that reminds me how little time I have left."

"For what?"

"To live my life the way I want. On my thirty-eighth birthday, I am duty-bound to serve my father, prepare to take my proper place and let go of my...passions. It's the agreement I made with him."

"So, you're saying titles and money and private jets aren't all they're cracked up to be."

"It's a prison I can't escape from."

"You said this before, the night we were at the races. There must be something you can do. I've seen how easily you wield power."

"Even with all that power, I really have none. The only time I feel in control is when I–" He stops abruptly.

"When you what?"

He shakes his head. "It's been difficult standing up to my father, to other family members."

"What would happen if you walked away? Seriously."

"It's not easy for a Crown Prince to abandon his birthright...but, my leaving would see it fall into the hands of my younger brother, and my father has no faith in him. Nor do I. Walking away would leave my people in the wrong hands."

His palpable sadness hits me. "I'm sorry," I whisper.

I discard the old dressing and wash my hands a second time. I squirt the cleaning solution into the wound and gently rub it from the inside out, fingers wandering further down his bicep, skin like smooth silk over steel muscles. Oh, the sinful things I'd like to do with him right now.

"How does this feel?" I try to adopt the throaty, raw sexuality of a Kathleen Turner femme fatale, but it comes out more like Kermit the Frog.

"Good," says Rashid and peers into the mirror to examine the wound. "It doesn't look like any of the stitches opened. You're an excellent nurse."

I study the wound from a closer vantage point, my fingertips brushing the skin makes me tingle all over. I breathe deeply, and his scent makes me want to devour him. I once read an article on hot sex maneuvers and how to make your orgasm last 15 minutes. It was all bullshit with a click-bait headline, but right now, I think a 15-minute "O" is *oh, so possible*. I close my eyes. "Rashid."

He responds with soft strokes along my hand.

Then I remember the photos and blueprints I scanned moments earlier. My addled brain fires a warning shot, reminding me of who I'm dealing with. My eyes fly open, and I pull away. "Who were those men?"

"I don't know."

Indeed, that may not be a complete lie. After all, Rashid may not know *who* they are, but I'm sure he knows who they work for. Despite what I first thought, I don't think he hired them to kill me. Something somewhere has gone wrong and smacked us in the middle of this maelstrom. I'd like to believe what Rashid told Jack earlier – that they were hoping to hold him ransom, but I know better.

"Have you seen them before?" I pull the backing off the new dressing and secure it over the wound.

He hesitates before answering. "Never."

Chapter 35

"**T**HIS IS UTTER MADNESS," says Jack. We are in front of the safe in Rashid's bedroom.

It was a spur-of-the-moment decision on my part, but this afternoon, when an opportunity to check the safe presented itself, I pleaded with Jack to come up without explaining why.

"No, it's not. Rashid will be gone for hours, and Hamed has stepped out," I say, my words low and hurried. My voice sounds unusual, weak and anxious in my ears, and my stomach is tied up in knots. I'm supposed to be helping Jack retrieve the painting, but nailing Rashid for it doesn't have to be part of the deal anymore, does it? He was genuinely wounded saving my life, and playing nursemaid to him last night has stirred up some feelings, confounding me. But then there was the blatant lie he told, and probably not the first time.

Jack says, "Who's that man standing outside your suite?"

"Don't worry about Omar."

"Are you sure no one is around?"

"Mmm hmm."

"What's in the wall safe?"

"I don't know," I practically shout, my voice strained. I continue, "Secret stuff. We're in this together, right? So, let's take down that ugly unibrow guy and get to work."

Jack turns to me, flabbergasted. "That's an original *signed* Picasso print. Those are incredibly rare."

My back stiffens, and my voice oozes sarcasm. "Really? You want to do this now?"

Jack averts my stare and clears his throat. He seems to admire the print and rubs his finger along the signature written in green crayon. Jack is in some trancelike state, wasting time.

"Do you want to be alone with him?" I say, arms crossed.

He shakes his head and delicately removes the print, leaning it against the wall on top of the dresser. "It's rarer than the Picasso in his office," mumbles Jack.

Sweat drips from his forehead onto his glasses, and he pulls them off, gently wiping them against his shirt tucked into–

"–Pleated jeans?" I say. "Did you iron your jeans?"

"What? Don't be ridiculous. The crease is from the folding."

My eyes glance over him. "I thought Jean burned your clothes."

"Really? You want to do this now?"

I roll my eyes. "825974," I say, memorizing the numbers from the video I shot.

Jack digitally taps the numbers and waits for a light beep.

I suck in a breath, anticipating an alarm to sound. I let the breath out, relieved by the quiet, but aware that there's always the chance of a silent alarm.

Jack pulls on the door but it won't open.

"025974."

"You said 825974 before."

"That was a guess."

"You dragged me here for a guess? I thought you said you have the number."

"Mostly," I say in a thin, defensive voice. "He blocked my view so I didn't quite get the first number. 025974."

Shaking his head, Jack keys in the number. "Any more guesses? At some point, the safe may lock us out."

"Do you think there's a silent alarm?"

"Well, I do now. Maybe we should forget this."

"No. Try 525974."

Jack presses the numbers, wraps his hand around the handle and pulls it open.

"What's in there?" I say in an excited tone, peering over his shoulder.

"I don't know yet." He removes a folder, slides documents out from envelopes and lays them out on the dresser. There are countless B&W images of paintings and artifacts, a blueprint of a building, and surveillance pictures of a middle-aged man. Jack retrieves the blueprint and studies it. "Does this mean all this artwork is located here?"

"Is it the blueprint to a museum?" I hope not. It would mean that despite the turmoil he's put me through, Rashid has no qualms about destroying more lives. I reach for some of the photos and fumble them with trembling hands. Jack snaps pictures with his camera phone, and I replace them into the envelope one photo at a time.

I hover and *tsk*. I'm irritating him, I know, but I can't control my anxiety. "This is nerve-wracking," I say. "Is there anything there?" Part of me hopes the answer is "no." I'd rather feel like a fool putting Jack onto this crazy assignment rather than find something.

"I don't know yet," he mutters.

Jack flips through documents and, angling his phone, snaps multiple pictures of the same page in sections. It's as though he's deliberately toying with me by taking his sweet time with our foray into larceny. Then again, is it larceny if we don't take anything? Is it merely a matter of breaking and entering without the criminal elements?

"This whole thing makes my stomach flip," I say.

"Why don't you keep an eye on the front door?" suggests Jack.

I open the bedroom door an inch and peer toward the entrance below. If Rashid returns early and walks in on us, what would I do or say to him? "I've changed my mind," I announce.

Jack abandons the safe and turns to me. "What is going on with you today? This was your idea."

"I know, it's just that, well..." My voice trails off. How can I explain to Jack that after spending a considerable amount of time with Rashid, I'm reevaluating my perception of him? Maybe I got it all wrong, and it wasn't Rashid who made me an unwitting participant in the theft of *Mistress*. Maybe I'm suffering from PTSD and somehow misconstrued meeting the Prince that night at the magazine's party with meeting the thief. Or perhaps those men on the boat forced him to steal the painting. That doesn't sound so far-fetched.

"What if I'm mistaken? I mean, Jack, this sophisticated, generous, wealthy man can't possibly be whom we suspect him of being." I abandon my spot at the door to plead with him.

Jack slowly blinks his eyes. "Charlotte, are you falling for the mark?"

I whip my head back and bellow in gross exaggeration. "What? No, it's just that he...isn't as bad as I initially thought..." I look up at Jack as the heat of a blush spreads over my face. "I'm not sure anymore. I've spent a lot of time with him lately. Sometimes I feel grateful that he's giving me this great life. Other times I feel I'm being held captive like that syndrome. You know when people feel they can't escape even when they can."

"Stockholm."

"Yes, thank you. Stockholm. See? This craziness is affecting me. Everything that I thought I knew is in question."

"How cruel the last week must have been for you. Races and dinner parties and shopping."

My eyes narrow.

"Oh yes," he continues, "I looked up your social media accounts. He's giving you quite a life."

Cocking my head to the side and shrugging, I say, "Sort of. His kindness has me all confused. He's given me house staff and a driver...but I'm sure it's all so he can keep an eye on me."

"This sounds dubious."

I blurt out, "He's killing me with kindness–."

"–And a black AMEX card." Jack finishes my sentence. When he looks at me, all I see is his disappointment. We were a team, and now I'm abandoning him.

"Oh Jack, please, I was genuinely scared but still kept my part of the bargain. When those men shot at me on the boat, Rashid tried to protect me. Whatever is going on, I don't think he's behind *all* of it. I've been thinking about that man at the races and what you told me in France about buyers already set up. What if *he*'s the buyer? What if something went wrong or Rashid changed his mind or...or...I don't know." My voice ends in a high pitch.

Jack looks like I just punched him.

I place my hand on Jack's, give it a light squeeze. "Don't give these to Favreau. I mean, you passed along the flash drive and, if he hasn't found anything yet, then maybe there's nothing to find."

"Charlotte, what did he offer you?"

I let out a forced laugh. "Nothing." Then in a low whisper, I say, "All I'm saying is what if there's nothing there, and it's all smoke and mirrors. Or maybe it's a one-time job. Or he was forced to do it by...by that scary dude at the races whose men are trying to kill me."

"Charlotte, just tell me the truth."

I can't escape his eyes. "I'm having second thoughts." I search his face for a hint of surprise, but find none. "Hear me out. After the theft, I felt like a total mess, and everything was jumbled – thoughts, feelings, memories. I'm not sure anymore that it was Rashid who...who–"

"–stole the painting and kidnapped you, then tossed you from a helicopter." His voice grows loud.

"I fell!"

"If you say so, but everything else I said is true, and you're not even refuting it. I can't believe this. He has upended your life, ruined your reputation, and you're perfectly willing to go along with what was supposed to be a fake life with him."

"My reputation has been repaired."

"What makes you think that? We haven't delivered *anything* to Favreau that's been worthwhile."

"Rashid set up new social media accounts for me, and the tide is changing. People wish me well in my new endeavors. I'm no longer a pariah."

"Do you mean to tell me you don't wish to pursue this any longer because you've been cleared via Trial by Influencers?" Jack asks, voice serious.

"What? No, that sounds so stupid." *But is it really stupid?* In a small voice, I say, "It's just that I used to have my whole life figured out, and not once did I stray from that path to success. Then Paris happened, and my friends turned out not to be my friends, and my career disappeared in minutes, the career that I gave up *everything* for. I know I'm placing too much importance on what strangers think of me, but..." I sigh heavily. "I'm just tired of trying to stop a tsunami with my bare hands."

Jack is quiet for a moment, and I wonder if anything I've said has expressed my emotional turmoil.

"Charlotte, do what you feel is necessary, but I'm doing this."

"What are you doing in my room?"

Rashid's tone is frighteningly calm and seething. Omar lingers behind him. Rashid's eyes drift from me to Jack to the exposed wall safe. The roguish grin on his face seems playful and expectant that this moment would come. "Omar, please cancel Ms. Milton's car for the evening. She'll be indisposed."

I clasp Jack by the arm.

Chapter 36

H UDDLED ON A SETTEE in the office, Jack and I stare at the painting propped against the sofa opposite us. The *Mistress* winks at me as though she, too, was in on this little joke of Rashid's. She had been under our noses this entire time. Tilting my head, I look at *Mistress in a Red Dress* from a different angle. Centuries later and she still has men falling in love with her.

"Is she the reason those men on the boat tried to kill me?"

"I'm afraid so," says Rashid, sitting on a modern, white leather chair between us and the painting.

"But why? I don't have the painting. I don't know anything."

"You're a loose end."

"A loose end," I repeat, and my voice cracks. "That's what *you* made me."

Finally, Jack draws his eyes away from the artwork. "Are they going to try again?"

Shaking his head, Rashid says, "I will protect you, Charlotte. You have my word."

I guffaw and glance toward Jack before returning my gaze to Rashid. "It's that man from the races?"

Rashid seems taken aback. "Levan, yes."

"You're the reason my life is in shambles," I say, staring hard at him. I'm disappointed in myself for letting my suspicions falter.

Rashid winces, the look of stinging pain on his face. In quiet contemplation, he knots his brows. "I'm afraid I've involved you in something quite serious. Believe me, it was not my intention to bring harm to you."

"I've lost everything. My job, my friends, my reputation. I felt guilty wanting to unmask you, but I *was* right all along..." I trail off. The part of me that had hoped myself wrong remains, and I'm not quite sure how to reconcile my emotions. "You stole that painting and had everyone suspect that I was in on it. Why me? Did you plan to use me or was I just convenient?" My voice rises until I become increasingly agitated.

Rashid looks away, too cowardly to face me.

"Take it easy, Charlotte," Jack says quietly.

"Take it easy?! I'll remember that the next time they try to kill me."

"They're done with all that," says Jack, his tone unconvincing. He places his hand on my back.

"Don't be condescending," I say, shaking off his hand. Silence fills the room. Jack seems to search for something to say.

To Rashid, Jack says, "By the way, Charlotte told me how you rolled up the *Mistress*, probably added more cracks in the paint. I hope you at least stored it flat in an acid-free box." His eyes land on the painting, then back to me. The painting. Me. "You know, now that you're both in the same room, I see an uncanny resemblance."

My gaze drifts back to the *Mistress*. "I should slap you."

"Me?!" says Jack.

"No. Rashid."

Rashid's eyes flick up at me with a look of resignation as though he's in agreement. I'd never slap anyone. I'm incapable of inflicting pain on another, even if it's deserved. With the painting within reach, I postulate a return to my old life. Surely, I can hand it over to the police with a perfectly logical explanation of how it ended up in my possession. *As though they'd believe you,* the *Mistress* says with an eye-roll.

"Where do we go from here?" I say.

Rashid practically rushes to me. "It should never have gone this far. I promise, I will fix this, but you must trust me."

"Ha!" I shout and look to Jack with an expression to impart my mistrust of Rashid.

"I understand," says Rashid in a low voice. His eyes lift to meet mine and he says, "But now you know the truth to do what you will with it."

I should despise him. Exposing Rashid and clearing my name is what I've been planning and hoping for, yet I read the anguished guilt expressed on his face and I can't explain how disoriented I feel at the moment, my emotions muddled.

"*If* I were to trust you..."

"Am I the only sane one in this room?" Jack says.

"I said *if*," I hiss. "Anyway, how will you fix the madness you created?"

"I'll show you." From the drawer of an end table, Rashid produces a remote. Blinds snake down, lights go dim, and a screen lowers against a far wall.

"Oh, look, a show," Jack says facetiously.

"If you give it a chance, you'll quite enjoy it, Professor. As an art historian, I'm sure you know of the painter, Karl Sonnenberg."

Rashid starts a slideshow, and a 1930s photo of a very rigid-looking man, with a large mustache obscuring his mouth, splashes on the screen. It's the same image we had pulled from the safe. Next up is a painting.

"Some of his work was smuggled out of Germany by his friends," continues Rashid.

"Why smuggled?" I ask.

"He was Jewish," Jack answers. "They smuggled works of art before the Nazis got their hands on them."

"To destroy them?"

"They wouldn't destroy these. Sonnenberg's paintings were too valuable, but they did burn lesser-known works of art and many books. The destruction of the Jewish culture began in 1930s Germany before the war," Jack says, and it sounds like he's giving a lecture. "At first, paintings weren't physically stolen from the walls of Jewish homes. Authorities stripped Jewish art dealers of their professional accreditation, forcing them to sell their gallery's assets in a climate when it would be sold for a bargain. Until recently, these forced sales weren't viewed as thefts at all, even though they were committed under Nazi coercion."

Rashid forwards through to other paintings and says, "The first two paintings have already been retrieved. They were sold on the black market several years ago when Interpol intercepted, and they now are on display at the Guggenheim in New York with the blessing of the family. These next paintings have never been found," Rashid continues as more paintings fly by on the screen in front of us.

"It's like finding a needle in a haystack, isn't it?" I ask.

"Depends. Some try to sell on the black market, like the Prince mentioned, and are discovered. Others turn up in an attic by the family members of the deceased. It's rare, but you never know when or where these will be retrieved."

"If ever," says Rashid. "Sometimes intelligence is received that can lead to the recovery of works of art." He flips to another painting, this time a self-portrait of the artist himself.

"Oh my God," Jack stands, moves in front of the slide; his silhouette distorts the portrait. "This? You're saying you've found this?"

I look from the shock on Jack's face to delight in Rashid's. "What is it?"

"This self-portrait is the only one in existence. It disappeared."

"Stolen by the Nazis," Rashid adds. "Sonnenberg was sent to a concentration camp where he died. His family has been trying desperately to retrieve his artwork ever since." Rashid steps forward, the light from the projector reflects off his face. He turns to the next photograph – a recent photo of a heavy-set man emerging from a limo and surrounded by personal bodyguards. The following picture has the same man exiting a European bank.

"This is Hector Banning, a very wealthy businessman in Luxembourg. He owns several high-profile businesses – shipping, banking, portfolio management."

The next set of images show Hector shaking the hands of various prominent European political figures.

"He's well connected, I see," I say. "Am I the only one not following where this is leading?"

"Seems our Prince hasn't finished yet, but I'm sure it will lead to something fascinating," Jack says.

"Oh, it will fascinate you, Professor. I believe he has the Sonnenberg self-portrait among other works of art. Krushek. Malone. He keeps a large cache of stolen art hidden in his private quarters. My source tells me he now holds the largest private collection of stolen work."

Jack arches his brows. "Source?"

Rashid remains silent.

"Is he being watched by Interpol?" asks Jack.

"Fortunately for us, no. As Charlotte noted, he's well-connected and keeps his distance, so no one suspects him."

"Like someone we know," I interject, eyes on Rashid.

"Yes, what does your cache of stolen art look like?" Jack asks.

"Let's concentrate on Banning, shall we?" says Rashid.

"You mentioned it's fortunate for us that Interpol isn't aware of Banning. Why is that?" says Jack.

"It will be easier for us to steal the paintings back, of course."

I laugh at Jack's incredulous expression. "Don't look so worried, Jack. He's only kidding."

With an intense stare aimed at Rashid, Jack says, "I'm afraid he's not, Charlotte."

My laughter abruptly muted, I turn to Rashid. "You have to be kidding."

"I have a crew nearly in place," says Rashid, "but I'm down two."

"Where's the target?"

"Jack!" His name explodes from my lips.

"I'm just asking," he says. Then, he shakes his head after a brief contemplation. "This is crazy," Jack says, prickling. "If Banning has what you claim, he'd have cameras, an impenetrable security system, armed guards."

"We can penetrate his vault," says Rashid.

"Vault?" repeats Jack. "I think I need a drink."

"I have a plan," Rashid says, "for us to break into Banning's home to retrieve the stolen artwork." Rashid stands taller, his chest puffed out slightly as though proud of his big announcement though I can't understand why.

"You want us to do what now?" I say.

"Break into Banning's..."

"Yes, we heard that part, but how exactly?" says Jack.

Rashid flicks the remote and a stunning, heart-shaped diamond necklace appears on screen.

"Woah," I breathe. "Diamonds. Now we're talking."

"This," continues Rashid, "is The Heart Diamond. Flawless. 6.07 carats in a rare blue color that will be up for auction. My source tells me Hector Banning will bid on it for his wife. Charlotte and I will also be in attendance bidding on the same necklace."

I swallow hard. "You're buying me that necklace?"

"I'll pretend to buy you that necklace. It will certainly get Banning's attention, and from there, we'll engineer our way into his upcoming Black and White ball which will be held at his castle."

"Where the stolen art resides. When do I come in?" asks Jack. "Am I bidding on the necklace, too?"

Rashid shakes his head. "You won't be at the auction, Professor."

"Where will I be?"

"Joining his household staff."

Jack's face flushes. "Oh, I see. I'm being removed."

A tight smile lands on Rashid's face. "No, you're needed at Banning's home. I know about his employees, his men, daily delivery schedules, but you, Professor, your job is to get the four-digit code, be our inside man, confirm the accuracy of my source's intel."

Jack nods, swinging his index finger back and forth between me and Rashid. "And while I'm out of the picture, you two will be together."

"Yes, Jack, bidding on the diamond necklace," I agree. "Keep up."

"Pretending to bid," corrects Rashid. "And while at the auction, Ms. Milton and I will retrieve Banning's fingerprints."

"What for?" Jack and I simultaneously pipe in.

"As a back-up plan to open the vault."

I sigh, "Again with the vault. This is beginning to sound like *Who's on First*."

"The vault," says Rashid as he exits the slideshow and clicks on a 3-D image of a vault door. "Through my source, I discovered that Banning had a vault custom-made. It's equipped like a fortress and guarded by a series of titanium locking bolts. It's fire and drill proof, with military-grade ballistic armor able to deflect bullets, and a bio-metric fingerprint entry with a four-digit code. It's also, booby-trapped with hand grenades contained to destroy the outside of the vault."

I'm startled by the exploding animation that follows on screen.

"You had me until the grenades," says Jack.

"This is too much," I sneer. "Why are you doing this?"

Rashid remains silent.

"Thomas Crown grows a conscious," says Jack.

I interject, "And you said the Thomas Crown persona was all Hollywood with no truth to it. We should take it to the police."

"Without evidence, police are bound by law. I do as I please."

"Let's go through this again," I say. "While Jack infiltrates the household staff at the castle to retrieve a secret code to the vault – good luck with that – we're going to an auction to pretend to bid on a diamond necklace."

"Correct."

"And we're somehow getting Banning's fingerprints?"

"Yes."

Jack's eye twitches. "This is giving me a headache. How are we supposed to carry out all that art he supposedly stole?"

"As I mentioned, I have a crew. We won't be doing this alone. During a fireworks distraction on the night of the Black and White ball, we will enter the vault via the waterway," explains Rashid. "No one will know the art is missing until long after we're gone."

"Famous last words," mumbles Jack.

I shoot my hand up as though in class, but don't wait for Rashid to call on me. "When we steal back the stolen art work, do we also steal the diamond necklace?"

"Charlotte!"

My head whips to Jack. "It was only a question. Besides, you're gaga over that weird guy's self-portrait."

I sigh heavily, contemplating the madness of this plan. Jack and I have been a team for a couple of weeks now, forwarding information to Favreau. And now we're to dig ourselves deeper into this criminal world and take part in an actual heist? Is that seriously what we're considering? "I need to clear my name."

"Absolutely. This is an opportunity of a lifetime," Rashid says. "We can be heroes."

"More like martyrs," I mumble.

Chapter 37

"ESTABLISHING SHOT. LUXEMBOURG. THE sun dips back into the horizon and casts a hue of semidarkness over the city. Limousines line up to the end of the block from the auction house and beyond–"

"–What are you doing?" Rashid says. He sits next to me in the back of the limo that creeps toward the main entrance.

My eyes hide behind oversized, dark sunglasses, and a (borrowed) diamond hair clip completes my white Versace dress. Rashid wears Armani, perfectly tailored to his fit body. I would have loved to be his tailor and take in an inseam here and there. I breathe in his cologne – a little bergamot oil, something citrusy and amber – it's warm and compelling. One more sniff, and I'll find myself straddling the guy. *Focus!*

I clear my throat. "Narrating. Or possibly voice-over, you know, like those bits in heist films where characters go over the details for the sake of the audience, so they know when things veer off course. Not an *Ocean's Eleven* fan?"

Rashid gazes at me. "Anticipating this to veer off course?"

"They always do in the movies. Hollywood loves to raise the stakes."

"Hollywood isn't real. If you always give an audience a happy ending, why worry about the stakes they raise?"

"Endings don't matter. It's how you get there that makes for an exciting journey."

"Hmmm," says Rashid.

The limo moves forward a few feet then stops. It's a constant motion of starting and stopping.

"I do enjoy George Clooney. *The Descendants. Up in the Air. O Brother Where Art Thou*," offers Rashid.

"*Out of Sight* with Jennifer Lopez and her gun. She should carry a gun in all her films. No one would mess with *The Wedding Planner* with a gun."

"You seem nervous."

"I'm not," I lie.

"Charlotte, I'm counting on you for this to work. Mr. Banning–"

"–Needs baiting. We all have a role to play. Frankly, I see mine ending with an Oscar for Margot Robbie playing me."

"My happy ending is a little different. Charlotte..." He leans into me, but his voice trails off.

Now would be the perfect moment to kiss, I think. Perhaps not *the* ideal moment but certainly *a* perfect one. Would I kiss him back? Over the past two weeks, I've spent so much time with Jack and Rashid that it felt like we had always been this group of friends. Then, when Jack left to fulfill his part in our scheme, something shifted between me and Rashid. He became more attentive. Rashid's confession has settled me and moved things forward on that front.

"Sometimes," he picks up again with a strange urgency in his voice, "I wonder about the decisions I made. What if I hadn't done that little thing of stealing a painting and bringing you along for the ride? What if I hadn't ruined your reputation?"

"But you did."

His face winces.

"What if we met on a friend's yacht in the south of France?" His hand reaches for mine, his thumb caresses my skin. "And we weren't us. I was a–"

"–Playboy," I interject.

"Racecar driver."

"Of course."

"And you were a Nobel Prize-winning scientist."

"Who cured cancer."

He smiles. "Who cured cancer."

"Hmmm, that works for a meet-cute."

"We'd be two ordinary people free to get to know one another."

Since when are a race car driver and a scientist who cures cancer considered "ordinary?" I'd like to ask him but keep silent. We can never be *those* people because Rashid did this little thing of destroying the life I had built.

"*What If?* is a fantasy," I sputter. "Are you doing George Clooney in *Out of Sight* or Tom Hanks in *You've Got Mail?* I suppose next you'll tell me it wasn't personal." My voice cracks, and I'm relieved when the vehicle comes to a complete stop, and someone opens the door.

Rashid removes his hand from mine. "I'm sorry, Charlotte. I will make this right."

Outside, a chaotic crowd has formed. The Heart Diamond, up for auction at this charity event, has brought a star-studded crowd. Hard, repetitive music blasts. Strobes light up the sky. Bulbs flash in my face, but I know it has less to do with me and more of a burning desire to get the photo of the glamorous woman with the Prince. At least I hope the photo editors use the word "glamorous" when describing me.

The entourage of body-guards trails behind us as we enter the warehouse space converted into the party venue. Inside, the atmosphere differs from the madness outside. Mundane, classical music infiltrates the room as reams of people – women in designer dresses and men in tuxedos – gather into cloistered groups.

Arm entwined with Rashid's, we seem to make a noticeable entrance. An attendant approaches to personally register Rashid and provides him with a numbered paddle.

"Oh, how cute. May I?" I say, already reaching for the paddle. I catch his slight hesitation before he agrees.

"Prince Rashid," a man's voice calls. Within moments, Hector Banning weaves through a crowd toward us until he's stopped by one of Rashid's bodyguards. Banning seems to take this as an affront. "Step aside," he tells the bodyguard. Then, from beyond the guard, he says, "Prince Rashid, I am Hector Banning. We met about two years ago at one of your father's races."

Rashid looks him up then down. Recognition doesn't settle on his face, and I see how this unnerves Banning beyond the bodyguard's actions. Stand-offish behavior is what we agreed would be what challenges our mark. Finally, Banning relaxes when Rashid waves away his bodyguard.

"Mr. Bal..."

"Banning. I don't expect you to remember me."

"His Highness meets so many, it's hard to remember them all," I say, trying on an accent, and immediately regret that decision. I figure I'll play it off as a mixture of my imaginary upbringing at various European boarding schools. "I do hope you'll be more memorable this evening."

Banning's mouth drops open, and his eyebrows shoot upwards. In a peal of nervous laughter, he says, "Now that we've met again, you'll remember me the next time."

Rashid doesn't comment, and I take my cue from him. *Let him squirm.* We stare at Banning with slight disdain to make him feel out of place in our presence. The awkward silence between us intensifies.

"Well," Banning begins but doesn't finish.

More silence fills the air.

"Well," Banning tries again, "is there something at the auction that has caught your eye?"

"No," says Rashid.

"Yes," I say at the same time. "The Heart Diamond."

Rashid wraps his arm around my waist, his fingers press in for a slight squeeze I know is for show. "Darling, you mustn't tell everyone why we are here. Mr. Banning could give us some competition for that diamond."

"And I'm afraid I will," Banning says, laughing. "To keep my marriage a happy one, I must bid on the diamond."

"Rashid?" I turn to him with mock concern on an entitled face. "You promised me I'd have it."

"Good luck at the auction, Mr. Banning. Keep in mind, I'm used to getting what I want." For the first time during this exchange, Rashid smiles at Banning.

"As am I," Banning laughs out loud. "As am I."

I abruptly guide Rashid away, leaving Banning laughing alone. From a few steps away, I turn in time to witness Banning rejoin his group, his body language animated, no doubt in the retelling of some fictional story about his dear friend, Prince Rashid. Without taking my eyes off him, I mumble, "Ass-kisser. How did you know he would take the bait?"

"Before you set any plan in motion, you must do your homework, study the person, know their likes, dislikes, understand what they desire most, whom they desire most. Eventually, you will uncover everything you need to manipulate them."

The confident tone of his voice startles me. Is this what he did with me? Study me and manipulate me into this charade? He had promised my name would be cleared. He had pledged to Jack a much bigger coup of stolen works. The answer, I know, is absolutely he did.

"You're a ruthless con artist, the quintessential bad boy," I say and maintain a smile for the sake of those around us. "You're a playboy," I add in a joking tone though I'm serious.

Eyes fixedly on me, he leans in and says, "I may like to play, but I'm no boy."

My face flushes, and I'm forced to turn aside to regain my composure. Luckily, an attendant appears to escort us to the front row, but Rashid presses a hand to my back and my body heat spikes. When we are seated, he leans close and quietly explains how the auction works. Only I'm not listening. Instead, I gulp in his cologne and lose myself in his eyes, his voice, his everything. It's play-acting, I tell myself, part of the role as his love interest though I'd go all in to turn this into a bodice-ripping adventure.

Mr. and Mrs. Banning appear from the back of the aisle. She's taller than her husband, perfectly tanned with breasts bursting to get out. I've seen her type in Beverly Hills and Palm Beach. He settles into the third row, but Mrs. Banning doesn't follow, and she points a long fingernail to the front row, whispering to him in quick huffs.

"May I have the paddle back?" Rashid says.

I break my gaze from the Bannings and down to the paddle in my hand. "Can I hold it until The Heart Diamond is put on display? I feel powerful holding it."

Before long, the audience settles, and the auction begins. The first item on the auction block is a pair of candlesticks that once belonged to a Duchess in Italy or England, or Russia. I'm not paying attention. My hand sweats, my grip tightens on the paddle, my mind fills with worry that things will go astray. It sounded crazy when Rashid first explained the plan to Jack and me, and it doesn't sound any saner even now that I find myself smack in the middle of it.

The auctioneer's shouts of "$25,000... $30,000... $35,000..." reverberate in my mind. I pay him no heed until I hear–

"And now, ladies and gentlemen, The Heart Diamond. This flawless diamond is 6.07 carats. Not only are blue diamonds scarce, but this particular hue of the diamond is rarer. Found in South Africa in the 1920s, it was worn by Princess Grace of Monaco. The bidding will begin at $3.5 million and move in increments of $100,000."

The lighting reflects off the diamond. The plan is for me to act as *if* I desire it, but I don't have to pretend. My heart speeds up as I stare, transfixed by the stone's dazzling perfection. Beside me, Rashid retrieves the paddle, and rubs against my arm as he lifts the paddle in direct competition with two other men. Banning isn't in the competition. What has happened to dissuade him from bidding on the prized jewel? Agitated, I shift uncomfortably in my chair, disquieted at a plan doomed to failure.

One of the men drops out when the bid reaches $6.7 million. The other man offers $6.8. Rashid holds for a moment.

"Banning's not interested. Was he teasing you earlier?" I whisper.

"Do I hear $6.9?" the auctioneer says and eyes Rashid directly. Calmly, he places his paddle across his lap to indicate that he's out of the competition.

"Going once..."

A paddle shoots up. The auctioneer points to Banning. "I have $6.9. Do I hear $7?"

Without looking in Banning's direction, Rashid lets out a slight sigh and lifts his paddle in the air.

Game on, I think.

The other man is now pushed out by Banning's entrance, and the competition remains fierce between him and Rashid. I can feel the eyes of all the women in the room upon me. *So, this is what envy feels like.* The bid stalls at $8.9 million. Rashid hesitates but then lifts his paddle. Banning responds by bidding $9 million. Rashid clenches his jaw. Quickly, he turns to stare down Banning. The crowd murmurs among themselves.

I lean into Rashid and, in an indignant whisper loud enough for the Bannings to hear, say, "What are you doing? Don't let *her* get it."

The gavel hits the podium, and the auctioneer shouts, "Sold for $9 million to the man in the third row, number 23."

Mrs. Banning gives Mr. Banning a peck on the cheek.

The auction over, Rashid and I join a small group congratulating Mr. Banning. But, the sudden departure of Mrs. Banning, who decided to join another circle, leaves Mr. Banning awkwardly holding two drinks.

"Your Highness, you gave me quite a competition. I went higher than I had anticipated."

"And yet you bid that one last time," Rashid says, his face empty of pleasantries.

"Well." Banning looks around before continuing. "I'll tell you my secret. I noticed you hesitated before your last bid." Banning's eyes fall on me. "This has caused you much unhappiness."

"You understate matters," I pipe in, my lips pursed. Banning offers me his other drink, which I take. We salute one other, down our drinks, and place them on the tray of a perfectly-timed passing waiter. I look past Omar, dressed in a waiter's uniform, to avoid intimating recognition.

In a low voice, Rashid says, "You must grant me an opportunity to win back my dignity, at least before Ms. Milton." Rashid reaches for my hand. "I'm afraid her unhappiness interferes with my own."

"I've experienced it many times," Banning says knowingly. "Perhaps I can make amends with an invitation to my Black and White Ball at my home in Switzerland where, I hope, you will come as my special guests. It's next month on the 18th."

"How very kind of you," Rashid says.

"Who will be there?" I say in a bored yet biting tone.

"Charlotte," says Rashid, admonishing me.

My eyes pounce on him, then turn innocent. "What? Remember Monaco? There was no one of importance, and we spent the entire evening with lesser-known royals."

"If I may," interrupts Banning, "the du Epps will be in attendance, as will the von Kleeps, the Swiss Finance Minister..."

Rashid says, "We'd be delighted."

I nudge Rashid and whisper into his ear with the full intention of having Banning overhear my tirade over not getting the Heart Diamond.

Rashid puts his arm on the small of my back and, in a gentle tone, says, "Darling, I will find you something better."

I acquiesce, and turn to Banning with a smile. "Switzerland is lovely this time of year," I say. Behind Banning, I spot Omar near the entrance to the ladies' bathroom. "Gentlemen, if you'll excuse me. I must powder my nose." Waltzing past Omar, I move down a corridor to a nook beyond the ladies' room. Omar follows. In one swift movement, I turn to him, open my purse, and he drops Banning's glass into it with his gloved hand.

Chapter 38

R ASHID SETTLES INTO THE comfort of the limousine next to Charlotte. There was a moment this evening when he feared he had been misled. But Banning did as expected, enticed by a bit of healthy competition to come out to play.

Next to him, Charlotte can't contain her excitement. "...Make him desperate to have us there. It was perfect. Did you like the accent?"

"Where is the accent from, exactly?" he says, a little amused, though he was thrown when she first spoke with it earlier.

"Oh, you know, a little from this country, a little from another."

Headlights bounce off the interior of the limo, momentarily blinding him, and he averts his eyes. "Do you have a mirror in your purse?"

"No. Why?"

Rashid turns his head slightly, tilts it toward her, and says, "A black sedan is behind us."

Charlotte shifts her body to look. "What's wrong?" She glances back at the next turn.

"It's been following for some time. Driver, take a detour. Make a right, please."

As their limo turns right, the car continues to follow.

"Left."

Again, the car follows.

"Are they Banning's men?" Charlotte asks nervously.

Rashid places a comforting arm around her. "No one is onto us," he says, though he doesn't believe his own lie. Could it be Banning? Certainly, but he would hope not. Levan also comes to mind. He can't determine which of the two worries him the most, but the consequences could be devastating either way.

"I worry about having Jack in Banning's lair. What if he suspects Jack is a plant?"

"Jack is safe," he tells her. He feels a pang of jealousy. Catching them at his safe proved what he tried to deny all along – that Charlotte and Jack have been working together. But is there more to the relationship? He's not sure... though he's seen the way she looks at Jack sometimes. Separating them has put him at ease. It'll give him a chance to connect with Charlotte without Jack in the way.

Rashid takes another look back. The car has now disappeared. "I'm sure I'm being paranoid. No one's following us," he says, but even he is not entirely convinced.

Chapter 39

"WHAT ARE YOU DOING here?" barks a male voice in a German accent.

Jack's first foray into snooping, and he's already caught. He hadn't gotten very far anyway, hitting a wall where, according to the blueprint, there should have been a set of stairs. Jack turns. His interrogator, the living embodiment of a villain from a 1960s spy novel, is tall and muscular. A scar extends above his eye and toward his cheek. If Jack wasn't unnerved by him, he would laugh at the absurdity. But this man isn't like the other staff members he's met at the Banning's castle in Switzerland, where he somehow talked himself into employment.

Earlier, when he sat in the kitchen observing the hustle and bustle of the kitchen staff, he thought it would be easy to slip away. They were too busy with their own work to fuss about the newest employee. He watched as someone accidentally let a dog in, but in the chaos, no one noticed until he was found sniffing a bag of potatoes. Laila, the head housekeeper who had let Jack in, shooed the dog out. She admonished the man who let the dog in, but he uttered something incoherent, followed by a half-shrug. Another young man, barely twenty by the look of it, lugged firewood. Among them, Jack would be practically invisible, scurrying around the castle unnoticed, spying on the comings and goings of everyone while searching for the stolen art. But he wasn't counting on this German to be alert.

"I'm afraid I've made a wrong turn somewhere and can't exit the premises... old boy." Internally, Jack winces at the put-upon manner that makes him feel like a caricature. Charlotte insisted he use that phrase, and when he pointed out his countrymen don't speak this way, she guffawed. "Non-Brits *think* Brits speak this way, and that's what matters," she retorted.

The German looks him up, then down. "This way."

It works—two points for Charlotte.

"Right-O. Thank you very kindly for rescuing me."

The German signals for Jack to walk ahead. He slips past the man casually and turns a corner. Down the hall, Jack comes to a fork in the road. Literally a fork, no doubt dropped by accident. A servant hurriedly enters from a door to Jack's right and looks about for the fallen utensil.

"Are you looking for this?" says Jack, picking it up.

"Yes, thank you, sir," she says quietly. Jack peers through an open doorway to Mrs. Banning sitting down to breakfast. She taps the top of a hard-boiled egg with a silver knife and peels it.

"Melanie, do be quick with that spoon," she shouts.

The young servant, with a harried expression, hustles past Jack.

"You there."

Jack whips toward Mrs. Banning's voice.

"Who are you?"

He points to himself like a buffoon. Of course, she's talking to him. Jack takes timid steps into the room. "My name is Jack Blunt. I'm a new employee. Mrs. Banning."

"You're British," she says in a South American accent. At fifty, she is every bit as beautiful as when she was a supermodel in Brazil. Her long, dark hair cascades around her facelift-free beauty, and she wears her trademark immaculate white shirt and pearls. "And where in England do you hail from?"

"London."

"Oh, I love London," she coos.

"Yes, it is a wonderful city. I do look forward to serving you, Mrs. Banning."

"As do I," she purrs, "as do I. You may go."

"Thank you," Jack says and stares at her for 8.4 seconds to make full eye contact. This is also Charlotte's idea. If the rumors about Mrs. Banning are true, then it will be easy to play her. It was Charlotte who researched her, then warned him about her discovery. Mrs. Banning's profile reads like one on the website "Who's Dated Who" – a string of famous and wealthy men and the occasional woman. Jack listened to Charlotte, nodded periodically, though he wasn't familiar with most of the names she dropped.

Before he left for Switzerland, Charlotte seemed a bit troubled and again warned him about Mrs. B. Did he detect a hint of jealousy on her part? He hopes so. Rashid's plan, though Jack thinks is a good one, has soured him. It's not lost on Jack that Rashid is attempting to rewrite the ending, paint himself as the hero in this movie that, by all accounts, is supposed to be co-starring Jack. Instead, Rashid has subjugated Jack into "servant" status. Shouldn't Jack be the hero in this tale? He's not the one who ruined Charlotte's life.

Nowadays, villains get the girls. It's all about the bad boys.

Jack wanders back into the kitchen. It's not long before Laila calls out to him.

"Mr. Blunt, today you have been assigned to driving duties."

He hasn't been there but one hour, and already the plan is falling apart. He's supposed to be scouting the place, and now they're sending him out. "But, I'm not a driver. My expertise is in the home..."

"You'll be driving Mrs. Banning into town... at her personal request. Mark is outside and will give you the key to the Bentley."

"Yes," Jack says, although Laila has already stepped away without waiting for an answer.

A back door leads outside to the stables and garage. Through that door, Jack finds Mark, the young twenty-something who had carried in the wood. Jack asks for the key to the Bentley.

"Which one," Mark says.

"I was told the Bentley."

"But which Bentley?"

Jack shrugs.

"The white one," Mrs. Banning calls out from behind.

Jack spins to Mrs. Banning, who stands there with some sort of fur tossed over as a shrug. Even this high up the mountain, it's too warm. She taps one foot, heels dig into the cobbled stones. "The car should have been ready. Let me make myself understood, Mr. Blunt, you wait for me, not the other way around."

"I do apologize," Jack says. "It won't happen again."

"It most certainly won't," she says. After a few moments, she glances at her watch. "Well? Get it."

Jack hurries off and finds the white Bentley at the end of the five-car garage. Inside, he notes a driver's cap on the passenger side. Is he expected to wear the ridiculous thing? He hopes not.

The drive into Ober, the tiny village at the foot of the mountain, is along a dangerous, winding, and narrow road. Jack is often forced to slow down and takes the curves into the roadway at a turtle's pace. If the tires were to skim the edge, he's not confident he could prevent the car from going over.

Silence fills the vehicle. Mrs. Banning sits behind Jack, where he's sure she catches his every glance. He should stop spying on her, yet he can't help himself.

"Where did you go to school, Mr. Blunt?" she says, breaking the quiet.

"Spencer Academy, Ma'am."

"Experienced, are you?"

"Yes, Ma'am. After Spencer, I interned at the palace." There is no need to add Buckingham. "Following my internship, I was employed at the home of one of the King's cousins until recently." He repeats the story he's been given, one that can be corroborated thanks to a favor he called in.

"We run a tight home. They've told you about our annual grand ball in a few days? Everyone will be over-worked."

"Understood. I have never disappointed the master of the house."

Through the rearview mirror, Jack sees her eyes bore a hole into him.

"And the mistress of the house?" she says. Her voice drops an octave.

"I have always satisfied my mistress." This is the kind of nonsense he's sure Charlotte was worried about.

"No, Mr. Blunt, I don't imagine you'll disappoint me. My couturier is just around the corner. There," she says, pointing to a discreet shop in the heart of the village. Jack pulls the Bentley up to the front, quickly exits, and opens the car door for Mrs. Banning. "I'll be a while. Don't leave your post," she orders.

Back behind the driver's seat, Jack scans the area – a water fountain in the center of a roundabout, a cheese store, bakery, a small mobile phone shop, a pharmacy. More stores line the side of the road he's on.

A rap on the window of the Bentley startles Jack.

"The lady would like you to accompany her," a teenage girl says before running back in.

The store is empty, and Jack wonders where the shop-girl has run off. To one side, a dressmaker's mannequin is swathed in a floral dress, short enough to reveal a black base. Behind it, perfectly lined shelves of hats, purses, and shoes come into focus.

"Ouch!" Mrs. Banning shouts from behind a curtain toward the back of the store. "I told you to be careful!"

Moving towards the curtain, Jack tucks the asinine driver's hat under his arm and, resting his hand on the curtain, says, "Mrs. Banning, you called for me?"

"Yes," she shouts back. "Step in here."

Pulling aside the heavy curtain, Jack enters. Towering on a pedestal in the center of the room, Mrs. Banning wears a nearly sheer black dress. Embroidery delicately covers her breasts, and the skirt swoops around her waist and hangs loosely to her feet. She shifts her left leg out to expose a thigh-high slit.

"Marta thinks the slit is high enough, but I say it should be higher. What do you suppose we do?"

Jack, unable to answer, simply stares.

Mrs. Banning smiles. "Jack? Higher?"

How wicked of her to call him in. "Higher," he says huskily. Embarrassed, he clears his throat.

Mrs. Banning grabs the fabric above the slit and tears, revealing far more than she should.

"This high," she instructs Marta. When she returns her attention back to Jack, there's such an intensity in the way she looks at him that he knows he's in trouble.

***

Exhausted after a 10-hour workday, Jack drives into Ober and parks near his apartment building. He has his cell phone already in his hand before he shuts off the ignition, dialing Charlotte's number. Twisting around, he scours his surroundings for prying eyes. No one had followed him from the castle, but he's cautious nonetheless.

Charlotte doesn't answer. Jack hangs up and dials again at a slower pace, careful to press each number for accuracy. The hollow tone rings endlessly in his ear. What has her so preoccupied that she's unable to answer? And how is there no voicemail? This troubles him. He hasn't been in contact with either Charlotte or Rashid since leaving Dubai. They spent the two weeks leading up to his departure together. Days turned into nights filled with planning, studying, and scheming. Briefly, he wonders if there had been another attack on their lives.

Jack tries to push aside these alarming thoughts, and it's not until he disconnects the line that he sees the two men. They sit in a black Mercedes nearby, watching him. The passenger lifts a phone to his ear and turns away. Jack tells himself he's paranoid, but still, he starts the engine and navigates his car away from his apartment, checking his rearview mirror periodically to ensure the black Mercedes isn't following.

Definitely paranoid, Jack concludes and returns home to his rented apartment on the top floor of a 16th-century building. His feet pound the hard, cracked stone of the narrow staircase, and he's exhausted by the time he reaches the fifth and final floor. Inside, he heads to the bath and starts the shower. The dangerous drive down the winding road from the Banning home, and the two men in the Mercedes, have caused him to sweat, aggravatingly. He pulls loosely at his tie and slips off his shoes when a knock at the door interrupts him.

"Yes?" Jack says, but he suspects it is too low for anyone to hear above the shower. He turns off the tap, rendering the apartment silent.

Someone fiddles with the lock of his front door.

Jack darts to the window and looks down. There, parked up the road a bit, is the black Mercedes. It's impossible for him to climb down from this height. He's not insane enough to crawl across the minuscule ledge to the apartment next door. Jack spins around and, hopelessly eyeing the old wardrobe in the middle of the small apartment as a place of refuge, grabs a poker by the fireplace, then squeezes himself in among the hanging clothes. One wardrobe door is left slightly ajar to offer him a view.

Two men enter the apartment. Jack recognizes the taller one as the passenger as he heads to the open window and peers down, shaking his head. His partner, wearing a rumpled suit, pulls out his gun and walks around, looks behind curtains. In the small kitchen, cupboard doors open and close.

The smell of mothballs overpowers Jack, coating his mouth, down his throat. Jack suppresses a cough. His breathing heavy, he knows it's only a matter of time before they find him, and a poker will not protect him against a gun. Jack pushes against the back of the wardrobe.

Creak.

Jack freezes and holds his breath, but his heart hammers loudly in his ears. Footsteps edge closer to the wardrobe. As a child, he was always the first found during a game of Hide and Seek. He can't hold his breath forever, but if he gasps for air, he'll suck in the pungent odor of the mothballs and cough. He envisions passing out in the wardrobe, smacking his head on the way down. The poker slips in his sweaty palms until the tip hits the floor with a small thump.

The wardrobe door flings open. The taller man waves Jack out with his gun and gestures to a chair. Jack lets out the breath he has been holding, unclenches his hand from the poker, and leans it against the back of the wardrobe. Stepping out, Jack stares at the man who discovered him, hoping to put him on edge, but it doesn't seem to have any effect. His face appears grim and focused and not frightened by Jack at all.

The other man walks around the apartment. He closes the curtains — the heavy fabric shuts out the glaring streetlights. He then turns on a table lamp near Jack. Up close, his tiny stature and large-eyed face remind Jack of Peter Lorre, entirely fitting with these criminals.

The tall man says something to the Peter Lorre guy, who responds in a huff, sounding very much like, "Why should I?" Then, he obliges and leaves the apartment. The remaining man says nothing, holsters his gun, and sits in the chair opposite Jack. He drums his fingers along the armchair, rhythmically thumping against the fabric.

The bright light of the lamp shines heavily on Jack. Is this an interrogation tactic? Jack can handle the heat and blinding light as long as they don't torture him. In the fifth grade, Luella Clemmons knocked him to the ground and jumped on his stomach. Jack threw up and broke a rib, so he's aware of his pain threshold. Really, it's limited.

Peter Lorre lumbers back into the room, struggling to carry a black case with him. Peter Lorre places it on the coffee table between themselves and Jack. Jack's sure he can take on the Peter Lorre one, slap him around a little like Bogey did, but the tall man is a good foot taller than Peter.

Torture it is, then.

The tall man turns the black case toward himself, opens it, fiddles with its contents, and removes a silver, razor-like object. They're going straight for the eyes. Jack squeezes them shut. Watching the razor come toward him is unbearable, and a sharp tool within two feet from his eyes will have him confessing to anything.

"Ok, I'll talk. Just tell me what you want to know," Jack sputters. He's a complete and utter failure, an antihero who doesn't deserve the girl. What is it F. Scott Fitzgerald wrote? *"Show me a hero, and I will write you a tragedy."* He was talking about Jack.

The two men exchange words in Arabic.

"Open." One man demands. Jack slowly opens one eye, then the other, to find the two men staring, looking absolutely dumbfounded. The tall man holds up the silver razor and points to Jack's chest.

"You put. We see. We hear," he says and gestures to Jack's eyes and ears. He isn't holding a razor at all, but a tiny silver object that turns out to be a wiretap and miniature camera. His partner adjusts the camera, masking as a tie clip, to Jack's loosened tie and snakes the wire carefully into his shirt. Peter Lorre unbuttons Jack's shirt to tape the wire to his chest, but the sweaty dampness renders the tape unworkable.

They are not here to kill him; they are Prince Rashid's men. Jack anticipated a meeting of some kind but didn't expect it would be a cloak and dagger event, but, given the circumstances, he should expect nothing less.

"More," the tall man says as he pulls out another item from the case. "Night vision." He puts it down and takes out a watch. "Careful," he warns before he leans forward to hand it to Jack.

Jack fumbles with it, tries to understand how to use the watch. Randomly pressing at buttons, Jack yelps as a sharp object juts out and cuts his finger.

"Careful!" the tall man snaps.

Later, once the men leave, Jack will play with the gadgets and practice in front of a mirror.

Blunt. Jack Blunt.

And he mustn't forget to make that critical phone call to one pissed-off Frenchman. Jack playing double agent is a betrayal to Charlotte – for she doesn't know he'll spill Rashid's plans to Favreau – but he had started this with Favreau and has to protect himself just in case it all goes terribly wrong.

Chapter 40

FOR TWO DAYS NOW, Jack has been hard at work driving Mrs. Banning, accompanying her from one appointment to the next. It's not supposed to go down like this. He must accomplish things inside the castle. He has secrets to uncover, photos to take, and codes to memorize.

Throughout the day at the castle, Mrs. Banning says little to him, but she gives him her undivided attention during their drives. Once, she reached forward from the backseat of the Bentley, ripped Jack's glasses from his face, and peered through them.

"How strong is this prescription?"

He side-swiped some bushes and had to pull over. "Mrs. Banning," he reasoned, "that was a dangerous move."

"Don't you like danger?" she asked him, her voice low and sultry. Mrs. Banning leaned in so close that he felt her breath on his lips. She rested the glasses on the ridge of his nose, and when her image came into focus, he saw that at some point, she had unbuttoned her shirt. Two rounded breasts were pushed together, a décolletage tanned and inviting as though they carried the hot Brazilian sun. Jack sucked in a breath. Mrs. Banning purred like a lioness.

Today, he's inside cleaning the silver but stuck in the kitchen with the old cook.

"There's no such thing as ghosts," sighs Jack after listening to her for a half-hour.

"Then explain how I've seen them."

"You were exhausted and your mind played a trick on you," says Laila, coming up from behind, carrying a basket of freshly laundered linen. "Don't let her tell you any ghost stories, Jack. And don't repeat that nonsense in front of my little boy."

"Maybe he should be scared to stop him from entering the secret passageways. You'll lose him in one of them someday."

"What secret passageways?" says Jack, suddenly interested in what the cook has to say and unable to believe his luck.

"The castle has many secrets, some I have yet to uncover, but that little boy of Laila's is so inquisitive that he's explored every inch of this castle." Then to Laila, she says, "Which he wouldn't do if he knew about the ghosts."

"Hush with your nonsense."

By late afternoon, Jack wanders the corridors of the Banning estate, playing a game of Hide and Seek with Laila's little boy, Christian. He spies the five-year-old child enter a small room off the main dining room, but by the time Jack follows, Christian has disappeared.

"Christian," he calls out in a whisper. "Christian. Where are you?"

"Boo!" The little boy shouts as he jumps out of a hidden pantry in the wall.

"Oh, what a hiding place you found there," Jack says. "Any more places for you to hide?"

Christian laughs and runs under the dining room table.

"That's not a good hiding place, now is it? Surely there are places more secretive than this that no one knows about."

The little boy pops his head out from underneath, peers up at Jack with skepticism.

"Come out here," Jack says and maneuvers the young boy toward the hallway that leads to nowhere where he knows a set of stairs existed at one time. "I'll close my eyes and count to ten while you hide."

Jack counts, fingers fanned across his face, and spies Christian press his finger to a knot in the floorboard. He then rotates it to the right, and the floor opens in. *A secret passageway in the floor!* No wonder Jack has been unable to find it. The little boy scampers down the hidden stairwell.

"Clever boy," Jack mumbles to himself.

A man's heated voice travels from the bottom of the opening. Jack falls back to hide behind a giant armoire and peeks around the corner. The same German from a couple of days ago climbs the steps and, gruffly admonishing the boy, pulls Christian alongside him down the hall toward the kitchen.

The little boy struggles. "Let go. I was only playing."

When the German and Christian disappear, Jack rushes toward the secret passageway, which the German left open. He looks back, catches Laila's voice apologizing to the German. He'll be back soon. Jack steps down. Darkness hits him at first, and he takes his time descending so that he doesn't trip and break his neck on the way down. Off in the distance, a dim light beckons. It's a small room he's led to with a single light bulb at its center, exposed wires running along the castle's vast stone wall.

Dripping water echoes, breaking the silence. An arched doorway serves as an entryway to a large cave connected to the moat outside that surrounds the castle. The area, dark and dank, is empty except for the waterway. It used to be that human waste was dropped into the stagnant channels, the same water mere steps from where Jack stands. A putrid smell inflames his nostrils, but surely, it's been more than a century since they ceased doing that. Still, Jack can't understand what's so secretive about this particular place.

Footsteps descend the hidden stairway, and Jack scrambles for some place to hide. He'd be exposed if he remains in this room. Jack moves forward as voices echo behind him. He spins, seeking some place to hide and finally darts in back of a pillar in a darkened corner. The German returns with another man Jack has never seen before, and a conversation erupts between the two in their mother tongue. It sounds very much like the grumblings of disgruntled workers.

At a set of large double doors painted in a color to blend into the stone that Jack hadn't noticed earlier, the two men pause, then the new man presses his fingers against a keypad. The pad makes an awful, buzzing sound, and the German, irritated, says, "Come on, come on" in broken English. Again, the first man presses the keypad, but it garners the same result. Finally, the German swats the man away and, in a brisk voice, says aloud four distinct numbers that he presses in the keypad.

Jack memorizes the four digits, repeating the German numbers continuously in his head until it's burned into his memory. He's spent some time abroad in Germany. Indeed, he remembers the numbers he learned by rote from that time.

Within moments of the men entering the vault, Jack follows. His hands clasp the metal knobs of the double doors, and he peeks through the one open door. The men sound far away. Jack sneaks into the large room and into an open area where he can potentially be seen. This won't do, and he sprints in the opposite direction away from the men. It's warmer in here than out there, and feels like 70 degrees Fahrenheit, a perfect temperature to store the art in what must be a temperature-controlled room. Hidden by tall shelving units, Jack studies a display of art clustered haphazardly on the wall near him. They appear to be undistinguished works, most likely from lesser-known artists. Some he perceives as personal, more family heirloom than anything else. Could this be the art Rashid is looking for? The art the Nazi's had stolen from the homes of prominent Jewish families?

On a shelving system that runs the room's length, Jack lifts linen cloths to unveil numerous artifacts underneath – bronze sculptures, wooden carvings, and jewelry. He feels the room get warmer, or perhaps it's just his nerves turning up the heat. He's seen enough to know what's down here and should get out before he gets caught, but a square item wrapped in velvet piques his interest. Wondrous things come in small packages. He plucks at the fabric, astonished to find *The Dawn*, the famous painting by a 15th-century artist stolen from a small museum fifteen, maybe twenty years ago. And here he is, holding it in his hands. He quickly takes a picture of it with his tie clip and continues to the next find and the next, slinking soundlessly through the vault. He uncovers antiquities he believes are priceless, all the while taking photos of the items and the room's layout.

German voices suddenly sound close. They may be in the aisle next to Jack's. He's unsure since he didn't hear their footsteps. He's been too engrossed in the find that he had nearly forgotten them. He looks for a way out, but one end of the aisle hits a wall and the other end would lead him to the open space. They'd find him within seconds. He plasters himself against the wall, his thighs screaming as he stays poised, ducked behind a giant stone sculpture. Jack holds his breath as the Germans pass. A box sounds as it scrapes along a shelf, items clinking beneath their voices. They're too close. Jack waits trying to control his breathing, desperate not to move, promising he'll do squats if he gets out of this, until the echo of the door locks him in the room.

Jack lets out a heavy breath and steps out from behind the statue, bouncing about to loosen his cramped legs. Near him, another velvet-wrapped painting rests against a far wall, the cover hanging loose at an angle, exposing a sliver of the image. Jack tugs on the velvet cover and, as it falls away, he's gob-smacked by the Sonnenberg self-portrait. *It can't be.* He analyses it more closely. Without the proper equipment, he can't verify its authenticity, but given that most everything else in the room appears real to his trained eye, he believes he's hit the jackpot. He clicks away with his tiepin, shot after shot.

This cache is much more than they've bargained for. It makes him giddy and light-headed. He'd love to camp out down here, spend days among the works, study them, sleep with them, but he worries he'll be missed upstairs and better go.

At the vault door, Jack keys in the four-digit code. It buzzes, but the door doesn't open. He waits several seconds and tries again. Another buzz. Another attempt, quicker this time. Did he misinterpret what the Germans said? Rashid reported the vault was fingerprint sensitive, yet Jack noted nothing of the sort when he entered. Besides, how did the Germans find their way in without Banning's fingerprints? Or was there a fingerprint pad that he hadn't noticed? He had slipped in so quickly behind the Germans. How is he supposed to get out now?

Jack sucks in a breath and closes his eyes, calming himself. Releasing the breath, he opens his eyes. He tries the numbers again. The door won't open. He looks around, panicked. How long will he be trapped? Jack pulls out his cell phone. Although he doesn't want to, he has to call Rashid. His fingers stab at numbers, but there's no cell service. He cry-laughs at his predicament, already calculating how long he can go without food and water.

Suddenly, the pad near him lights up, the numbers flashing as they're pressed from the other side of the door. They've come back. The door unlocks and slides open. Jack bolts behind the door when the Germans re-enter. Their disgruntled banter continues and Jack wishes they'd take it elsewhere but they haven't moved from the entrance. What if they close the door? There's no place for him to hide. He'd be caught and fired. No, they wouldn't fire him for being in the vault. They'd have no choice but to kill him now that he's seen everything. Finally, they move away. As soon as their footsteps sound more distant, he peers out and sees them round a shelving unit. Jack darts out and races upstairs.

Chapter 41

Rashid and I arrive among a deluge of fanfare. We've barely stepped into the manse when a crowd forms around us. Someone the Third says he knows Rashid's father but it seems pretty evident to me that he does not. Then there's a Sir and a Lady and a Count from Italy or Germany, I can't quite place the accent, who won't stop chatting to us about race horses.

"All this attention just won't do," Rashid whispers to me.

It will indeed make it difficult to blend in with the crowd before setting our plan in motion. "It's still early," I whisper back. My hand tucked into the loop of Rashid's arm, I unclench my sweaty fist and remind myself to breathe and relax but I fidget anyway. Besides, it's hard to hear myself think above my skirt's rustling. The detachable voluminous taffeta skirt hides sleek pants underneath. "So much for picking a gown by a young, hot designer. Honestly, I feel like it's prom night circa 1986 and I'm not even *Pretty In Pink* Molly Ringwald. I'm Duckie before he cleaned up for prom."

"Which one am I?" asks Rashid.

"Oh, you're definitely James Spader."

"Your Highness," someone calls from behind us.

Turning, I spot the Bannings in the center of a hall, greeting guests like they're the Royals in Buckingham Palace.

"Mr. Banning, thank you for having us to your lovely home," Rashid says.

"My pleasure. May I properly introduce my wife? My dear, Ivonete, please meet Prince Rashid Mohammed al-Zayed and Ms. Charlotte Milton."

"How do you do?" Ivonete says, eyes squarely focused on Rashid. Around her neck rests the Heart Diamond, glistening with the sparkle of a million stars.

"Lovely necklace," I say. My tone is biting but with a subtly that I've only seen perfected by Meryl Streep. Perhaps I should consider a career as an actress.

Mrs. Banning turns to me with a slight tilt of her head and, in a sultry tone, says, "Thank you. It was a gift from my husband."

"Perfection deserves perfection," Mr. Banning chimes in, then gestures to the next room. "Please make your way into the ballroom and enjoy yourselves."

I have seen plenty of chateaus in France that this grand ballroom is modeled after, but none of them are as stunning. The crystal chandeliers sparkle; black chairs surround white-clothed tables, and tiny bouquets of white tulips hang in black cones from the centerpiece candelabras. Over to one end, a quartet plays, while at the other, a large band sets up.

Introductions are made. Faces blur from one to another. Some behave as though they know Rashid personally, most likely having seen a biography about his family on PBS. Others try too hard to impress, failing miserably. Then there are the one or two who pretend his title is inconsequential.

In the midst of yet another group of hangers-on, I excuse myself, in search of the ladies' room. But I really just want to find Jack. We haven't been in contact since he left Dubai, and this leaves me feeling discombobulated. I wanted to reach out to him, but Rashid worried any unnecessary contact may expose him in this crazy plan. While there have been moments within this amateur hour of espionage when I found myself questioning everything, I never wavered from clearing my name.

By the time I enter the corridor leading to the ladies' room, I still haven't spotted Jack, and I need confirmation that everything is in place. Inside the elegant powder room, I dampen a small cloth towel with cold water and pat my neck. My nerves are getting the better of me. My fingers tremble.

Be cool, I tell myself. Everything will work according to plan once the fireworks set off. *Or even better*, I add as a precaution and send this out to the universe.

Chapter 42

A BLACK CUBE VAN with the words "Specialty Fire Displays" sprawled on the side idles outside the servants' entranceway. When the front gate had called earlier, Jack confirmed them as part of the festivities, then waved the van over. It looks ordinary, like any other cube van a business would use. This truck, however, is a specially-made armored vehicle complete with bulletproof exterior and smash-proof windows. Jack tries not to think about *why* they need to protect themselves against bullets, but he's not an idiot. He's fully aware of the danger they've put themselves in. The men, dressed in all black with "Specialty Fire Displays" in small lettering on their T-shirts, unload straight away and blend in with the other workers traipsing in and out. Other than Peter Lorrie & Co. back at his apartment, he hasn't been in communication with anyone else, aside from emailing them the vault photos.

Inside the kitchen, Jack swipes a tray topped with champagne flutes and glides past other waitstaff through a door and into the ballroom, his eyes on the prowl for Charlotte and Rashid. He meanders through the crowd of men in black tuxedos, and women in black ballgowns, a handful in white. There are too many of them that he's jostled about and nearly drops his tray. He holds it steady in both hands. It's a monotonous and torturous job. Empty the tray, pick up empty glasses and return to the kitchen for more. Each time he cuts a path through a crowd, his eyes skitter in search of Charlotte. Finally, on one of his many returns from the kitchen, he spots her with Rashid and the Bannings.

God, she's beautiful. He misses her laughter that sometimes ends in a snort. He misses her humor even when it's unintentional. But mostly he misses that brief intimacy they shared on the boat when he thought he had lost her. The two weeks he's spent here working his way into the Banning home has made him nearly forget what the very essence of her does to him. He thinks back to that night at the police station when her eyes first landed on him. How she rejected him at first, then changed her mind. Even now, he can hear her heels clickety-clack their way back across the cobblestone to accept his offer of a ride back to her hotel. And he can still feel her hips grinding into him that night at the vineyard, her lips thirsty for his, his hands roaming over her body.

Jack is irritated by the way Charlotte stares at the diamond around Mrs. Banning's neck. When this is over, he half expects Rashid will surprise her with the necklace. And where would that leave Jack?

The Bannings walk away, leaving Charlotte and Rashid alone. She whispers something, he bends forward, her head tilts up, and together they share a laugh. He notes the gentleness in how Rashid wraps an arm around Charlotte's waist.

Charlotte breaks away from Rashid and heads toward a corridor. Jack follows and whispers to himself, "Be cool."

Chapter 43

"CHAMPAGNE, MA'AM," A MALE voice offers as I exit the bathroom. The tray hovers beside me, and I can't help notice how odd it is to be nabbed like that outside the ladies' room. I'm about to decline when I look beyond the flutes to the waiter's face.

"Jack," I say, but it's whispered in such a breathy tone that it comes out more a sound than anything resembling a name. My eyes caress his face. I certainly didn't think the two-week absence would be this impactful. "You had me so worried when I hadn't heard from you." I glance at partygoers within close proximity, coming and going into the bathrooms.

"Are you having a wonderful time, *ma'am?*"

The emphasis on his last word suddenly annoys me, and, hearing him use it twice now, I wonder if he's insulting me on purpose. He has a few years on me.

Jack steps in close and mumbles, "I knew you weren't paying attention when we went over the plan."

A quickened *oh* follows, my body in betrayal mode. I clamp my mouth shut. It embarrasses me that I more or less forgot the code word that encapsulates everyone is in play. Still, I can't let on that Jack caught me, nearly upending our plan. "I'm playing my part as you should be. Help shouldn't be communicating with guests," I say in a hushed tone. I glance at our surroundings, but it doesn't appear that anyone is paying attention to us.

"This servant is troubled carrying a gun in the midst of this."

I whip my head towards him. "Where'd you get the gun?"

"Rashid."

"He didn't give me one," I say, feeling left out, though I wouldn't know what to do with a weapon anyway. Still, it irks me that this so-called team is a boys' club.

"One of his men slipped it to me yesterday. We never agreed to an armed heist. Champagne?" Jack's tone changes quickly as he offers a glass to a passerby.

"No, we didn't." I lift a glass, drain it, and replace the empty back on Jack's tray. "I need to find Rashid," I mutter and leave.

Rashid has abandoned the spot where I had left him moments earlier. Perhaps he's gone off to our meeting place, or he's been whisked away by someone ingratiating themselves into his circle. I float through the ballroom at a steady pace, careful not to draw attention to myself as I scan the surrounding faces in search of Rashid. A light touch on my arm brings me relief. Rashid has found me, and I spin to–

My breath catches in my throat.

"Miss Milton." Levan's voice is nasal and not at all what I had expected.

"Hello." The small word sounds fragile out of my mouth. My eyes dart about. As long as I remain within this crowd, there's no harm that he can impose on me... but I've seen enough films where murders occur in public.

"My name is Levan. I'm an admirer of your work."

He looks like a rat when he smiles, and a chill shoots down my back.

Recovering from the shock, I purse my lips and say, "Really? You've read my magazine articles?"

Levan pauses for a moment, his rodent eyes settling on me. "Your *other* work."

My face is most likely ashen in color, and I'm afraid the champagne I knocked back moments ago will come back up. Fighting the urge to be sick, I smile and, in a clumsy manner, reach out to shake his hand. "It's a pleasure to meet you, but I'm in the midst…"

"I'm afraid you have something of mine," Levan says and suddenly latches onto my hand.

"Sorry?" I attempt to pull away but he tightens his grip. Whatever shade is paler than pale must be on my face now while a dark shadow crosses his.

Levan's rat-like lips turn upward, and he indicates to the small of my wrist. "Your bracelet is entangled in my cuff link. Allow me." He unwinds my bracelet and frees me. "Voila. Until we meet again, Miss Milton."

Carefully, he brings my hand to his lips for a kiss.

I fight the urge to scrub him off.

Chapter 44

Leaning by a brick wall in the rear garden, Rashid inspects his watch for the time, precisely set and impeccably kept. Charlotte is nowhere to be found. It should have been a quick trip to the ladies' room, and he tries to tamper his concern.

A patio door swings open, and he glances, expecting to find Charlotte, but it's a couple he met earlier whose names he's forgotten. He acknowledges them with a smile. When they pass, he wipes at a bead of sweat behind his neck. He usually doesn't get this way, with nerves eating away at him, but she's been gone nearly fifteen minutes now. He could go in looking for her, or–

"Rashid," Charlotte says in a low voice. She descends the stone steps and rushes into his arms.

He knows it's for appearances' sake – two lovers in need of seclusion – but a small part of him, no, a big part of him, wishes it were true. Without uttering a word, he wraps his arm around her and guides her to the lower grounds. Quietly, he whisks her away toward the waterway that leads back into the castle through a moat running underground. The noise of the revelers fades in the distance.

Footsteps hit concrete then soften against the grass. In his periphery, Rashid sees a security guard following; their cover is undoubtedly blown. He immediately pushes Charlotte against the hard, cold castle wall and presses himself against her.

By the look on her face, he can tell she's surprised, yet she brings her arms to his neck when he leans in for a kiss. He's wanted to do this for a long time now, but each time the mood seemed right, something unexpected happened – like Charlotte falling off a boat or Charlotte accusing him of ruining her life. Which he did, but, in the end, doesn't the fact that he's trying to rectify the situation matter more than the mistakes he made? Though he's made plenty of them, with one mistake far outweighing the next.

A sweet moan escapes her lips. He pushes his hand across her bottom, fighting to grab hold against the slippery, voluminous fabric.

The guard's footsteps break into his thoughts, then scurries in another direction. Rashid tilts his head, gives the guard a sideways glance until he disappears toward the castle. Perhaps embarrassment overwhelmed him.

"We're safe now," Rashid whispers in Charlotte's ear, then brings a hand to her neck and his lips back onto hers. He should stop, but where would be the fun in that?

"Rashid," she pulls away slightly, then returns her lips to his and moans. "Hmm. Levan's here," she whispers after thrusting her hands between them to push him away.

His mind spins at the thought of Levan. He hadn't seen him, but he should have known.

Pop! The sound startles them, and Charlotte jumps. Looking back toward the castle, a fireworks display is being orchestrated to Switzerland's national anthem.

Rashid disentangles himself from Charlotte, but she seems reluctant to let go. Even with all their planning, they knew time would be tight. The fifteen-minute fireworks show is enough to get them inside, with another distraction planned to get them out and down the mountain unnoticed.

In the moonlight, Rashid and Charlotte jog along the water's edge toward a hidden entrance, Charlotte holding the skirt of her gown. A light shines on Charlotte's face, and she shields her eyes. The light repeatedly flashes in code. It's Rashid's men in the boat, but where are the others? Rashid guides Charlotte in their direction and helps her board; the hem of her dress drags in the water. Only two of his men are here in the boat – Amir and Rami, the same ones he had sent to act as a conduit between himself and Jack. Amir signals behind them. Someone flashes in return. Once in the boat, Rashid scours the floor, fingers dance until they lock on a knapsack. He swings it over his shoulder and onto his back. Oars cut through the water, and they glide into the waterway beneath the castle while the fireworks drown out any noise they make. It's an ingenious distraction meant to keep everyone preoccupied, including Banning's men.

Rashid hopes.

Chapter 45

J ACK LOOKS AT HIS watch. The fireworks display has entertained the guests for three minutes now, and it's his cue to leave. He deposits a tray on a back table, scoops up dirty glasses, piles them on, and then floats through the ballroom. He hears guests outside *oohing* and *aaahing* over each *pop* and *bra-ta-tat* on display. He spots Mr. Banning and, wherever he is, Jack assumes so is Mrs. B.

A guest congratulates Mr. Banning on the entertainment, but the host assures her it wasn't his doing; it must have been a surprise from his wife. He looks around. "Ivonete? Ivonete, where have you gone?" To the person on his left, Mr. Banning asks, "Have you seen my wife? She was here moments ago."

Jack escapes the crowd mesmerized by the lights in the sky and sneaks back into the kitchen, where he abandons the tray, then down the corridor to the hidden passageway. He turns a corner – *almost there* – his heart quickens, and a tingling sensation travels through his body. So this is what adrenaline feels like.

"Mr. Blunt."

"Yes." Jack spins on his heels.

Mrs. Banning stands in the corridor behind him.

"Where are you going?" she says.

"I was..." Jack attempts at a laugh, "going to take a break while the fireworks entertained the guests. I'm afraid you caught me."

"Yes, I did catch you," she says and saunters toward him, hips swinging from side to side. On anyone else, the movement would be an exaggeration, but for Mrs. Banning, it's simply her nature.

"I know what you're up to," she says, her voice clipped.

Jack is speechless, astonished that of all people, it would be Mrs. Banning to catch him, but how? And what exactly did she see him do?

Jack stutters, "I...I can explain..." He stops and stalls for time to invent an explanation to God knows what.

"Mr. Blunt, how can you explain hovering by the ladies' room when you were to circulate the party?"

He briefly pauses and searches for a compelling lie. "There was a guest who fell quite ill, and I wanted to ensure she was fine."

"Hmmm," she mumbles and looks him up and down with penetrating eyes. "And was she?"

"Was she what?"

"Fine?"

"Yes. Her husband arrived, and when I saw her in good hands, I left."

"I would think she'd have been better served in your hands." Mrs. Banning leans in closer.

Instinctively, Jack edges backward until he hits the wall. "Well, I should return, Mrs. Banning." He steps to the side to walk around her, but she throws an arm against the wall, trapping him. His eyes roam to the other side where he could escape, but she'll probably block that exit, too.

"Do you like it here?"

Jack nods and offers a playful smile. "Of course. I am very grateful to be here."

"Do you enjoy our rides?"

Oh God, this is torturous.

"Chauffeuring you is one of my more pleasant duties."

"Well, I certainly would like to return the favor and ride you tonight," she whispers in his ear. "Where are you staying in the village? I can meet you later. Say around 2 am?"

"I don't get off until three."

She slams him hard against a wall, presses herself into him. He worries she'll find the gun holstered beneath his jacket, and he tries to sidle away from her. "I suppose I won't get off before three, either."

"Ivonete!" Mr. Banning's voice booms from somewhere down the corridor. "Where are you?"

"Damn," she mutters. "Coming, darling," she calls out to him.

Mrs. Banning pulls back from Jack, giving him a long, hard stare and then follows her husband's voice. In the distance, Jack hears Mr. Banning thank his wife for the fireworks and her stuttering response.

Relieved, Jack continues to the hidden passageway and presses the secret lever. Down he goes, closing the entranceway behind him. When he arrives at the vault, a noise in the water startles him. He ducks behind a column, realizing he isn't alone.

Chapter 46

THE CAVE IS MORE extensive than Rashid envisioned. Once inside, he has Amir ramp up the light, and a glow casts an orange hue on the stone wall.

A face peers at them then pulls back behind a column. Rashid shoots his hand up to warn his men, but when the man moves in front of the column, Rashid realizes it's Jack. The Professor draws closer as their boats bump alongside the water's edge. Jack extends a hand to Charlotte, who scoops up her voluminous dress and steps, awkward and unsteady, onto the cobblestone walkway.

"Wait," she says. Charlotte unclips the skirt from her waist, slips it off, and tosses it back into the boat. Underneath, she wears slim black pants. "Okay, ready."

"This way," Jack tells them.

The second boat pulls in, and while Tavi tethers a rope through a metal loop, the younger one, Kassim, jumps out. This band of thieves makes for an unusual group.

At the vault, Jack punches a code. A red light blinks, flashing three more times and returns to a solid red when it should have turned green. A heart-pounding buzzing sound follows. Jack tries a second time. He runs his hands through his hair, stares at the keypad as though time doesn't exist.

"Have you forgotten the code, Professor?" says Rashid, his voice unreasonably loud and irritated.

"No, it worked yesterday."

Again, Jack punches in a code. The light flashes red, then solid red.

Rashid feels time and opportunity slip away. "We'll compensate for the failure."

"I didn't fail. It's the correct code I witnessed just the other day."

"Does the door open?" says Rashid, his voice strained.

"No," Jack mutters.

"Then you failed to acknowledge they changed the code. Kassim," Rashid calls for one of his men and steps aside.

Kassim tosses his backpack to the ground before him, kneels, and pulls out a grey device to crack the code. He secures the gadget to the keypad and inserts it; a display of combination numbers spins through.

When Rashid first learned to crack a safe, he did his homework, and verified the manufacturer, memorized the model's default code. As Rashid discovered in his younger days, a startling number of people either used their birthdays or didn't bother to reset their security code from the default setting. That isn't the situation here. The device should beep whenever it determines a coded number, but, for now, it remains silent. Patience, Rashid reminds himself, but time is not on their side. He glances at his watch. They're five minutes behind schedule.

The device beeps once. They let out a collective breath—three more numbers to go.

Beside him, Jack wipes sweat from his brow. He removes his glasses, rubs them with the edge of his vest, and inspects them. Clearly dissatisfied, he repeats the cleaning. Rashid tries to concentrate on Kassim's actions, but he can't pull his eyes away. Finally, Jack replaces the spectacles on his nose, and his eyes land on an irritated Rashid.

"What?" hisses Jack.

A second beep breaks the awkwardness.

Charlotte bounces from foot to foot, mumbles, "come on" under her breath.

Third beep.

Rashid steadies his breathing, something he learned in meditation long ago to help calm his nerves in heightened situations. Even now, he's unflappable.

Kassim's device sounds and locks. He turns to Rashid, his eyes wide, and says, "Booby trapped. Their system has detected the machine."

Above them, a woman's automated voice activates over a loudspeaker. "Code denied."

Jack's head whips towards the speakers. "This is new. Now what?"

"Fingerprint access is required for verification. Thirty seconds."

"Thirty seconds for what?" Jack says, his voice agitated.

"Twenty-nine. Twenty-eight."

"The grenades," Charlotte reminds everyone.

"Twenty-five. Twenty-four."

"Stop counting down," says Jack, hopping from one foot to the other.

Tavi heads to the boat, muttering his children's names.

How long before the system alerts Banning and his men? Rashid digs into his knapsack and produces a black leather box. Opening it, he slides his hand into a glove, the tips encoded with Banning's fingerprints taken from the stolen drinking glass.

"Everyone, step back," Rashid commands, his voice strained.

"Fifteen. Fourteen."

Amir blocks Rashid and says, "Your Highness, let me do it. If the grenades..."

"Ten. Nine."

Rashid pushes past him and places his gloved hand on the screen.

"Five. Four."

The countdown stops. An orange light scans Rashid's gloved hand on the board. Seconds pass, but they are no nearer to opening the vault door. For all they know, it could reset the code. It could restart the countdown from thirty seconds. Or trigger the grenades. Rashid turns back to Charlotte, who is pushed behind Jack while he covers her with his body. Rashid should have thought to place her the farthest away. She stares back, her eyes wide, her breathing quick.

What if he had just left her alone at the Lumière show instead of involving her in his madness? All along, he had convinced himself Levan was the real threat against her, but it was him all along. And now he will cause their demise, and, of all the people on his crew, hers will be the last face he sees if they fail.

A light shines green in his peripheral. Rashid returns his gaze to the vault door, and it unlocks, gears grinding into place. Around him, everyone lets out a collective breath, but it's short-lived as they move into action. Everyone has a mission: Amir, the artifacts; Kassim, the jewels; Jack and Charlotte, the art; and Rashid, the Sonnenberg self-portrait. But when Rashid finds himself in the middle of the room and scanning shelves filled with artifacts and paintings hidden beneath cloth, he's uncharacteristically overwhelmed.

"It is greater than I had imagined," Rashid says in hushed tones. "All these years, these works have been hidden away in this dark place where no one can see them." He shakes his head in obvious disgust.

"How is this different from the people who pay you for the stolen artwork?" Jack says.

"My clients appreciate the work, and while it may be for their private viewing, it isn't hidden away in a place like this. This is disrespectful."

Amir says, "Seven minutes before the fireworks end."

Rashid's men go to work, move quickly to grab oversized items while pocketing the smaller ones. They work in tandem transporting the items to the boats back and forth – three bronze sculptures, paintings flat against the bottom of the boat, jewels tucked in pockets.

It's a casing in the middle of the room that stops Rashid, and, despite the ticking clock, he moves ever so slowly toward the display, for inside rests the golden salt cellar he stole many years earlier. How it ended in Banning's possession is a mystery, but somehow the two are connected by a client. This is his for the keeping, and Rashid slips it into his crossbody bag. Coming out of the spell the salt cellar had placed on him, Rashid sees Jack with the Sonnenberg in his hands. The Sonnenberg was *his* to take, not Jack's.

"Leave that, Professor. I'll take it," Rashid says.

Jack looks up at him. "I already have it."

Rashid puts his hands on the painting. "I said I'll take it."

"You sure do like to take things that aren't yours."

"This doesn't belong to you, either."

Neither man lets go. Beside them, Charlotte scurries here and there, grabs what she can.

"You two, knock it off," she admonishes while slipping past.

Jack lets go. "I'll help Charlotte."

Rashid considers Jack's look as rather smug. They both understand the Sonnenberg isn't the real prize. He's not blind to the fact that Jack is in pursuit of Charlotte, but she must see that between the two men, Rashid is the better choice, doesn't she? Then again, it's Jack she's working with at the moment, grabbing pieces and working in tandem, so perhaps it's not as black and white as he suspects.

Rashid says, "Two minutes."

Their quickened movement leads to clumsiness, and a bronze sculpture topples over from the boat, hits the water with a splash, and sinks before Rami can catch it.

"Forget it. It's lost," Rashid barks. "One minute. Get in the boat now, Charlotte."

"What about the rest?" she says.

"We've taken the more valuable pieces. Everything else will need to be left behind," Jack says, siding with Rashid.

"You weren't so complacent to the plan earlier. You objected to leaving anything behind," says Charlotte.

Jack says, "That was in theory. We've got to go."

"Twenty seconds," Rashid says, and shortly after that begins the countdown from ten. "...three, two, one. Everyone to the boats. Let's go. Jack, go in the other boat; it's better that they carry even numbers."

Jack looks from Rashid to Charlotte to the other men.

"We're seven. How is that even?"

"Our boat carries more artwork," Rashid grumbles and moves past him into the first boat with Charlotte.

Swiftly, the boats glide across the water back where they came, then out of the mouth of the cave. They take the waterway east, toward their vehicles parked elsewhere away from the partygoers back at the castle. Behind them, the fireworks display continues.

When they are close to land, both Kassim and Amir leap out, dragging the boats alongside them, and beach them on the sandy edge. The cube van of the fireworks company that Jack let in earlier is backed up near the water, the back door rolled all the way up. Two more of Rashid's men jump out from the truck's cab, and one scrambles into the back of the van, ready to load items.

Rashid looks to their getaway car. "A white Bentley, Professor?"

Jack gives a sheepish grin. "Mr. B. won't miss it."

With the two additional men, it doesn't take long for them to unload the contents from burdened boats into the truck. With everything now stored in the van, Amir closes the back door while Kassim heads into the driver's side and starts up the truck. A loud, cranking noise sounds as it turns over.

On their way to the Bentley, Rashid notices Jack linger behind, squinting into the darkness surrounding them. "Do you see something, Professor?"

Jack turns to him, looking a little unsettled. "Uhm, no."

"Come on," Charlotte says. "We need to get out of here."

She hops into the passenger side of the Bentley. Rashid stands by the driver's side, stares at Jack, at his continued slow movements and nervous disposition. Following Jack's gaze, Rashid stares into the darkness, where he captures movement among the trees. Did the leaves flutter? Or is it just the wind? Finally, Jack takes a step toward the Bentley.

From the darkened space in-between the trees, someone claps. "Bravo, bravo," a man's voice says as he emerges from the darkness.

Banning.

Chapter 47

"DID YOU REALLY THINK I wouldn't know?" Banning asks. "My wife would never bother with a random act of kindness, let alone a fireworks show."

Seated in the Bentley's front passenger seat, I twist around to peer out through the open door.

Banning continues, "And then I thought, who would arrange such a thing and why? One of my men mentioned he spotted you with Ms. Milton in a restricted area. It's been amusing to see you work like busy little bees." He smiles his terrifying grin at Rashid. "Now, if you'll please tell your men to step out of the truck."

"I'm afraid that's not possible," Rashid says.

"Oh, everything is possible. Especially when one's outnumbered as you are."

At his cue, several armed men step out from the darkness behind the copse of trees. One moves toward the Bentley, his gun aimed at me. I gasp and step out of the car, hands raised. I look over at Rashid, who has a peculiar smile on his face though I can't understand what he has to smile about unless... well, surely, he must have a plan B that I'm unaware of.

"Out of the truck," Rashid orders his men. Kassim and Amir slowly descend from the cab, arms up.

"And the men in the back," Banning reminds Rashid. Amir heads toward the back door to let the other men out, and they emerge one by one. He rolls the door back down.

"Slowly remove your weapons," Banning orders.

I can't help notice, despite the situation, Banning's calm and polite tone. There's civility among thieves.

Rashid nods to his men, and they obey Banning's instructions, reaching into their back holsters and holding their guns in a non-threatening manner.

But when a shot ricochets off the top of the bullet-proof truck, Rashid's men scatter for cover behind it, guns firmly held in their hands, and aimed into the darkness.

Rashid pushes me to the ground and covers me. I hadn't even heard his footsteps coming at me. A few feet away, Jack drops to the ground.

"What's happening? Who fired? Who fired?" I scream.

Chaotic whispers surround me. It seems others are just as unsure as I am about our circumstances. Beside me, Rashid squirms, looking this way and that, peering into the darkness. Soon, the figure of a man appears where the shot originated. Others fall in line around him, and soon, there are enough, perhaps twenty of them, to outnumber and surround Banning's men.

"Mr. Banning, tell your men to drop their weapons."

In the darkness, guns are lowered and dropped to the ground.

I wonder how we became trapped in a reverse babushka doll where, instead of getting smaller, the group of armed men grows. The mystery man steps into a sliver of moonlight. My mouth drops open when I recognize Levan.

Levan continues, "I do apologize, Hector, for intruding, but I believe the Prince has something that belongs to me." He glares toward Rashid. "Please bring her to me."

Rashid lifts me to my feet. I suck in a breath, eyes on Levan, and say in a low, strained whisper, "Does he mean me?"

"He means the *Mistress*," Rashid quietly assures me.

"But it's not here."

Banning's voice booms above the quiet chatter and startles us both. "I won't stand for this, Levan. I have business to take care of here. You can have the Prince when I'm done with him. All else belongs to me."

"Hector, you're still standing because I've decided not to have my men kill you, so if..."

A shot zings off a rock near Levan. He dives for cover as an array of bullets fly in the darkness.

I scramble to hide behind a nearby tree, calling to Rashid and Jack to follow. Bullets ricochet around me. Curled with my face against my knees, I cover my ears, the sound of gunfire drowning out my whimpers. From the shadows, I spot an armed man approaching.

My hands raised, I stumble off the ground and cry, "Please, don't."

A gunshot rings, dropping the armed man to the ground. The silhouette of a second person, gun in hand, draws closer. I scream, my voice raw, my heart pounding, the noise of the gunshot still reverberating in my ears. It's not until the person wraps his arms around me and pulls me close that I relax just a bit.

"Are you okay?" Jack whispers in my ear.

I nod – *yes* – then shake my head – *no* – then nod again. I don't know if I'm okay or not. How can I be when we're in the middle of this crazy world war? "Where'd you learn to shoot like that?"

"High school skeet club."

My body quickly shifts from trembling in fear to shaking from laughter. I'm losing my mind. It's as simple as that. "Wow. Skeet club and botany," I say, sounding rather flippant though that's not what I mean to convey. Still, skeet club is not cool. But I have to admit, Jack looks badass caressing that gun in his hand. Single-handedly taking out someone trying to kill me *is* badass and, right now, at this very moment, I conclude Jack is the sexiest man I've ever met.

"Jack," I whisper after I gain control of my misguided giddiness.

If this was a romance novel, this is the part where the hero would sweep me in his arms, kiss me passionately. But, this is my life, and it never comes close to a romance novel. My life is more of a situation comedy, and not the highly-rated, funny kind either. I would play on a Friday night with the other duds.

Suddenly, Jack lands on the ground with a thud, a stranger on top of him, fists raining down.

"Jack!" I scream and attack the man. I claw at him to stop him from pummeling Jack, pulling his hair and his ears, but I'm nothing more than an irritating fly he can swat. Finally, I sweep the ground around me and spot a fallen tree branch. I lift the branch and bring it down on the man's head with all my strength. He goes limp.

Beneath him, Jack doesn't move. I throw myself next to him and roll the man off of him. Jack's eyes are closed and he remains motionless.

"Jack." I shake him. "Jack," I say again, caressing his face.

Finally, he opens his eyes, looking stunned. He points to the man passed out on the ground next to him. "How did you do that?"

"Tennis club captain," I say. "Let's find Rashid and get to the Bentley."

Together, we skirt the trees that line the open area. The Bentley is within sight, but getting there may be a problem. We locate Rashid near the water, struggling against one of Levan's or Banning's men, who can tell in this mess which bad guy belongs to which bad guy?

"Get to the Bentley," says Jack, turning away. "I'll get to Rashid."

"Jack!" I shout after him, leading him to turn back. "Be careful." I charge for the Bentley and fall into the driver's seat. I crank the key already in the ignition. Someone thumps against the back of the vehicle, startling me.

Through the rearview, I catch sight of Jack and Rashid in combat with an armed man. Jack has him in a chokehold while Rashid struggles for the man's weapon, but then all three drop to the ground and disappear from view. I peer out the window, but all I can discern at the back of the Bentley are three pairs of feet on the ground, rolling on top of one another. Someone grunts.

"He's out cold," I hear Jack say then watch as Rashid and Jack scramble to their feet.

Suddenly, Rashid jumps into the passenger side of the Bentley, and Jack opens the back door. A spray of bullets whips past them. Someone yells *Go!* But I've already got the Bentley moving.

A bullet cracks the windshield.

Chapter 48

J ACK GRABS THE DOOR handle, but before he can throw himself into the backseat, the Bentley speeds off.

They left him.

No, not *they*. It was Charlotte in the driver's seat. How could she leave him?

A bullet zips past his head, and he drops to the ground. From his position, it's unclear who's shooting at whom, but what's incontrovertible is that the battlefield is moving toward him. He's in a dangerous spot, exposed in No Man's Land. Half crawling, half running, Jack scrambles for cover toward the water, but someone's onto him and a bullet ricochets beside him. If he doesn't sprint now, the next slug will hit him.

Racing across, Jack leaps into a boat and ducks. Bullets hiss by and land in the water near him. A shot blasts through the boat, narrowly missing him. Around him, the disorganized shooting gallery between Rashid's, Banning's, and Levan's men, ensues. And what the bloody hell is Levan doing here anyway?

An interlude of quiet follows. Jack pops his head up. Perhaps no one knows he's there, and they're not intrinsically shooting at him; he's merely stuck in the crossfire, an accidental hostage.

A bullet strikes the back of the truck.

"The art," he whispers to himself, then remembers the truck is bullet-proof.

Flood-lights illuminate the darkness, blinding him.

Over a loudspeaker, a male voice shouts first in Swiss-German then English, "Police. Hold your fire! Hold your fire! You are all surrounded." The voice is faint at first, growing into a crescendo until, little by little, the shooting subsides. Continuing, the male voice says, "Put down your weapons. Toss them. Hands up high. You, there. I said up."

Jack reaches a hand up against the blinding light, and his eyes adjust to the scene. Uniformed police are everywhere. The gunmen, pushed to the ground with legs spread wide, are frisked and cuffed.

Jack recognizes the uniform: Swiss police. *Not them, again!* Why is it that every time they're involved, something goes horribly wrong?

"Professor, where are you?" calls Capitaine Favreau, who stands among the Swiss police.

Unsteadily, Jack lifts himself on his feet, the boat rocks beneath his clumsy attempt to stand. "What the hell was that?" Jack shouts. "I could have been killed."

Favreau moves toward the water's edge and shrugs. "I'm afraid I'm not in charge and only came along for the ride. It does seem, however, that your friends have left you, Professor."

"Yes, well... to get away from all these bullets. And..." Jack stutters, "...and you French have no sense of time. I told you it was going down at midnight. You're late, *Capitaine*."

Chapter 49

TREES BLUR PAST. THE moon plays Hide and Seek between treetops. The Bentley swerves down the mountain, back tires skidding close to the edge, fishtailing. Hands tight on the steering wheel, I flatten my foot on the gas pedal and push the car away from the drop and back onto the road. I throw it into the next gear, gun the engine, and accelerate. Beside me, Rashid struggles to put on his seatbelt.

In the distance, a siren sounds. I look through the rearview.

"Keep your eyes on the road ahead," Rashid tells me, his tone on edge.

"Is that a police siren?" I don't get an answer, so I repeat the question, shouting.

"Perhaps. Yes, it sounds like one, but they're far behind us."

I glance his way and lift my foot off the accelerator.

"We should stop."

"No, they may be on Banning's payroll. We can't trust anyone. Pick up the speed."

The car swerves around a bend, narrowly misses a sign that warns of steep cliffs ahead. In the dark, I'm not worried about the hairpin bends of the road, the same ones that terrified me earlier when we traveled up. If I can't see the plunging chasm, I figure it's not there. It provides for a bit of comfort, better than visualizing a plummet to my death.

A niggling sensation grows, and I glance into the rearview again. "Where's Jack?" I tore down the driveway so quickly that, amid the chaos, it has taken me this long to notice Jack's absence. I'm mortified. "We left him?! How could we leave him?"

"I don't know."

"Where did he go? He was about to get in the Bentley, and then the shooting started. Someone said 'go'. I thought it was him! Oh, God. Oh, God. What if he was shot?"

"He's fine."

"How do you know?"

"Charlotte, we can't go back. We'll head into Ober."

"And then what? Tell me what we're doing!"

"The only thing we can do. Keep going."

"What if I had been left behind? Would you keep going then?"

"Of course not. You're not expendable."

"Neither is Jack."

"I didn't say he was."

"You implied it."

"Charlotte, please, you're not thinking with any clarity. We have to keep going."

The Bentley zigzags, its back wheels losing control until I steer into a straight run and pick up speed. Ahead, we escape into a darkened tunnel, and though I can't see the police, judging by the sounds of the siren, they are moving closer.

The moment we come out of the tunnel, a police helicopter ascends from the side of the mountain.

"Stop the vehicle," a voice commands from the chopper.

"Damn it," Rashid says through clenched teeth. "Do as they say."

I slam on the brakes, the tires screeching to a stop. My breaths are quick and loud over the sound of an engine left idling.

"Put your hands where we can see them," the voice booms.

We do as we are told.

"Now step out of the car one at a time."

I turn to Rashid. "This is it," I whisper.

He nods his head in agreement, yet neither of us moves.

A warning shot hits the ground near the Bentley. The irate voice says, "Place your hands where we can see them. Up. Up."

I suck in deep breaths. Our hands move up at a steady pace.

"Now step out of the vehicle, one at a time."

I step out first, and Rashid slides out behind me, both with our hands firmly up in the air. I turn my head away from the blowing dirt kicked up by the hovering chopper.

Police cars arrive on either side of the Bentley, and the chopper moves away. Our plan to be heroes made sense at the time, and Rashid was right about the law handcuffing the police. Retrieving the stolen art was a coup that only we could accomplish, and it would have been the evidence needed to bring the police in to retrieve the rest. It was a good plan. Or a stupid one. Standing there with my hands up in the air, surrounded by police, I'm undecided. Besides, who would believe us now that we're caught?

"Charlotte."

I turn to the sound of my name. Jack stands beside an open door of the police vehicle.

"Jack!"

"That was exceptional," says the uniformed man standing next to Jack.

My gaze travels from Jack to the uniformed officer. Favreau. What's he doing here? He's Javert to my Jean Valjean.

Favreau continues, "Absolutely astonishing. Between the heist and the shooting and the escape, I don't know which was the most exciting. You can tell me your favorite scenes at the police station."

Chapter 50

A T THE STATION, I slide out from the backseat behind Rashid and Jack. My head hangs low, eyes focused on a ground that turns from asphalt to concrete to speckled tiles. With Favreau pulling up behind us, we follow the driver into an office; a sign on the door reads "Inspector Fricke." It's a small room, stark with four chairs on this side of a grey desk that we would-be-heroes take while Favreau pulls his chair ahead of us. Through an open window, I hear the media frenzy outside, and I flash back to the first night I met Jack and that drive to the hotel. It seems like a lifetime ago when this all began.

The driver makes his way to the Swiss Inspector's side of the desk, rubs his eyes, and mutters, "This day will never end." *He* is Inspector Fricke. He hangs his cap on a coat rack next to his desk and takes his time settling into his chair. Elbows on the desk, fingers intertwined, he leans forward. "We're combing through the truck, taking inventory of the art found there and on the premises. We've only begun, yet we see it is quite a find – provided it's authentic – Monet. Fraisson. Sonnenberg. Several have been missing since the Nazis stole them during World War II," says Fricke.

Favreau adds, "And *Mistress In A Red Dress* was also recovered from the truck, which now closes my case."

"It was?" I say in astonishment and quickly look to Rashid, who gives me a knowing look. "I mean, yes, of course, it was."

"Gentlemen, I'm afraid there's been a misunderstanding, which can be explained completely," Rashid says with easy confidence. "We retrieved the stolen work from Mr. Banning to bring as evidence to..."

Favreau waves his hands in the air, cutting off Rashid.

"No need to explain anything. Jack has already kept us abreast of the situation," says Favreau.

"He has?" I say, wondering what deal Jack worked out for himself at my expense. I was unaware Jack was still feeding him information once we switched gears and boarded Rashid's plan.

"Yes," Jack pipes in. "I notified the *Capitaine*, informing him of our highly... top secret plan to break in and...and retrieve the stolen art from Mr. Banning's, um... gang... and hand it over to the Swiss police." Jack struggles to tell the story, emphasizing certain parts. "You know, from that lead we received which we knew would be useless to the police without concrete evidence."

Favreau says, "Yes, Professor, you were supposed to do some recon, not take matters into your own hands. Though when he informed me of the plan, I immediately told the Swiss police to put an end to this nonsense. We tried to stop you before you went ahead, but alas, it was too late. Legally, I'm not sure where this puts us."

"Legally," Jack says, "the Swiss police were called in because a robbery was taking place."

"Yes, that's very true," remarks Favreau.

I look from Jack to Favreau and consider them both liars. I wonder how long Favreau has actually known about our plan. Of course, they wanted to catch us in the act to retrieve the goods.

"Yes, yes," says Frick, staring at the paperwork on his desk with a look of contemplation. "However, I must say no one suspected that such a respected businessman would hold these works. Well," Fricke says and stands, "you must be exhausted. I suggest you remain in town for a few days while we continue to uncover the cache of stolen art. Come back tomorrow, and we will continue our conversation. We have booked you rooms at the Hotel St. Moritz, courtesy of the Swiss government. It is our way of thanking you."

"You mean it's all over?" I say in dismay.

"In a few days, it will be. We will make a joint announcement, both the Swiss and French police, about the recovery. This is the result when several agencies work in tandem. And you, Ms. Milton, will be fully exonerated at that press conference," Favreau says, then, turning to Jack, he adds, "as promised."

Jack didn't abandon me after all. I offer him a feeble smile, little compensation given that I left him back on the mountain when the shooting started.

Favreau says, "It will take a while, but many of these works have reward money attached. It should be a significant amount."

"Whatever is coming my way should be given to Ms. Milton," Rashid says. "After all, between the three, she's the one who had her reputation wrongfully damaged by all this."

Jack fidgets in his chair, and his eyes flick to Rashid. "And mine too. She can have it all," Jack says, straightening himself in his chair.

I feel as though I'm sitting between two peacocks. I turn to Jack again. Then the Prince. I feel a headache coming on.

***

"Well," I say once I'm alone with Jack and Rashid in the corridor outside Inspector Fricke's office, "you have some explaining to do, Professor."

"Yes," he whispers and looks behind us. "I'm afraid I had no time to notify you of what was going to happen. I had to think fast and make a deal with Favreau, bring him into the fold. I had no idea it would go as far as it did with all the shooting.

But it's over now, and your reputation is intact." Jack looks past me. "Favreau is calling me back. I'll see what he wants," he says, departing.

"Which means we can get back to the business of our magazine," says Rashid.

I hadn't thought about the magazine since we started working on the heist. In fact, even now that my name will be cleared, I'm not interested in asking Pierre for my old job back, either. Saving my career and reputation were the impetus behind this entire scheme, and yet the last few weeks have shown me an alternate to that life. "Let's put a pin in that. I'm exhausted and could really use a vacation."

Rashid says, "Let me take you away on a journey through Africa while we put the magazine on hold. You'll love it there. Think of it as a sabbatical...for the both of us," Rashid says, cocking an eyebrow playfully. "We can run with the elephants, live with the gorillas..."

I picture myself trampled by the elephants and eaten by the gorillas. "Do you ever stop with the adventures?"

Rashid looks at me hard and, in a quiet tone, says, "If I stopped, I'd die. I'm a few months away from my thirty-eighth birthday then...I...I..."

"You join your father."

Shoulders lowered, his voice softer, he says, "I join my father and behave like the Crown Prince I'm supposed to be."

He's surrendering to the life his father set out for him, giving up who he is to become the man he's expected to be, yet I know the reason Rashid's sacrificing himself is for his people. He told me once that he had no power, and I thought him wrong, that he was strong enough to fight against that belief. But it was me who was wrong. I didn't fully understand the pressure he was under to conform, and a lifetime of being told he had one path.

I chose my path. But, for years I hadn't noticed when, bit by bit, my job took over every facet of my life. I watched from the sidelines as old friends from university married, had children, and drifted away. I'd love to drop everything and not think about the future for a while, disregard schedules and deadlines. But I'm a grownup with a mortgage to pay, and if I don't settle down soon, I may miss out on the family life I've always wanted. And really, what's Rashid offering me anyway? What Rashid hasn't said and what I know is that he'll also choose a wife approved by his father. Spoiler alert. It won't be me.

I bite down on my lower lip. "I'm afraid your adventures may just kill me. In fact, I think I've had just about enough adventure to last a lifetime or two. I need space to get away from everything and…" I look from Rashid to Jack speaking with Favreau down the corridor. "Everyone." It's not until the words tumble out from my mouth that I realize I've made my decision.

I choose me.

"Well," Rashid says, a look of dismay on his face, "not being with you is an immeasurable loss but there's no blame in this. My responsibilities, my birthright…"

"Will keep us apart," I finish. "Like star-crossed lovers."

"Have I missed something?" says Jack, returning.

Neither Rashid or I respond to Jack's question.

"I'll see you both tomorrow." Rashid gently brushes up against my cheek and kisses it. He steps toward Jack and extends his hand. "It's been a pleasure. I much prefer you as a partner than a challenger."

Rashid walks away. He does not turn back, and everything that we had been, or that we could have been, vanishes. Journalists circle him the moment he's out the door.

Jack stares after him. "Hmmm, I was hoping we'd save on a shared ride to the hotel." Turning back to me, he says, "You look exhausted. Ready to go?"

I nod then follow him through the same crowd of shouting journalists to a waiting taxi. We sit quietly on the way to the hotel. There's so much to say, and yet we are too exhausted to say anything. Besides, I'm not sure where to start. My eyelids flutter. I lean to the side and nestle deep into the crook of Jack's neck, and drift off to sleep.

"Charlotte, we're here," he whispers, nudging me awake. I mumble something incoherent and open my eyes, disoriented by the ordeal. Jack pays the driver and exits, holding the door open for me. He leads me to the front reception and arranges our check-in. With no luggage, except the small bag of toiletries we purchased from the gift shop, we head to the 5th floor, Jack with determination in his step, me lethargic. He opens the door to a hotel room and steps inside with a strange smile on his face that I read as victorious. I snatch the key from him.

"I agreed to share a taxi with you. Not a hotel room."

Jack looks embarrassed.

"I didn't mean to imply anything," he says and holds up another key. "My room is right next door." He clears his throat. "Let me know if you need anything, and I'll see you in the morning."

Jack disappears into his room and I'm glad to be alone. I don't want to deal with any more boy drama, don't want to agonize over who I should or shouldn't have chosen. Given everything that has happened, I can't imagine making a decision about anything except which beach to plop my ass down on, even if it means walking away from someone who may just be *the one*.

I turn the television on, scan for an English-speaking channel, and sink into the bed. My body yearns for rest and relaxation and a hot shower. The threat is over. No more falling out of helicopters or being chased by men with guns. No more running and hiding. No, this is precisely what I need.

Still, I wonder what Jack is doing next door. Will he call me? Knock? I bet he's ironing the towels. I shake the thought of Jack from my mind. I've made my decision to choose neither men, and it's the right one. I *need* to be alone.

My stomach growls. I can't remember when I last ate and decide to order some room service. The food is impeccably timed and arrives the moment I exit the bathroom, dressed in the hotel bathrobe, my hair towel dried after a shower. It takes two to deliver my food and I'm surprised because I didn't think I had ordered that much.

The two waiters look from me to the rest of the room, eyes skirting about. One says, "We will uncover the food once your guests arrive."

Guests? When I scan the number of domed covers, the cutlery, the bottle of pinot noir, I'm embarrassed. "He's here," I announce, and hurry to the door for the adjoining room, and knock loudly. "Jack, our food has arrived."

Silence. I look back to the waiters with a weak smile. "He'll be right out. In the meantime, if you can open the wine, I'd appreciate it." Returning to the door, I knock again. "Jack!" I say in a louder tone.

He opens the door quickly.

"What's wrong?" he says, looking into my room as though danger lurks in the corner until his eyes settle on the waiters.

"Room service has arrived," I say in a lighter tone while noting his disheveled hair and that he, too, is wearing the hotel bathrobe. I have obviously woken him.

"I can see that."

"Well, thank you gentleman," I say, pull some tip money from my purse and usher them out. Pivoting back to the room, I find Jack sitting at the table and studying the bottle of wine. I suppose I'll have to entertain him now.

"Good vintage," he says and pours out into two glasses. "You've ordered a lot of food for the two of us. Thanks for thinking of me. I'm famished, but I was knackered, too, which won me over."

"Well, I know what's best for you," I say as though sitting in my hotel room, eating and drinking with Jack was my plan all along.

We dig into the codfish, served in butter and walnuts, gnaw on the quail with truffles and mushrooms. I sniff the duck liver and pass, sticking my fork into a stuffed artichoke instead. At some point, a second bottle is ordered, though I barely remember finishing the first.

"I'm so glad we're doing this," says Jack. "It's a great idea."

I swallow the bit of food in my mouth and smile in agreement when it hits me how much I've missed him during the time we separated. I mean *really* missed my heist partner because somewhere in all this, while I played this persona created for Banning, I lost the old me. And, well, I can be the real me around Jack, something I couldn't be with Rashid. "I'm full of great ideas." I want to list all the great ideas in my head, but things are a little fuzzy at the moment with the alcohol consumption. *Oh, yes, Italy!* "For example, I just decided I'm going to eat and drink my way through Italy when we're done here. And you know what I'm going to do after?"

"Eat and drink your way through Spain and Portugal?"

I look at him intently. "You know me so well." He does know me well, doesn't he? After all, I didn't know I was planning to eat and drink my way through any country until ten minutes ago. The idea wormed into my mind and just like that, it became a plan.

The voice of the newscaster bursts into my thoughts: "...Carey plans to lengthen his time in space next week."

Jack's head shoots up toward the television screen.

I follow his gaze, which is fixated on the newscast. "Ugh," I groan, "just what we need, another billionaire taking yet another trip into space."

"My brother has always been the adventurous type. I barely trust airplanes."

"I know what you mean...wait, what? Sir Richard Carey, the eccentric billionaire, is your...brother?"

Jack nods.

Slowly, it dawns on me. "That means your family owns Carey Enterprises, the international conglomerate. You're one of *the* Careys?"

"Yes."

"You Oliver Twisted me," I say a little stunned.

"I'm pretty certain you can't use a name as a verb."

"The English language is fluid."

"Not that fluid."

My mind races. "We had it all wrong in *Ville de Loire*. This makes you Claudette Colbert and me Clark Gable. You could have told me."

"When?"

"Whenever! Like when we were at the casino and you didn't give me enough money for the table."

"That wasn't my fault."

"Or when you bemoaned using your credit card points for train tickets."

"It's not appropriate to discuss how much money one has."

"Says rich people. Oh. My. God. Your wardrobe."

Jack sits up straight in his chair, a perplexed look at his face. "You can't seriously bring up my clothes again."

"I thought maybe they were all you could afford on your salary, but no, you just have horrendous taste. That settles it."

"Settles what?"

"The Eating and Drinking Tour of Charlotte Milton now includes a shopping trip for Professor Jack Carey," I announce. Then in a mischievous tone, I add, "We'll start in Milan if that's OK with you, Claudette."

A smile works its way on his lips. "That suits me just fine, Clark."

"You know," I say, leaning towards him until we're mere inches apart, "someone once told me they fall in the love in the end."

THE END

Acknowledgments

I MET AUTHOR JUDY Blume when I was nine years old and told her I wanted to be a writer. Her response to my ambition was encouraging, and now years (read: decades) later, I finally achieved that dream. So, thank you to every author whose books I read as a child for your works nurtured my love for reading and fed an overactive imagination.

Thank you, dear reader, for choosing my debut novel. It's been a long, sometimes lonely road from the moment I conceived of this story to the finished book. I certainly didn't do it alone and am indebted to many wonderful people who took the time to read and edit and made this book into what it is today. Quite frankly, they all have been so generous with their time.

To my agent, Logan Harper, who supported and championed my work over the years. Your insight, editorial notes, and guidance have proved invaluable. Every writer needs a group of author friends to lean on, and to commiserate with during those months (and years) of torturous submissions to publishing houses. I was lucky to have found Amy Suiter Clarke, Libby Hubscher, and Richard Scarsbrook. To Sharon Pelletier who had me throw out the entire second act and start from scratch.

What can I say to my beta readers except *Sorry*? Sorry that I made you read those horrendous early drafts (you trashed those copies, right?). Sorry for all my neurotic texts and emails as I worked through ideas and had you as sounding boards. To Doris Montanera, who, despite suffering the most exposure to all those appalling drafts, still talks to me. As an editor, you were the first to accept my short story for publication all those years ago, and your edit notes and encouragement on this have been immensely helpful. And Ivonete de Sousa for designing an absolutely kick-ass cover. You are the best. To Kathy Paljus, Dawn Kuisma, Catherine Kunz, and Mark Sonnenberg for your enthusiasm for this book. It takes a village to coddle an insecure writer.

Thanks to my late father, Angelo, for regaling me with stories about his life and the odd characters he knew. You were the original storyteller in the family, and I somehow picked up the torch and ran with it. To Michel for always asking if I need the time to write on any given day, then leaving me alone to do it. And thanks especially to my boys, Julian and Christian, who have grown into incredibly wonderful young men. Follow your hopes and dreams wherever they may take you, and enjoy every amazing moment life offers.